To:

Leonor Aureus Briscoe

All the characters in this novel are fictitious; the setting, San Francisco, is real.

what the hell for

you left your heart

in san francisco

a novel by

BIENVENIDO N. SANTOS

New Day Publishers
Quezon City
1987

1

IF THIS STORY were to begin, as it ends, with Estela, the invalid in a wheelchair, in the mansion on Diamond Heights, I might find a thread that would tie these random notes together. You see, she had a strange fascination. On evenings before she would allow herself to be tucked in bed, she had to be given time to look down at San Francisco below the Heights, blazing up at her. The sight seemed to soothe her of all the ills that infested her misshapen body and mind, enough to give her the peace she needed to sleep at night.

But Estela came too late, almost too late, just shortly before all my hopes had been dashed, near the fading of the dream I had held on to while I walked the streets of San Francisco. She must have had things to say, too, but she had no words for whatever was locked behind her bulging eyes that saw more than what was given to the naked eyes to see. She will never find the right words for the thoughts that live only in her mind, unable to shape them into human speech, to describe her needs and name the burden of her laments or what sounded like laments as her head gyrated loosely on her neck, her spindly arms swinging wildly in bursts of uncontrolled passion beyond entreaty and prayer. Yet there is a thread, there must be, somewhere among these disparate events, which I have to find.

I am also looking for words to name what I see and hear and feel as I go about these now familiar streets. Surely there is a way of surviving for me and others like me in this city— without compromises and betrayals, without anchors.

My name is David Dante Tolosa, a Filipino, born on February 14, 1938, on the outskirts of the American naval base near Subic Bay in the Philippines. An oriental with broad hints of Malay-Indonesian, perhaps Chinese, strain, a kind of racial chopsuey, that's me. Better yet, for historical and ethnic accuracy, an oriental omelette flavored with Spanish wine.

My American friends call me Dave. Estela's father, Dr. Pacifico Sotto, calls me "Mister Editor" and never by name except when we are alone. Then he calls me David, broad *a*, accent on the last

1

syllable. Dr. Sotto is a urologist who specializes in vasectomy. He heads a group of wealthy Filipino medical practitioners and businessmen who are interested in publishing a magazine for Filipinos who live outside the Philippines.

Dante is my mother's family name. When she died while I was in high school, I was the chief and only mourner. My father left for the States shortly after the outbreak of World War II. I don't think he ever wrote home. Maybe he didn't know how to write. But he sent Mother various sums in postal money order which helped assuage, no doubt, her grief. Before long, she was living with another man whom I knew even less because he joined the U.S. Navy soon after and, like my father, disappeared from her life. However, the money orders kept coming for a long time. There must be something good in a man like that, I thought, who kept faith, in a sense. Then the money orders stopped coming. But Mother, in her desperation, continued to drag me to the town post office. It seemed she aged visibly after every frustrating visit. I still wonder what she kept mumbling on the way back home after every futile visit to the post office.

Wherever I go in this country I carry my passport. I feel threatened without it here in San Francisco where we, who are obviously Asians, have to be ready at all times to prove who we are and what our intentions are, at least, for the day. Even with a "green card" certifying that "the holder has been duly registered according to law and admitted to the United States as an immigrant," we get paranoid every time a stranger looks at us with more than passing interest. He could be an immigration officer or, worse for the overstaying or illegal alien, a fellow national, a *paisano*, acting as informer for a substantial fee. These informers are clever, resourceful, and hungry.

I cannot imagine my father without his passport wherever he went. After all, I am supposed to have taken after him. In her lonely moments, my mother talked about him, saying repeatedly how I had taken after him. He had a winsome smile, a "school girl complexion," and except for a tiny growing mole, purplish brown, where a dimple should have been, his skin was smooth and unblemished. I, too, like my father, have smooth skin (I have often wished it were thick instead); no wrinkles yet. Clean shaven, a young David in a season of Jesus freaks. I'm not too muscular, except for the right arm, from tennis. Nice and warm to fondle "like a young pigeon." The simile from a girl whom I still remember for her immoral legs.

2

Until I was stranded in San Francisco, on my way back to the Philippines from New York through the Midwest, I thought the only women who liked me were those beginners with whom I played tennis because I was patient with them; and some of the girls who wanted their pictures in the popular magazine I edited in Manila, a song and movie monthly with literary pretensions.

Visitors straying into the editor's office sometimes called me Boy, asking, is your boss in? I must have been young-looking. I kept healthy, that's why, and, in my younger days, I was quite vain and shamelessly open about it. I was fastidious, too, about my teeth and I used to carry a toothbrush and a small tube of toothpaste because I had a compulsive need to brush my teeth even after a mere snack. I don't recall when I stopped the habit, which was often inconvenient. According to my mother, my father carried a toothbrush and a tube of toothpaste wherever he went. He didn't smoke either and Mother hoped I would not take up the bad habit, which I never did. I drank an occasional cocktail, usually available and free at parties, but no cigarettes. I made sure I had at least eight hours of sleep, which was not difficult for me except when something truly sad or cruel bothered me.

Like in those days after Richard Nixon resigned. I could see and hear in my dreams the clatter of thousands of framed pictures of the man being removed from the walls of Federal Office Buildings across the nation and in the offices of United States embassies, consulates, and missions all over the world, and dumped into garbage cans and I wake up, my throat dry with a bitter taste in my mouth as if I had jogged more than I should have. Or the last time I saw him on television, trying to smile himself out of his predicament while his wife and daughter watched him, trying hard not to cry themselves. It's so painful, I feel like crying myself every time I see the scene repeated in my dreams. With Marcos, the man in power in my country, it's an entirely different matter, but a similar pain, more intense and intimate, assails me. I console myself, saying, even this shall pass. Besides, my teeth are too good to risk grinding them in my sleep. And all for what?

Other things just as personal should cause me loss of sleep but don't. Like not having a steady job. Or getting stranded in San Francisco. This magazine which I am working on and trying to help publish before my backers change their minds. I can

3

see the signs already from the questions they ask and the answers they give to my questions. But what the hell, the more I work on the magazine and see it taking shape on the drawing board and in my mind, the more I love it, the more worried I become, afraid it won't ever come out, or if it does, probably not beyond one issue or two.

It would not be true if I said I came to America to look for my father, but it had crossed my mind. Just thinking of the possibility of meeting him excites me. Those money orders came from all over California and most of them from right here in San Francisco, arriving with astounding regularity until they stopped quite abruptly. My father must have walked these streets. Does he still walk them now?

Suppose, just suppose, we met. How would the meeting come about? After these many years how would I recognize the man whom I never knew that well? How would he know I was his son? I like to think I had really taken after him. Shall I know him by the sparkle of his eyes (oh, how well my mother remembered)? By the toothbrush in a plastic tube peeping out of the rim of his breast pocket? Whatever, it had to be melodrama. The ultimate reunion. Add to the scene the other man in my mother's life and what do you have? Fiction most contrived. Human interest material for the magazine on the dreaming board.

2

ON MY WAY to San Francisco I stayed overnight in Salt Lake City with a friend from the Philippines, an American born and raised in Utah in the Mormon faith before joining the Associated Press in Manila where I met him. There was not much else to see in Salt Lake after a glimpse of the Tabernacle from the outside and the Angel Moroni with his golden trumpet glistening in the sun. My friend seemed embarrassed when he took me to see the Great Salt Lake as though it were his fault that it was not a field of diamonds. I was leaving early the next morning for San Francisco. He must have noticed I was feeling low. "Help yourself before going to bed," he said and gave me a number to dial.

4

When I did later that night, more out of curiosity than actual need, I heard a prayer of hope and humility, of thine-will-be-done-not-mine stuff. I laughed so much my eyes filled with tears. I knew I could depend on my Mormon friend.

The first few days in San Francisco I stayed in a crummy hotel room downtown. I was looking for my favorite professor in the University of Santo Tomas in Manila who, I heard, now lived somewhere in San Jose. In my ignorance, I thought San Jose was a suburb of San Francisco like Daly or Berkeley and Oakland. No, San Jose was not really the suburb that I thought it was. My professor was supposed to be on the faculty of a school in the city so I kept calling the personnel departments of local colleges and universities, but without success. I might never find my professor, the one man who could help me find employment.

That noonday I stayed in my room listening to the radio in bed. I should have gone out to lunch, but I was not hungry. When I'm worried I save on food. At first I couldn't believe what I was hearing. I must be hallucinating. Had I gone mad from despair? I shouldn't have left the Philippines. Out there I could have kept my sanity if nothing else. At least, there I had a job.

The woman's voice over the radio was soft and easy. She was describing in detail her favorite sexual position. A man's voice was urging her on as she ohhed and ahhed and grunted. The woman was telling the world about a very private act! How could she, right here in San Francisco and to thousands of radio listeners like me? The longer I listened the more certain I was that I was not hearing things. I was sane. I should have felt embarrassed but the talk was too interesting for embarrassment. One girl after another, with short intervals of commercials advertising waterbeds, described what turned them on about men and where and how they enjoyed sex best. They spoke, proudly, it sounded to me, of sex acts even an Olympic gymnast or acrobat would have difficulty performing. They called themselves "California girls." My worries dissolved with every sexual revelation. Asked by the male emcee, the girls gave the exact number of men they had had sex with. They must have kept a score card or tallies on their panties in pencil or indelible ink. One girl could not keep count. Sweetheart, the emcee cajoled, try to remember. Fifty? A hundred? Yes. No. Maybe. Oh, yes, more or less, a hundred. And how old are you, honey, the man asked. Nineteen, the girl answered quite distinctly and went on with

5

her story. So I began laughing. Aloud. Like in Salt Lake City. This beats a prayer any time for getting a hold of oneself again which I needed to do.

3

AFTER A WEEK of searching, I finally tracked down my old Professor. I didn't have to go to San Jose to see him. I found out that he was teaching at City College so I took the bus to Ocean and Phelan Avenue. He was in his office waiting for me. I remembered that, in my student days, he always sounded excited whenever he talked. Now I noticed that he still did.

"You have just come on time," he said, shaking my hand vigorously.

"No, sir, I'm late by about fifteen minutes," I said.

"You have just come on time," he repeated, ignoring my statement. It was fifteen minutes past ten, the hour I was supposed to see him. "You're heaven sent!"

Professor Arturo Jaime looked thinner and a bit older, but he had not changed much. He still didn't know how to tie his neckties. He was wearing a faded blue shirt which I thought I had seen on him before when I was still his student. He must hate ties and wear them only out of resignation. His pipe was as smelly as I remembered it to be. It must be the same pipe, too, God, how many years ago?

"You haven't changed, Professor," I said. But he was not listening. He had exciting news.

A group of very wealthy Filipinos in San Francisco was looking for someone to edit a magazine for Filipinos in the United States which they wanted to publish. They were willing to finance it. They had heard of Professor Jaime and thought he would be interested. But hell, it was a full-time job and he had just gotten tenure and a promotion to full professor in Philippine Studies. But he had promised them he sould look around for an editor.

"And here you are! Heaven sent, what else? " He beamed at me. The man acted as though he was turned on. Perhaps, after all, the California girls were for real.

6

Professor Jaime assured me I had no idea how fabulously wealthy these countrymen of ours were who wanted a Filipino magazine. Most of them were in the medical profession, surgeons, specialists in open heart surgery, kidney transplants, vasectomy, which all involved expensive operations. Some were in private practice and had controlling interests in medical centers. Dr. Sotto, who headed the group of would-be magazine publishers, was a urologist and derived his lucrative practice from vasectomy. He was married to another medical doctor. There were four other medical couples in the group.

"You have no idea how rich they are. I don't even know who they were in the Philippines. Complete unknowns. Some of them are so young they could be my sons. You should see the houses, actually mansions, where they live, located in exclusive residential districts in San Francisco. You'll see one. Soon. Dr. Sotto is throwing a *luau* party over the weekend as a kind of thanksgiving for the couple's safe return after a month's visit to the Philippines. Sometimes they just give parties for no reason at all."

"But I'm not invited."

"Now you're underestimating your old professor." He smiled as he worked on his filthy pipe. "What do you think? As soon as I heard from you, I din't waste time. You and I are attending the party. Dr. Sotto has asked me to bring you along. He wants to see you and introduce you to the others."

"But I have no Hawaiian costume," I said, wondering why a group of Filipinos away from home should prefer a Hawaiian party to something more native to the Philippines.

"Wear anything. In these parties there are always those who come in business suits. But a *barong* will do. I'm sure you have one."

"Sure," I said. Foolishly, I wanted to add, I also have a genuine visa and passport.

4

THE SOTTO RESIDENCE on Diamond Heights didn't appear imposing when Professor Jaime pointed it out to me as we rounded a curve near the peak of the hill overlooking the city. It was later afternoon but the sun was still way up over the bay. Close to the top of the hill no less than three separate constructions were going up and I wondered whether there would be enough space for all of them on that bit of rugged peak we were slowly approaching. Just then the Sotto place came into full view, a brownstone structure surrounded by scattered trees. From our side of the hill, it was hard to guess where the main gate was, if there was one. At first the house looked inaccessible from any angle and then, suddenly, it seemed open and could be reached from any direction. It was not until much later when I had the leisure to look around that I realized that the various levels of the house fitted into the natural breaks on the sides of Diamond Heights into which the mansion was pressed, a massive insertion to fill the ugly gaps on the terrain. There were at least three levels, perhaps three and a half. Each level except the topmost, was ground level any way you looked at it. On a fair day, every floor had an unobstructed view of the city below which spilled beyond the surrounding suburbs, far off into the mists over the well-known picture-card bridges spanning waterways dotted with specks and lined with what seemed like dull colored boxes crowding the tops and sides of other hills and valleys.

As we stood tentatively at what we surmised was the main entrance, a pretty, doll-like Philippine girl in heavy mascara approached us with leis in her hands. She was so short I had to bend over low as she tiptoed to place the lei around my neck. As she passed it over my head I caught a whiff of lotus and sweat from her exposed armpits. Thanks, I murmured, but she was already putting another lei around the professor's neck.

We thought we were late but the place didn't fill up until an hour later. All evening I felt self-conscious because I was the only one in a *barong*. Everyone else was dressed in Hawaiian costume. Where were those who usually came in business suits? I wished someone in the course of the evening would come dressed in something else other than Hawaiian. No way. Even the waiters and barmen wore Hawaiian shirts. Soft music seeped through some secret crannies in the mansion. It was pure Hawaiian, voices and strings, honey and gall and a smattering of bitters, mostly wailing, long drawn out. I thought of little hurt children looking for their wayward mothers but this was adult pain and joy, hope in the midst of island despair. It was everywhere. In the indoor gardens with fountains, birds in silver cages and fish in well lighted aquariums, around the busts cast in bronze, on the oriental furniture

8

and tapestries, wood carvings on the walls, bamboo dancers in petrified grace, armed Ifugao warriors in mock belligerence, and Igorot women with exposed breasts, brown and wooden. I thought the guests turned for a second look at me, a stranger in the wrong attire which clashed with the music. I had never felt so alien among my own countrymen.

The feeling passed gradually as the professor and I walked to the bar. After taking a few sips of the double scotch and soda in my glass, I no longer felt embarrassed but actually resentful. Perhaps if I had another double scotch I might even be moved to vent my hostility by belting an impassioned rendition of *Bayang Magiliw* or recite "I am a Filipino." Maybe I'd get myself thrown out for misplaced patriotism. Later, after more drinks, I began to feel so good I wondered what the hell for I had gotten so damned mad about earlier. I felt right at home here and all the rest were interlopers in my domain.

Dr. Sotto was shorter than I had expected. Barely five feet two. But then for his specialty he didn't have to be tall. He was good looking, almost cherubic. Imagine an angel snipping away at something inside your scrotum.

"Welcome, Mister Editor," he greeted me even before the professor could make the introduction.

"The others will all be here soon," he promised as he pulled a stately woman in a long, deep-purple dress by the arm, and presented her to me.

"My wife, Dr. Imelda Sotto," he said and turning to her, introduced me, "Mister Editor."

"David Dante Tolosa, ma'am," I said, bowing low because I felt I was standing in the presence of royalty.

At the first opportunity, I asked the professor, "That lady, the wife, what's she in?"

"I don't know," he said, "maybe pediatrics. Most women doctors I know are."

"Not vasectomy, I hope," I said.

The professor hee-hawed, spilling the bloody mary on the carpet. Quickly recovering, he pulled me aside as he whispered, "So you know the husband's specialty. I must have told you, right? But there's something you don't know. You should visit his office one of these days. There's always a long line of American males waiting to be snipped."

My imaginative mind was quick to grasp the picture. But there was the doctor again introducing me to "the others" who

9

had just arrived. This time he called me, "*our* editor."

In between introductions and tentative attempts at conversation, Professor Jaime stuck to his often interrupted story. "No less than ten males a day and at a hundred fifty per, minimum, plus other things besides, you can almost see, can't you, the very foundations on which this house is built."

"Of course," I said, sorely tempted to add, "and what a shaky foundation."

"What do you know about vasectomy?"

"Well . . ."

"Everybody's talking about it."

"Well . . . we are."

"The greatest thing since sliced bread. That's the way it's advertised."

"Really?"

The Hawaiians had taken over Diamond Heights. They were everywhere, walking desperately, I imagined, into the groove of the music, spilling all over the mansion with the peculiar foundations. The professor was still talking about vasectomy.

"A simple 15-minute operation with local anesthesia, often with only a tranquilizer. Snip, snip and the patient's back home within a half hour."

"A castrated male," I said, wanting to touch my crotch for a bit of assurance.

"No, no, nonononono!" Professor Jaime intoned, turning the monosyllable into a verbal centipede. "Let me explain."

"You don't have to explain," I said, not wanting to hear another word about vasectomy. At this point, every time I heard him say the word, I pressed my legs together involuntarily.

What was there to explain? For God's sake, this was a party the likes of which I had never seen before. It was a glittering bore, but the place fascinated me. I wished someone would talk to me and make me feel truly at home. I just couldn't keep drinking and eating. I wanted to talk to "the others," the backers of the magazine I was supposed to edit. Get acquainted. Enjoy. But it was all Drink and Eat. There was a long table in another room where food of all kinds lay tastefully arranged, most of it imbedded inside cut-out pineapples of all sizes. Peeled jumbo shrimps lay on banks of ice. Huge pink salmons, said to have been flown in from Alaska in a private plane, were at both ends of the long table. Suckling pigs, the way Hawaiians roast their pigs at luaus, lay prostrate on banana leaves. I moved towards the table, but

10

Professor Jaime held me for a moment. "Oh, I forgot to tell you, it's tax deductible, you know," he said, smiling.

"What is?" I asked, not catching his drift.

"Vasectomy."

5

FOR NO REASON OTHER than that he used to be my professor in the Philippines, I had a hard time calling Professor Jaime by his first name, which he wanted me to do.

"You're so damn formal, Deedee," he remarked as he drove through the highway to San Jose. "Call me Art. Everybody does. Even my daughters, the two younger ones who were born here. You'll see them if they're home. They're . . . well. . . different."

He had insisted on my checking out of the hotel and staying with him until something turned up. He had six children, but only the two youngest ones in junior high were living with him and his wife Felicia. It was a big house, he said, two stories. There was a guest room on the first floor. His last guest over the weekend was a priest, a former classmate of his in the seminary who had come to solicit funds for his impoverished parish in the Philippines.

I told him I appreciated his concern, but I could not stay with him even if I wanted to. It was likely, or so I hoped, that if the project progressed well enough, the backers would give me some kind of allowance or stipend, pay necessary expenses and I could stay in some apartment in San Francisco where I would be conveniently available to them. San Jose was too far.

"You don't have to stay in the house. Live somewhere close by. Rent's relatively cheaper in San Jose than in San Francisco, especially around where we live. You can drive with me to City College every week day. Weekends I'll show you around. You'll be interested in what Felicia—have you met her? —is doing."

"I'm not sure if I've met her. It has been so long ago. What does she do?"

"You'll see."

"Does she know I'm coming?"

"Of course. And I told her you're staying."

"Oh, no, please, but really, I thank you. I'll stay overnight.

11

Okay? Meanwhile perhaps you can help me locate myself in San Francisco. I also want to teach, you know. Perhaps in your department?"

"We'll see, we'll see," he nodded, his head bobbing up and down over the wheel.

"Don't you get tired driving this far every day back and forth?" San Jose was much farther than I had imagined.

"I used to make better time, but this dumb energy crisis limits us to . . . well, you know."

Glancing at the speedometer, I noticed it was closer to 65 than 55.

"You drive a car like this and you think you're just cruising along, but you're really going 65 or more. It's a crazy law," he said.

Their house stood in a shady residential neighborhood on a street named Quentin. We didn't have to pass through the downtown area but he wanted me to see what he meant by San Jose being the fastest growing city in the United States. Unfortunately, I couldn't see any of that. I didn't know what to look for in the first place. What were the signs anyhow? I thought it looked like any other city of its size that I had seen in the United States. Pretty dull and, at that time of the evening, quite sad as though this so-called potential for growth people were talking about, was a burden it could not live with comfortably.

Nobody met us at the door. I had a suitcase and a valise which I could have carried easily myself, but the professor wanted to help so I gave him the valise which was smaller although it contained some books and magazines. The door was not locked so there must have been somebody home. Then the familiar scent of Philippine foods cooking hit my sensitive nose.

"Adobo!" I said aloud without intending to.

"Fely?" Professor Jaime called as I followed him to the kitchen after putting down my luggage near the foot of a stairway leading to the upper floor.

Fely was a tiny woman, thin, and light complexioned. She couldn't have been more than five feet tall. She spoke like someone I had known all my life. Hers was a familiar face although I doubted if I had seen her during my student days. I felt right at home with this small woman who had a gentle voice and the kindest smile.

She asked whether I was one of the students in her husband's classes at the University who used to visit at their home in Manila.

12

No, she didn't remember ever meeting me. Did I know the others? She mentioned names and it disappointed her to realize that I didn't recognize any of them. She wondered what had happened to them especially after martial law was declared in the Philippines. How did I get away? When? Thousands lined up daily in front of the U.S. embassy on Roxas Boulevard seeking entry into the United States even before martial law. It could be worse now, she imagined. I agreed. Oh, was I so lucky? Deep in my heart I felt I could use some luck these days.

"David was one of the shy ones," the Professor explained.

" Not really," I said, "but remember I was a working student."

Fely remembered the articulate ones who were politically oriented and often spoke of freedom and love of country. Where could they be now, Fely wondered.

The adobo was as I thought it would be, heavily seasoned and utterly delicious. There was no need to say how much I enjoyed it the way I gobbled up the pieces and mixed the sauce in my steaming rice.

"I love the way you eat," Fely said, piling more food on my plate. "My children don't . . ." That was as far as she got because the door opened noisily as two creatures—how else could I call them? —rushed towards the dining table. I sat there wondering who had attacked us, remnants of a decimated army of stragglers from outer space? After a while, I noticed they were a pair of little dark brown girls with afro hairdo that covered much of their faces. They were shabbily dressed in jeans and nondescript blouses and reeked of cigarettes. They put their fingers on their snub noses and exclaimed, "Yucki," no doubt referring to the aroma of the fabulous adobo I had been devouring. Both parents made futile attempts at introductions. The girls ignored me completely.

"Izzat all we're having, ha?" one of them said.

The mother turned to me and said, "They hate Philippine food."

"They prefer hamburgers or hot dogs," the Professor said.

"There's something in the fridge for you," Felicia said, standing and walking towards the refrigerator to show them. "Come, help yourselves."

The girls picked up their plates and practically pushed their mother as they crowded in front of the open refrigerator. When they returned to the table they had sliced bread and something that looked like spam and dill pickles. But they didn't remaim seated

13

long. Carrying their plates with them, they danced their way to the living room to some imaginary music. Soon loud rock filled the air and we could hardly hear what we were saying around the table. I thought the couple would at least ask the girls to turn down the volume, but they didn't. We had to talk above the noise.

After dinner, I had a glimpse of the girls seated on the rug on the floor, eating and smoking while their bodies swayed to the beat of the music.

"That's all they do when they're home," their father said as he and I helped with the dishes in the kitchen.

"Surely, they help around the house sometimes," I said.

"Never!" the father said.

"Oh, they're young. They'll change as they grow older," Fely said.

As though they read the questions in my mind, the couple explained that in the beginning they tried to discipline the girls, but it was useless. There was no peace in the house and, worse, both girls threatened to run away if their parents kept "bugging" them.

"Grow up," both girls told them once.

The older children didn't live with them. The Jaimes owned two apartments called residential care homes which took in boarders, young and old persons of both sexes in the care of the government. Fely managed these homes.

The rock music was getting louder and the couple were obviously worried for my sake. Art wanted to ask them to turn the volume low, but I told him it was all right with me. If they didn't mind, I surely didn't either.

"I don't know why these girls are this way," Art said shamefacedly.

Both of them were born in the United States but that didn't explain anything, or did it? It could have been the company they kept, their so-called "peers," the kind of young people they spent time with all day in school and on the playgrounds and wherever they met outside of school hours. I wanted to say that my impression was that the children in American homes helped around the house and had their assigned chores. What was so special about these young girls? I wanted to know, but to ask would not only be impolite but tactless.

The eldest daughter in the Jaime family was married and taught school in San Francisco's Unified District. Her husband, a Filipino immigrant, was taking graduate work in economics.

14

They visited regularly every month. I was shown a picture of the couple. A beautiful pair.

"She's as lovely as you are," I told Fely and she blushed.

"She was Miss Philippines-America during the Fourth of July celebration in her junior year at City College," the father said proudly, quickly adding, "I don't think any of these two rock-crazed girls would make it in any beauty contest. Maybe, Miss Shabby. They would tie for first place."

"Oh, don't be too hard on them, Art. They're young. They will be just like the others when they grow up," Fely said, scrubbing the sink.

The second child, Art Junior, lived in one of the residences and the third, Bob, in the other home. Bob loved to paint and was still in school unlike Junior who was a dropout. Quite religious, Junior heard mass every morning no matter what the weather was like. Both were single. There was another Jaime son in the Philippines who never wrote letters but sent Christmas cards regularly, even if he didn't write anything on them, not even "love" or his name. The couple forgot to mention his name. They were eager to talk about Junior and Bob.

"Bob may yet get married, but I doubt that Junior ever will. He could be a priest, though," Fely said, looking at her husband. "Perhaps he would be making up for you."

Art smiled. "Do you want me to tell Deedee why I dropped out in my last year in the seminary?" he asked.

"If we're going to show David the residential homes, we better hurry, it's getting late." Fely ignored the Professor's suggestion.

As we were getting ready to leave, I noticed that neither the Professor nor Fely bothered to peep into the living room if only to say we were going some place. I was not too keen myself about seeing the apartments or meeting the residents. I was tired and after that heavy meal I just wanted to go to bed. But they were so sincere in their invitation and so enthusiastic. It seemed they wanted to impress me. They were proud of what they were doing. I went with them quite willingly, considering the visit as an escape from the noise in the living room.

Professor Jaime's statistical explanation of how they operated their residential homes didn't brighten my low spirits. But it helped pass the time. I remained attentive and polite through the tour, although my thoughts were on the magazine I was going to edit if everything went well. What sort of maga-

15

zine was it going to be? The group backing it were all serious men. They showed no sense of humor at all. They were all business, stiff to the point of hardness. What sort of material would they want the magazine to contain? Photos of beauty queens from the islands now in residence in this country, well groomed and heavily rouged and definitely past their prime if they had had any prime at all? Good looking tots of obvious Philippine descent in their Sunday best having a birthday party? A seemingly endless listing of names in bold type throwing parties of all sorts, anniversaries and *bienvenidas* not to mention *despedidas?* So and so has just arrived from the Philippines or leaving for the islands on a visit. This dull-faced youngster has just passed an exam where a thousand others have made it? The high and the mighty, names evoking power and wealth? Oh, God, no! I might just as well start looking for another job. Material, material! It was here right under my nose. Filipino families like the Jaimes, their tribulations and triumphs, trying to make it in this land where the streets have never been paved with gold, but is still, thank God, a land of opportunity. Yet one must have sensitive ears to hear opportunity knocking. Not only does it knock once only, but it knocks too softly and there are other sounds in the air. Like rock music.

Yet somehow I had to listen. Even as a student in Professor Jaime's class, I never paid attention this closely. I looked around.

A maximum of two residents to a room. Each room was just big enough for two narrow beds, no better than army cots actually, a common dresser, two built-in cabinets. During the year each apartment had an average of fifteen to seventeen patients, most of them on their feet, but barely. A TV room wide enough for a couple of second-hand sofas and easy chairs in front, and a magazine rack beside the set. An unused fireplace, old framed prints on the walls, a pay phone booth. The entrances and exits allowed for the use of wheel chairs. A dank shell of decay and age filled the apartment. It clung to me as soon as the door opened. There was no escaping that stranglehold.

"We serve a varied menu," Professor Jaime explained while Fely disappeared somewhere inside the house presumably to tell Junior there was a visitor from the Philippines. I have been told he occupied the room closest to the kitchen all by himself and did the cooking whenever his mother was delayed elsewhere. "Canned tuna, cold cuts, juices, cofeee, eggs, buttered tcast, waffles, pancakes or cereal, bananas, oat meal cream of wheat,

16

hot dogs, ham, chicken or roast beef, rarely steak on Sundays, and ice cream and cookies always," the Professor droned from memory.

A young man was sipping coffee when we entered. The blotches on his face and arms were crimson and he looked like a red man.

"Jim was a mental patient," Professor Jaime said in a low voice. "He practically grew up in institutions. Used to be afraid to go out. Sometimes he can't even turn on a faucet. Seldom talks. Never had a visitor. He doesn't seem to care."

Looking at Jim, I thought to myself, "And why shouldn't you be afraid out there, why should you care? " I was beginning to feel crazy myself.

"What does a day look like, an average day, in this home? " I wondered aloud.

"Like a day in a big family," Professor Jaime said. Breakfast at 8:00, lunch at noon and supper at 5:00 p.m. Like in most homes, the daily routine is staggered. "Fely spends the day preparing the food, washing dishes, and cleaning the premises. Junior helps, of course, but that boy locks himself up in his room for hours, meditating or praying perhaps. I call him the resident priest—not to his face, of course. He is very kind. Sometimes he reads to whoever asks for it. He has a soothing, gentle reading voice. They love him here."

I remembered the two afro-haired girls squatting on the floor, their bodies twisting to the beat of some jungle music.

"The guests, as we call them, usually stay home watching TV and listening to the radio. Otherwise, they take time preparing for bed. Some of them go out for walks, window shopping or sitting around in nearby cafes, sipping coke. They're free to come home any time they want to. Each one has a key to the main door. We don't have too many rules, but we try to train them to be considerate of the needs of others and live together in harmony. We feel that allowing them to make decisions helps them live a more normal life."

Again I thought of the Professor's rock-crazed hippies—they wouldn't make it here. They belong to some other place.

"On special days like Christmas or Fely's birthday, we include them in our family celebrations. During my eldest daughter's wedding, we took all our residents with us. They came all dressed up and the other guests couldn't tell that they were not our close friends. They looked as if they were an extension of our own family."

17

I could see Jim preening in front of a mirror, wondering why his face was so scarred and all the others' faces were smooth. He would want to touch their skin. It must feel nice to his fingers.

"Most of our residents are former mental patients. Half of them are young, in their early twenties, usually damaged by drugs. Many have been diagnosed 'paranoid schizophrenic.' About a third of them are on tranquilizers. Some can handle their own allowance, but one or two may need a public guardian or conservator. A few still have families but they are hardly ever visited by their folks. Except for the 'family' they have in our home, they usually have no one else to care for them. They get very depressed and may get drunk. Usually, though, they are not a menace to society. Fact is, they feel more menaced by so-called normal people like us."

While the professor talked, not too unlike the way he used to in our class many years ago, I was thinking what a wealth of human interest material there was in his family life in San Jose. Would my magazine have any use for such material? If the magazine covered much more than social goings-on among Filipinos in the United States, this information the Professor was giving me should be grist for it.

An old man with a leathery face and what looked like a boil on one cheek limped towards us and extended his hand, open palm up, to Fely. They talked for a while. The man's jacket was too thick for the mild season.

"He says he needs money, an advance," Fely told her husband.

"What for?" the Professor asked.

"He wants to go downtown to buy a birthday card and other things."

"Can't it wait till the end of the month? That's less than a week from now."

"It might be too late for the birthday perhaps."

It was more of the same in the other residence where Bob was in charge. His room served as a studio. It was cluttered and he kept apologizing for the mess.

We were back to the Jaime residence before the 11:00 o'clock news which I didn't want to miss. There was no sign of the two girls. It was so quiet after all the noise earlier in the evening. When I finally fell asleep I could see them gyrating and clicking their fingers to jungle sounds, rhythmic and maddening, while a cigarette hung loosely between their lips.

18

6

DR. SOTTO wanted me to be in close touch with him, at least during the preliminary phase of the magazine project. For this reason he offered me the use of his basement. I couldn't think of what else to call it since it wasn't really below ground level and yet seemed to be in relation to the other floors of his mansion. He was home only nights so I could, when necessary, stay out all day doing research in and around San Francisco. The nearest bus stop was a mile away, maybe less.

I didn't have to report to Dr. Sotto every night. He talked to me as often as he considered necessary. The Board had left everything to him so he suggested this living arrangement which he hoped would be all right with me. He would give me some kind of petty allowance I didn't have to account for. As a matter of fact, he said if I needed more all I had to do was ask him.

"I want you to meet the others on the Board as soon as you have something concrete to present. I want you to impress them and, I tell you, they're ready to be impressed. I want you to show them what the magazine will look like. I have a few ideas myself which I want to discuss with you—that's why I want you around."

Even Professor Jaime, who sincerely wanted me to stay with him in San Jose, saw the wisdom of the arrangement. I liked it myself. Very much. It somehow dissipated the doubts I was beginning to feel about staying on in San Francisco with very limited funds and no job.

What I called the basement was the lowest level of the house on the hill. It had a bedroom, a work room, a combination kitchen and dining room, shower and bath. The plumbing shone like silver under the indirect lighting. The telephone close to the bed lighted up when in use at night. I felt like a prince in royal surroundings. Luck appeared to be turning well in my favor. The first time I was left alone I touched the walls, felt the rug under my feet, soft like an overlay of leaves in a dense forest. I passed my hand over the clean sheets. I sang in the shower, listened with delight to the authoritative flush of the gleaming toilet. Then I remem-

19

bered something more crucial to my well-being than these luxurious appointments.

I rushed to the refrigerator. It opened easily with a dull sound, vapor issuing from its depth. There were fruits and vegetables, canned and bottled drinks, a double row of eggs looking like monster's odd dentures. The freezer was stacked full of meat and seafoods. I couldn't tell exactly what they were because a layer of ice covered each packet.

After a few days I felt quite at home, discovering new delights. With a push of my glass in a compartment in the refrigerator, water flowed or ice cubes fell into it in a cascade of sound, rich and thrilling to this new Filipino immigrant to America. You lucky son of a gun, Deedee, I told myself, smiling into the mirror over my dresser. I wanted to scream, whoop it up, but I realized I was not alone in that huge mansion. I remembered the young man and his mother who kept house for the Sottos. Why didn't they look happy living in a house like this? I would be. They had the use of a car, even if it was an old one. The Sottos each had one, a red Porsche for the man and a light blue Mercedes for his lady. The boy attracted me most; he looked so sullen and spoke in a low hesitant voice, his English heavily accented with what sounded to me like Visayan intonation. His mother, perhaps in her fifties, spoke in Pilipino. She never smiled and looked even more sullen than her son. I felt like an intruder in their presence. They must live on the same floor as the couple in surroundings even more fantastic than mine. So why did they look so miserable?

But what the hell, I was happy. The work ahead was cut out for me. There was no question in my mind I was going to impress the Board.

7

WHAT TO CALL the magazine was the first question we discussed during my first informal meeting with the all-Filipino backers of the project. It seemed that as far as they were concerned, the nature of the magazine in general terms was already quite settled in their minds. A monthly magazine for Filipinos abroad.

20

Something slick like *Ebony* or *Sepia*. All they needed now was someone like me with experience as magazine editor.

"And who needs the job very badly," I said, chuckling nervously.

My remark was greeted with laughter. The way they looked at me made me feel good. They were nodding as if to say, nice guy, good sense of humor and who cares whether he's telling the truth or not?

"*Sepia* would have been perfect," I said, "but we're a couple of years too late."

"Have you seen, Mister Editor, that new magazine called *Oh You I?*"

"What are you talking about?" chorused a few from the rear.

"I believe the gentleman means *Oui*," I said, pronouncing the French word correctly and spelling it out.

Everybody laughed. Even the guy who asked the question joined in the laughter, saying, "How the hell should I know?"

One of the doctors, a Dr. Tablizo, and by far the youngest looking of them all, said loud enough to be heard in the noisy room, "It's a good thing he didn't say I O U, which would have been understandable in his case, being a businessman."

"You're damn right," the businessman agreed. He looked familiar. I must have seen his picture in one of his ads in a local Philippine paper, a smiling face, all teeth. Like now.

"What about *Kayumanggi?* That's brown, light brown in Pilipino."

The suggestion caused a mild flurry.

"Not in my dialect, it isn't."

"Your dialect don't count anyhow."

"I don't know the word. It sounds funny."

"No less funny than . . . say, is that a French magazine?"

"*Oui?* It's a girlie magazine. Like *Playboy.*"

"Wow! Our wives gonna kill us."

"Your wife only."

"What about calling the magazine *Brownie?*"

"That's a dog. I got a dog named *Brownie.*"

"That's a camera. Like Kodak."

"Isn't that a cookie? Something chocolate — sweet? "

"My daughter's a Brownie. I think. She's a girl scout."

The discussion was lively and confusing. Nothing came out of it as far as naming the magazine. At first their levity worried

21

me and made me doubt the seriousness of their intention to support the project. And I had thought they had no sense of humor. Later, however, I realized that that was the way they did business. Finally, they suggested that I should keep thinking of a good name. I was assigned to present the magazine's format and a detailed organization plan at subsequent weekend meetings for their consideration. Other details, including an estimate of the necessary funding, could come later.

There were fourteen or fifteen men present, most of whom were prosperous medical practitioners in and around the San Francisco area. They wore expensive suits and spoke English rather self-consciously as if they were trying hard to sound American. I think they knew their accent showed. All of us. Young, in their early thirties. Some were actually fresh graduates from Philippine medical schools, although baby-faced Dr. Tablizo looked young enough to be a mere high school student.

More conservatively but just as expensively dressed were the three or four businessmen in the group who were much older. Unlike some of the doctors who wore their hair long in the latest style fashionable these days, the businessmen had crew cuts and were balding. They sounded even more uncomfortable with the English language. When they had to talk at length, they spoke in Pilipino with a few English cliches and colloquialisms thrown in. But all of them knew what they wanted, a slick magazine for Filipinos abroad, expensive, dignified looking.

"Something to be proud of in a country well-known for its slick magazines."

"Attractive. With a personality."

"The Filipino personality."

8

ALL I THOUGHT of the next few days was *the* magazine, as yet nameless. I jotted down ideas, plans. There was work to do. Research. In those days I had moments of doubt about my ability to push through the project. One fact stood out clearly in my mind. I could not, and would not, do it all by myself. It was a business venture that ought to have specialists on the staff. As editor, with the approval of the Board, I was merely to point the direction it should take, its scope and coverage, and all those elements which I knew would make it stand out and eventually make money, not to mention the outstanding reason I had been hired: write for it. Yet even this, I would not be able to do alone.

With my limited allowance, I bought current issues of magazines I could draw inspiration from and studied them. I collected and carefully read available Philippine publications in the United States. I visited the public library and the Philippine consulate library in San Francisco. I took long walks trying to find out where Filipinos usually gathered, through the so-called Little Manila section in Chinatown and similar places. A local Philippine newspaper published fortnightly listed a calendar of events of Filipino happenings in and around the city. I went to as many as possible, trying to look inconspicuous and harmless, and not the gatecrasher that I was. I dared not introduce myself as the editor of a non-existent magazine for Filipinos. From here on there would be no idle moment for me. I had work to do and I was determined to succeed, even to the extent of neglecting my weekend tennis. Jokingly, I told myself that meanwhile I would restrict my physical exercise to crossing my fingers. A hell of a joke, I know. I know.

A cursory glance at a typical issue of two of the most widely circulated Philippine publications in this country showed practically everything my magazine should *not* contain.

Start with pictures: photos across an eight-column page of convention delegates of varying intentions and persuasions, beribboned shriners in their typical headgear, Philippine-American community organization officers, their right hands raised in the act of being sworn into office, usually by a diminutive consul or ambassador of the Philippine embassy or consulate or someone pinch-hitting for them; men and women receiving plaques, trophies, ribbons, cups or other emblems of appreciation and recognition, usually surrounded by smiling relatives and well wishers, including babies. Weddings where even the bridegroom smiles, lifting the bride's veil for a not so chaste kiss, or the bride shovelling a piece of cake into the groom's wide open mouth. A christening party where everybody's name is printed, occupation, regional ancestry, from left to right.

The advertisements, principal source of income for all these publications, are unique in a Philippine paper. We should be able

23

to carry more substantial accounts without catering to individual egos and publicity-seeking businessmen. Samples of what I have seen: most advertisements of business firms, shops or banks, fish markets or similar enterprises with goods to sell or services to offer, include a photo of the Filipino manager, proprietor, president, or the prize agent in the case of insurance companies, often with a phone in hand, receiver close to the ears, eyes smiling into the camera. Each picture bears the person's name and additional information such as: "I speak Spanish and most of the Philippine dialects." Sometimes an additional message is appended to the picture: "Baldomero *(Bald* to you) Sumira is your countryman, friendly and eager to help and serve all your (transportation, funeral, or whatever) needs."

One Filipino funeral home advertises its specialty: "Shipments to the Philippines."

A Filipino-Chinese owner of a fish market has his picture in an ad, smiling affectionately at a huge fish he could hardly carry.

And the *personals!* Says one: "Attractive oriental registered nurse age 48 desires marriage. Applicants are urged to write to the California Association of Companionship and Marriage Bureau."

For immigration problems, one ad offers:

"Reasonable monthly payments. Owned and operated by a well-known specialist in immigration laws in the United States and a former officer of the U.S. Immigration Service (no photo included in the ad)" for the following services:

* Arrangements for permanent residence or American citizenship
* Deportation problems and trips to other countries
* Invitations for relatives
* All types of visas

If I could have my way we would have to establish a policy of steering away from politics, the so-called New Society in the Philippines that the martial law government was supposed to create. The question was at best divisive and would hurt circulation one way or another. Concentrate on human-interest stories, toned-down success stories, no superlatives and embarrassing assumptions that sound like bragging. All features would have to be relevant to the life of the Filipino in America, particularly the new breed of Filipino immigrants like the members of the

24

Board, with an occasional special about old timers, their little successes and big problems, the more factual, the more effective (no sob stuff). Helpful hints covering the more prevalent needs and problems of the Filipino in the States. Profiles on those who have distinguished themselves in whatever field, no matter how humble. Movements, worthy causes that need to be sponsored. Seemingly perennial problems of the new, and sometimes ignorant, arrivals. Solutions or attempts at solutions. Get experts to contribute articles with corresponding payments or honorariums. Interviews. Fiction? Maybe. Poetry, rarely. Fillers.

Excellent professional photography. Very essential. Get an experienced (preferably Filipino) photographer-artist for the cover. Vary each issue. Not too arty, something with a punch, even a message, why not? A montage of the Filipino face, racial types (what about that for the first issue?). Occasionally, a Filipino beauty set against a familiar background of harvest time, Mount Mayon, the rice terraces, the zigzags of Baguio, Kennon Road, the Luneta; panel shots of Filipinos in America in action, in laboratories, in the fields, factories, classrooms, clinics. . . everywhere.

Caution: Don't let the magazine look and read like one of those expensive slick magazines the government of the New Society puts out (Hosanna in the highest to Malacañang!) Keep it from looking like a travel brochure.

A minimum of columns. Maybe none. Or just one. Mine. Certainly no proliferation of columns and space-consuming letters to the Editor, usually unedited and self-serving and without any news value, which are characteristic features of local Philippine publications.

Nothing religious or irreligious for that matter. Much as I detest inspirational pieces, we should use some of that stuff on certain occasions. Interesting, readable, that's all I require. Dat's all?

What official name shall we give the so-called Board of Publishers, that body of men and women who are financing the venture? I included the women because I got the impression that the members of the Board who were all male would not make any financial commitments without the approval of their wives. Quite a few have admitted this openly.

Determine the utmost minimal composition of each department: business (circulation and advertising) and editorial (that's me to begin with). Work up from this skeletal staff as the need

25

arises. I should have in due time a staff to work with who will help with the writing. We must get the best printer money can buy. That's thinking big, but that's what I was supposed to do.

But what to call the magazine?

Perhaps if I didn't try too hard, forget it for a while, take it easy, sleep on it, get as many suggestions from the members of the Board and their wives and their children and friends, we would hit upon a name we would all like very much.

However, the question consumed me, awake or asleep. I just couldn't let go. Hell, how did I ever get into this?

9

THE FIRST FEW NIGHTS I spent at the Sotto residence, the doctor came down to see me, as he had promised, practically every night although once or twice he came quite late, past midnight and I was already in bed. Our talk always drifted away from the problems of the magazine to his own personal problems. He appeared on these nights rumpled and ruddy from too much liquor.

"May I call you David?" he asked one night he was down in the basement. I didn't say anything because I felt he didn't need my permission and, of course, he knew I didn't mind, but I kept calling him doctor.

There were nights when I wished that he would talk less of himself and more of his wife, but he didn't and I was curious. I saw her only once and that was at the Hawaiian party. At our few conference meetings it was always someone else's wife who played hostess. That his wife's name was Imelda meant a lot to me.

The only woman I have truly loved was named Imelda. Face of an angel. Inconspicuous, without wings. Quiet, not too smart, always asking me to help her. Funny, all those years I had known her I had not even kissed her, not even on the cheeks. She looked frightened and trembled a lot whenever she was with me. But she loved to be with me. She needed me, oh, how she needed me! She sought my advice for every little thing; she wanted my approval. The last time I saw her, she was in the arms of a man who was running towards a waiting ambulance. I no

26

longer loved her then. She was in a crumpled heap, barely conscious and seriously hurt, her slim ankle showing beneath the hem of a yellow skirt. At that particular moment, my heart went out to her; she was my Imelda again before the big change caused by fortune and circumstance turned her, in my eyes, at least, into a creature, hard and greedy.

Imelda, Imelda, I cried after her, recalling that soft day in December when I took courage to hold her hand, pressing it long and gently as I studied the sadness in her eyes, wanting to say something I didn't know what until years later. Imelda was saying goodbye not only to me but to innocence, goodbye to the simple life. That was what her eyes were saying as she held me in those long gone days before she became what she was and I, what I am now.

At the height of her glory, everybody seemed to love her, including the miserable fools who adored her like a goddess, her picture radiant on the crumbling walls of their nipa shacks, the one bright object they worshipped, forgetting their hunger and deprivation in their worship of her beauty. The fanatics, the idolaters among them must have lighted candles and burned incense as on an altar at the foot of her picture.

I burned one picture. I spat on another.

I pasted one on the lid of the water tank so that every time I lifted it to relieve myself some of the urine splattered on her face.

Could I have hated her that much or loved her even more?

And now when a girl, among my amazing lays, grips my hand with some sort of ardor, all I feel is a hardon coming.

10

SOMETIMES while walking through the streets of San Francisco, I felt no sense of direction. It mattered little whether I was going north or south, east or west. I was going nowhere and yet I wanted to be somewhere but I didn't know where. All I wanted was the movement, the seeming progression into what lay ahead, which somehow calmed me down and there was less clutter in my mind. All I could think of was the magazine. The magazine!

It was during these aimless walks that ideas came to me piecemeal about what it was going to be, what it would contain. I made myself believe that from here on, my life would be dedicated to that end, the production and the success of the magazine. Now I would go through life open and susceptible to whatever looked or sounded like possible magazine material. I carried a little notebook I filled with words. More words seemed to burst out of my mind. At times I felt tense as if I were on the verge of a discovery whichever way I turned. Every street I walked was a rainbow's end. The colors glowed and I walked on air but how quickly they disappeared, leaving a sudden brownness where sparklers used to be. I felt like I was floating in a vaccum, and I had nothing that my fingertips could touch, no solid ground on which to stand.

What was I looking for anyhow? I didn't know what I really wanted except in a vague sense. It seemed I had no idea at all, which was not true because I had an idea that haunted me but nothing specific. And I had fears about the demands the magazine would have on me. What if I couldn't make the backers see that all I wanted to be was editor-in-chief, not circulating manager or advertising solicitor? I would not be able to contribute much to the business side of the magazine. As editor I would try to put out a magazine good enough to make it easy for the business department to sell.

I walked on, aimlessly, meeting all sorts of people, but what interested me most were the orientals, the Asians, the Filipino-looking faces. I hoped—vaguely and without much reason—to meet someone I knew back home in the Philippines. The truth was, I was feeling quite homesick and alone, left too much to myself, not a new and strange feeling, actually more familiar by now than I wanted to admit.

Whenever Professor Jaime suggested that I spend the weekend in San Jose with his family, I felt eager to go, but didn't show it. I even tried to banish from my mind the impression his teen-aged daughters had left on me. They had become more real than ever, and when I thought of them, I felt sad. Lila was the younger of the two and the only way I could tell her from the older one named Donna was that she didn't wear glasses. Donna wore oversized ones that covered whatever part of her face her afro hairdo didn't hide.

There were successive weekends when I didn't hear from Professor Jaime and on these days I walked the streets of San

Francisco. I noted that the streets bore singing names as if they had been culled from religious songs or missals, mostly Spanish, quite familiar and welcome. Esmeralda Avenue, a realm of enchantment. Quintana street. Moraga, a plaza in an old city back home. Valparaiso. An alley named Malden. Dolores and Dorado, the sorrows and the gold; bells ring in my head as I go down Mission Street, Escolta, too, and Clementine with the upturned lashes — many many more, all singing and sometimes gold.

Sights impressed me like the completely shaved heads of men, and I suspect, women, too. A few of them were black. They sold sticks and danced to their chanting accompanied by drums not far from Woolworth's on Market Street close to the Emporium. I gaped at the skyscrapers like the Bank of America where, I was told, a very wealthy Filipino who was sick and dying lived in a penthouse suite. What a way to die in spite of his millions and all that luxury.

The sound of sirens screaming always startled me. I had a compulsion to trace the source of the alarm and get carried away in a rush of people towards the unknown, whatever it was, smoke and fire and gore, slow or sudden death, the tail end of a violence or a death watch that dragged for hours.

The animal odor in crowded buses and coaches gave me a sense of life but not well being. What happened to all those crazy commercials selling body deodorants?

Strange sight: A drunken woman walking unsteadily, teetering for a fall because her panties had fallen down on her ankles. Pedestrians laughing over her predicament. This couldn't be real, I said to myself, looking around for hidden cameras grinding away. Must be a scene on location on the streets of San Francisco.

11

DR. SOTTO visited me for the first time in my room, in the middle of my first week on Diamond Heights. He looked around as though he was seeing the premises for the first time. "This is good, not bad at all," he said. "This is really for guests and you are our first. We want you to have everything you need to be comfortable while you're here." He paused and looked at me inquiringly. "Well, what do you say?"

"This is fine. Beats anything I've ever been in," I said.

"Who can have everything? Tell me, do you know anyone who has everything?" He slumped in a chair, sighing heavily.

"You," I answered without hesitation. "You have everything or seem to, anyhow."

"I seem to. There's a difference." He looked much younger, so much more youthful and vulnerable when he smiled. Who cared to pursue the point? At the moment, I didn't.

"This is really fine, it's superb. I even like the view from here."

"That's right," he said, "this is one basement with a view instead of the usual feet and legs and dogs and cats that basements offer." Jumping from the chair, he drew the curtains aside.

"Look, the city's blazing. Even with a thick fog you know it's there, blazing."

"There's another hill, too. Over there," I said.

"Do you know what that building is?"

"It looks like a prison, or a hospital. What is it?"

"That's the mint," he said as he went back to his chair. "I wish you would ask me more questions."

But I had no questions to ask that were relevant to my being there. About the magazine. I really wanted some time to think the whole thing over and when I had something definite I promised to inform him.

"You're new in San Francisco although you've been to the East and Midwest. This is your first visit here. Right? Well, take your time. Look around. You'd love the place. Imelda and I used to think we would go back to the Philippines after a while, say, a few more years, surely when all that mess out there is over. But we've changed our minds. This is a fantastic city to live in."

"I thought in your last visit a month ago, you had glowing reports of what you heard and saw."

"That's right, but that was because we were in the right places. Maybe the right places were the wrong places. Depends on what you are looking for. Even now I wonder where the truth lies. Were we looking for it? Were we looking for assurance that all's well in our country even with martial law?"

"Now about the magazine . . . "

"With my specialty, I would be a pauper in the Philippines in no time." He was obviously not listening.

"On the contrary, I thought that with the current birth rate soaring along with the price of foodstuff and everything, a doctor like you in vasectomy. . ."

"No. No. Not vasectomy. Not me. I would starve. The Filipino male is a funny guy. If he can't make a baby, he thinks he's a faggot. Besides, vasectomy is permanent. Up to this point, we believe it is. And that scares them. The fact that they'll never be able to father a child. They'd feel queer. Like they belong to a condemned species of mankind."

"Suppose President Marcos, in an effort to stop the population explosion, signed a decree . . ."

"That's a joke. He's too smart to do that because if he did there would be a revolution. All the men would be up in arms."

"I thought our people were too meek, too faint-hearted."

"Not when their *cojones*, I mean, their balls, are concerned."

"You sound convincing. Maybe our predominantly Catholic faith has something to do with that objection."

"Don't be funny. Most Catholics in the Philippines go through the motion of their so-called Catholicism: a hurried mass, an occasional communion—for appearance's sake—in various stages of mortal sin. They practice, I mean they indulge in practically everything that the Church considers a mortal sin. Then they show up in church on Sundays—those who still do. And there's still a lot of them. There's nothing more crowded than a Philippine Catholic church on the sabbath. Yet if a poll were taken, it would show that more than 90% of churchgoers don't know a damn about the meaning of the mass, or for that matter, give a damn."

Dr. Sotto had no doubt the Filipino male's objection to vasectomy had nothing to do with religion. Superstition was more like it. Or was it machismo? The Filipino man is so damned proud of his sexual prowess, nothing can convince him that vasectomy will not impair his virility. He thinks vasectomy is a form of castration which would change his voice and make him talk like a eunuch, or behave like a homosexual. He thinks he would become impotent.

"Remember the saying, it's all in the mind? A lot of it is, really. But let's not talk about the Philippine situation. Hell, today I had eight patients, half of them scared to unconsciousness. You should see me working on them one of these days when you find time. Just now, let's just talk. Do you have any more questions?"

I had questions but they would sound crazy if I asked them.

31

Do you know that your wife looks like a twin sister of another Imelda whom I once loved? Yes, loved even when I hated her most?

Who plays that grand piano in the spacious living room on the top floor? Why doesn't anybody ever play it? And why is it open all the time, the keys exposed like gargantuan teeth in a perpetual grin?

Why is the boy who helps his mother with household chores so sullen? Why do mother and son talk in whispers?

As time went on, I thought of other questions and there were times when I thought I had the answers, too.

Sometimes Dr. Sotto would come with a bottle. He seemed delighted when he learned that I, too, liked to drink. But he did most of the drinking and the talking. I listened and nursed my glass. Always he asked the same questions: how was I getting along with my research? When would I be ready with the first detailed report on the magazine? Was everything all right? Did I have everything I wanted?

Once or twice when I stayed out late or spent the night elsewhere, usually in San Jose, he asked, where the hell have you been? Are you working too hard, man? Why don't you drink, relax? Most weekends, nobody's home. Go on up and do anything you want. Help yourself to the refrigerator. There are pastries, local and imported, in the cupboards if you have a sweet tooth. There's food and drink. Turn on the stereos. When the boy and his mother are around ask for anything you fancy.

May I play the piano? I wanted to ask, which was silly because I didn't play the piano. I just wanted someone to play it. It bothered me that the piano sat there, open, and nobody touched its keys except accidentally when a drunken guest stumbled and had to hold on to the piano.

There was always the view of the city from my window. A blazing city, to use the doctor's term. Later when I learned more of the city, I saw the people who inhabited it, Filipinos among them, the very old and the very young, the lost and never found, their exposed lives beyond the blazing view. Candle-lit lives or what one saw under a dust- and dirt-coated bulb or what one sensed in total darkness. There were those that carried this darkness as they walked the streets of the city or sat on park benches wondering why no birds came, only stray dogs that littered the streets with their shit.

32

I had plans which kept changing as I thought them out again and again. I took notes and jotted down ideas. If I was going to give the Board a picture of what the magazine was going to contain, I ought to concentrate on the contents and leave the business angle to others, the organization experts. I would be ready with a few recommendations of my own. I wished Dr. Sotto would give me a chance to try them on him, but, alas, in his visits, the bottle and his confessions took precedence.

A business consultant firm should take over the initial business aspects of the magazine, advertising, circulation, promotion, office space, supplies and personnel with a summary of an estimate of costs for at least one year. Determine whether it was going to be a monthly or a quarterly, number of pages, etc.

My sole responsibility would be the magazine material.

The articles would be serious without being too ponderous and dull. There would be interesting studies into the psyche of the Filipino, his peculiar predicament as exile arising from cultural and historical accidents, and always pegged to current events. In other words, articles had to be meaningful and immediate, offering something personal and intimate to every reader. Articles that directly address the reader and make him feel they had been written for him. Not only the men, but the women of all ages as well should feel so addressed. The variety of materials would appeal to the new breed of Filipinos in the States, particularly those who resent being called Philippine hyphen American, because they believe there is no such animal, only Filipino. There was also a sizeable percentage of Filipinos that had to be served, those who belonged to the first and subsequent waves of immigrants around World War II, before and a little after. The oldtimers. And let no one on the staff forget the growing number of young ones, born of Filipino parents in this country from the fifties down to these blazing (really) seventies and well into the eighties. They read, too, didn't they, between trips to the mirror where every time they saw themselves, the way they looked, the way they sounded, their family names, those oddities they called mom and pop, they would ask and keep asking, who am I, what the hell am I, really?

The magazine should attempt at every opportunity to answer some, certainly not all, of their questions. They would not always be pleased with the answers and this should result in on-going discussion, a taking of sides, which would keep them reading and buying, looking forward to each issue. At this point in my thinking, it dawned on me that the magazine should be called simply: FILIPINO. Whether the initial letter was an F or a P didn't really matter. Anyhow some of us have difficulty distinguishing one from the other when we said the word.

The magazine was coming alive in my mind. I had notes on pad paper, notebooks, memo sheets. Clippings were all over my room. I had articles, rough drafts, columns, panels of photos with telling captions, sometimes lyrical and dripping with sarcasm, enlivened with humor, and others harsh, abrasive but true.

I told myself, get lost in the city, sniff around those places like a puppy where Filipinos live and die, introduce yourself to the new breed, get invited to their private clubs. Watch the guys play no-limit poker, their wives, high-stake mahjong. Listen to what they say above the sound of shuffled cards and tiles. Find out what they want to read in a magazine meant for them. What were they before they came here, before the goddess of good fortune touched their shoulders with her magic wand? What do they remember of their past in the homeland? Ask them: are you going back to visit only or to return for good? Whatever the answer, ask and keep asking why, why?

I got lost in the city all right. I learned something of what the Filipinos were before, a hint here and there of bitterness and frustration, sometimes a desperate struggling to attain the dream, the ultimate dream of wealth and luxury and ease. But I never learned what they wanted in a magazine. I don't think they ever bought a magazine to read except to look at pictures of beautiful men and women wearing the latest fashion or wearing nothing at all. Oh, I had accumulated stuff I would never be forgiven for if I published it in the magazine.

Thank you, Dr. Sotto, for letting me loose in the city.

Damn you, Dr. Sotto, for not warning me. Unless you yourself didn't have any idea of what I was bound to see. Unless you didn't suspect that even I, such as I was, could still be hurt. After a while, Dr. Sotto, this beautiful room you lent me to live in, on top of Diamond Heights, wasn't any good for anything except for writing my heart out, for crying quietly, for God's sake, while I gazed down the hills and valleys of your blazing city and saw old men waiting to die a long, long way from home; and angry young brown boys and girls who cursed their parents and spit on their own images, confused and secretly frightened.

12

DURING MY OCCASIONAL VISITS in San Jose, I realized that Professor Jaime was as much involved, although in a different manner as his wife was, in her business of providing homes for welfare recipients. Personally, I was more interested in his work at City College. I wanted to find out if there was any possibility of my teaching even one class only in the Philippine Studies Department which he headed. Yet no matter how hard I tried to steer him away from his favorite topic—his wife's business—he always came back to it. At first, he impressed me with his eagerness to pay tribute to his wife's business acumen and industry. But that was not all as I surmised later.

On one such visit, Professor Jaime droned on about the way the business was run.

"We used to deal directly with H.E.W.—that's Health, Education, and Welfare, in case you didn't know. But beginning January this year, our residents were handled by the Social Sexurity Service under the A.T.D.—that's Aid to the Totally Disabled. The funds come from the federal, state, and country coffers, but occasionally, we get residents on General Assistance who need temporary quarters, then their funds come from the county alone. These residents are referred to us by social workers. Prospective residents are taken around to look at three residential homes before they decide which place they prefer to stay in. An eligibility worker decides how much stipend each resident is entitled to, and many residents are assigned a social worker and a doctor to look after their needs. They are also given free medication and some pocket money amounting to $41 a month. Those who need more personal supervision now get as much as $229, while others get $190 a month for board and care."

"And Fely is in charge of all these?" I interrupted, trying hard to sound interested. It was all very dull and boring stuff, and I asked a question merely to break the Professor's monologue.

"Right," he said with enthusiasm. "I myself try not to get involved in the business."

35

"Doesn't your school work take up most of your time?"

"That's right, so I really try not to get involved too much. I mean, what the hell, it's business. We're able to pay the amortization on these two homes and then some. In these days of inflation, Fely has been a great help. She has always been. And she enjoys it, too."

"Why didn't I ever get to meet her in the Philippines?"

"You never visited us."

"I wasn't one of your brighter students."

"You were, too. You were not book smart, but you could write. You had a way with words. I'm proud of you, you know?"

"Thank you." I shouldn't have paused. I should have continued talking, asked him about his work. My chances of teaching a subject or two at City College. But I let the opportunity pass, and the Professor was back to his favorite topic.

"Now, if I may resume. Once the welfare patient decides he wants to stay in our home, we enter into a formal contract with him, sanctioned by the Welfare office. The contract requires us to provide board and lodging, as well as medical health supervision. We have to get clearance from the fire and health departments to obtain a license to operate a residential home. They come and look into the sanitation, food preparation, comfort and satisfaction of the residents. Twice a year, the licensing agency visits us to check and make sure we comply with their requirements—otherwise they revoke our business permit."

As the Professor talked, it occurred to me that perhaps I could use some of his information in my magazine.

"Some of your residents must have interesting case histories," I said.

"You bet," he replied with such vehemence that he snuffed the light from his pipe. "Fely had a hard time with most of our women residents. They were always complaining and behaving very badly among themselves and with the men. There was one particular girl. Patty. She was as close as I ever got to getting involved."

36

13

ONE NIGHT Fely came home visibly upset over a problem resident. It was not like her to get disturbed easily and show it. She was efficient in her job; her understanding and patience always carried her through many a crisis of one sort or another. Art sensed immediately that it was an unusual case. After all, the couple knew they had problem residents on their hands. All of them, without exception. That was the special nature of the residents in their care. But this case concerned a girl named Patty Grand. Art was not sure he knew her.

"What's her record like?" he asked Fely.

"You won't believe it. I shouldn't have admitted her. But she seemed all right in spite of her record."

"Maybe she isn't as bad as you think she is."

"I doubt it. No other home would have her."

"Then you had no choice but to take her in."

"But now look at all the trouble she has been giving me."

In something like a shock of recognition, Art remembered Patty. She was not bad looking in spite of the acne on her face and the scars on her arms. She had a high I.Q. and wrote poems, religious, crying poems. This was not the first time she had misbehaved and it looked like there would be no end to her capers.

Patty had been in mental institutions most of her life. At age 13 she had a son by her mother's husband. They had to marry her off to a sixty-year-old man, an ice-cream vendor, so she could have her child. At 14 she became officially a juvenile delinquent and was committed to a mental hospital. Her mother took care of her son who was made to believe as he grew older that Patty was his older sister.

She was barely twenty when Fely admitted her. She had finished at the top of her class in high school at Agnew State Hospital where she was a patient.

The first time Art saw her, she was pushing an elderly resident in a wheel chair. Now and then she stopped to arrange the old woman's dishevelled hair. Patty reminded Art of a student of his long ago at the University of Sto. Tomas who had acne,

37

too, and scars on her arms. They had the same smile, so innocent and shy and quite captivating.

Patty had problems in the worst way. She had a tendency towards nymphomania and because of it, she had extreme guilt feelings that drove her time and again to try to kill herself. Luckily, every time she felt suicidal, Art happened to be around, and he managed to talk her out of it. Sometimes, past midnight or in the early morning hours, the couple would rush to her side when she felt very depressed and suicidal and asked for Art. She had attempted suicide so many times that doctors thought she was just using it as a tool to manipulate others. But Art took her attempts seriously. A week would not pass without some kind of crisis in her life and she would send for Art. Some of these crises were real, others were only in her mind.

Her trust in Art must have started that day she showed him the poems she had been writing.

"You are a professor?"

"Yes, Patty."

"I want to show you some stuff if you promise not to make fun of me. I call them poems, I want them to be poems, but maybe they're not."

"Let me be the judge."

Art still had those poems. He kept them among his valued papers. Now and then he showed them to friends who might want to read them.

They were, indeed, as Art called them, crying poems. The imagery was unvaried: death and pain, the cross, calvary, skulls, temptation and remorse, with death as the irresistible temptress of all.

Art would get them from a folder when he remembered Patty and read them softly to himself or whomever he considered an appropriate listener. Like me. I jotted down some of the poems.

Starlight, star bright
Who will bring me home tonight?

    * * *

I believe, I believe
Yet I grieve
This life I live
Take me in your arms
My lover Death.

* * *

On the stone above my head
Carve my name in one day bread

* * *

Mirror mirror on the wall
Which skull is the prettiest of all?

* * *

Sweetest lover
Seducer Death
Thee I seduce
Ha, ha, ha, ha!

* * *

Forgive me, your straying lamb,
There are no pastures would have me
I don't deserve to live
I don't deserve to die.

* * *

Is your cross compared to mine
Heavier than all my wickedness?

* * *

Art asked her, "When do you write these poems?"

"Oh, so they're poems, the professor thinks they are.
Goody, goody!"

"Of course, they are. When do you write them?"

"Like when . . . any time, but especially after . . . after I've
been bad."

"You aren't bad."

"You're sweet. Fely's a sweet woman, isn't she now?"

"You are, too."

"You're joking."

"I'm telling you the truth."

"What do you think of my poems?"

"They're good. They move me. I feel I know what you're saying."

"Do you? How strange. Sometimes I don't. The words come out different from what I want to say."

"But they're sad. They're crying poems."

"Ha! My tears."

"Better than tears."

"Read them to me. Please?"

"My accent will ruin them."

"Go ahead. You can't ruin them worse than I have already."

Art had a sort of "contract" with her: that she would not attempt suicide without telling him when she felt like doing it.

"But I failed her, you know," Art confided. "Or she failed me. We failed each other. Not long after she left the home— Fely couldn't take Patty's problems any longer, my poor wife was becoming a nervous wreck—we learned that she had hanged herself from her bedpost in a hospital, in a town called Oroville, some thirty miles from Sacramento where she had been taken for observation. She knew she was going to die young and once she asked me if I would attend her funeral and I promised. I did, too. Fely came with me. She cried more than I did, but my grief was deep because it was tinged with guilt."

Art sincerely believed he had failed her. He could have found more time to be with her. Once she told him, "You're the only person who has reached me."

But what good was that now, Art kept telling himself. He was sure she had written other poems, but where were they? And who cared? He did. Very much.

14

DR. PACIFICO SOTTO and his wife, the former Imelda Valdez, left the Philippines for San Francisco soon after passing the medical board examination. This was in the sixties. No one in the circle in San Francisco to which they belonged knew much or anything about them, or so the couple hoped. In the Philippines, they didn't have too many friends either. They called their trip to the Philippines a delayed honeymoon which they richly deserved. And after their last visit to the homeland they decided to become U.S. citizens and stay here for good.

In those early years as young medical doctors in San Francisco, everyone who knew them assumed that they were childless. Dr. Sotto suspected that his friends, mostly other doctors like them practicing in the Bay area, joked behind his back about his being unable to father a child. The couple appeared out of place among their friends with families crawling with infants and toddlers. They must have surmised that Imelda couldn't have been the reason. A successful pediatrician with more patients than she could handle, Imelda looked like someone who would make an ideal mother. She looked so fertile, Mother Earth in person. She couldn't have been barren. She exuded an air of inexhaustible sexiness which she carried about her with gracious abandon. The fault must be in the urologist himself. Perhaps he had asked a colleague to do a vasectomy on him, or he could have done one on himself if that were possible.

But what a pity for such a beautiful couple not to have any offspring. How sad that the Sotto mansion on Diamond Heights did not resound to the patter of little feet. It was silent like a museum on a holiday and dark much of the time except during dinner parties when it blazed with lights and hummed in a babel of voices against a background of piped-in music. Much of the time it remained a crypt with lights turned low or pitch black, where the ghost-like presence of an old woman and her son moved about the indoor gardens, strange and unsmiling. So everybody who knew them or thought they did, sympathized with the Sottos in secret.

41

On nights when he came down to see me, Dr. Sotto seemed high on much more than the liquor he brought along with him on these visits. Even when his talk sounded serious, he remained jovial as if he really didn't want to be taken seriously. On such occasions, the best I could do in recording such moments was paraphrase what he said.

Perhaps you wonder how I can drink so much. I really don't. Or maybe I do, but it doesn't affect me at all. I don't touch a drop all day. I have work to do and I do it well. I know my responsibilities. Look at my hands. How steady. Let's see yours. Oh, well . . . I don't drink before dinner time except on weekends when I have no evening appointments at the clinic. Perhaps a wee bit of an aperitif, no more. But I have to, I gotta drink before going to bed. Makes me sleep like a . . . well, like a drunk. But of course! Before you came, David, I went out with friends, but I was careful. I knew I had to drive myself home. Imelda asks, why don't you just drink at home? Hell, she doesn't even drink tea. And I can't invite just anybody to drink with me here night after night. I hate to drink alone, don't you? I love to talk while I drink. The words come easy. That's why I'm glad you're here, David.

Are you comfortable? If there's anything you need, speak up. In your case, you don't need a damn drink to get at the words you need. Words come naturally with you. No, no . . . don't deny it. You're a writer.

God, I don't know why I feel so damned alone when I have so many friends. I'm not boasting, but I circulate in what you may call an international circle. But how many of them can I talk to? I don't even like their faces. Ugh!

Unlike other doctors, I seldom have to be on call twenty-four hours. Although I have patients every day, my Saturday schedules are full. Like today, I had fifteen. You have no idea. That's why you must visit me. What about next week? Put me on your calendar.

When you get down to it, it's no worse than a visit to the dentist. Yet even in this enlightened country some of my patients have to be persuaded to get rid of their funny ideas about the operation. Of course, some of them are just plain yellow. Chicken, I mean. But we all got yellow streaks, don't we? Except that some are better than others in hiding it, a kind of camouflage like loud words, belligerent gestures, braggadocio. Is that the right

42

word? You're the writer. I can only get drunk with this stuff. You can get drunk with words.

Anyway. . . so I spend more time talking them into it because at the last moment they get second thoughts.

"Are you sure, doctor, my sex life won't be affected?"

"Of course, it will be," I tell them. As I watch their faces get that funny oh-my-God expression, I add, "It will be better. No worry. No messing around with fertile periods, douches, the last-minute panic at the precise moment when the minutest interruption destroys everything that had been building up, with a frantic search for the diaphragm (Oh, my God, where did I put it? Hurry . . . hurry . . . turn on the light, I can't see a damn thing!)"

Then they start laughing. "You're a cunning oriental, doc. Go ahead!"

They submit timidly.

15

NOTES TO MYSELF:

Regular departments: what will they cover?

Profiles: don't be too New Yorkerish. Nobody will read that stuff. You're trying to reach readers who don't really love to read. They'd rather watch TV. Pictures, they'd love candid shots, photos that tell stories.

Articles: on a wide spectrum of current topics of interest peculiar to the Filipino away from home. Where will you get the writers? You can't write the whole damn magazine. It will smell of your sweat, babee!

Maps and charts (specify)—showing density of Filipino population in any number of counties in the U.S.A. Should be helpful to circulation department and promotions, but would the reader be interested? Dullsville!

16

ONE NIGHT Dr. Sotto talked of nothing else but Imelda. He started by complaining that she didn't have time anymore to relax on weekends and holidays. She was constantly on call. It was different in his case. None of his patients so far needed hospitalization. If the operation was performed as was usually the case on a Thursday or a Friday, the man experienced nothing more than some kind of discomfort and was able to return to work on Monday. The only advice—and often the last—he gave the patient was to avoid lifting heavy objects and to refrain from sexual intercourse for, say, ten days or two weeks.

On the other hand, Imelda was continuously on call. Her little patients were in different hospitals, often attended by high-strung parents who would send for Imelda (her beeper sounded like a broken record) at the least sign of restlessness or a fever that would not abate, a cough that sounded flat and dry. He, the poor husband, had to accompany her on these calls at night whatever the hour. In some cases when he was fast asleep (or dead drunk), she made excuses, gave instructions to nurses, promising to see the little one first thing in the morning. In very serious cases under such inconvenient circumstances she would drive herself with the houseboy sitting, usually asleep, beside her in the car.

Imelda got along better with their fellow doctors. She was charming where he was often petulant, intractable.

"I can't spell most of them," he admitted. "You know how most Filipinos are, sensitive, extremely so, what we would call onion-skinned—*pikon*—can't take a joke, and they're so paranoid, quite roundabout in their ways and suffer from an inferiority complex. What the hell, they've been in this country much longer than we have, they should have overcome by now these weaknesses. Why do we keep beating about the bush and playing games of evasion? Get straight to the point, say what the hell you don't want. I much prefer our American colleagues. Sport *lang.* No grudges."

I must have looked worried, thinking how I would manage if the members of the Board belonged to this type and he read my mind.

44

"The members of the Board are a fine lot. Make no mistake about it. They would know what I'm talking about. We get along fine."

He had yet to meet Filipino, American, or whatever nationality, in whatever occupation or persuasion, whom Imelda could not charm. Everybody adored her. In their minds she stood on a dais, royalty herself. They had her enthroned, as it were, crowned her Queen of Pediatricians, U.S.A.

Without attempting to hide his true feelings under a veneer of lightheartedness, he poured out his thoughts (as he did the scotch) while I listened, no longer envying as much as pitying him.

Imelda deserves all the accolade and perhaps more. After all she's truly a beautiful and generous woman. She thinks of our profession as a service to humanity, however trite and corny that sounds. She wants to give all her patients the very best she can. She wants to give them all her time. She doesn't have to answer every call at the most unholy hours of the night, but she does. She is a caring woman. But there is a point in our life together when she should learn to banish all professional cares and problems. God, we have problems of our own. She just can't let go. I know why. . . but even then. Well, what happens is she brings the hospital to our home. We discuss her patients. She talks about taxes and investments. It's like going to bed alone or, just as pathetic, with one of my colleagues in the clinic. But I know why she hates to talk about ourselves. She used to have such a healthy sense of humor when we were still in the Philippines before . . . well . . . before we decided to immigrate and try our fortunes here. Her laughter soothed me like a salve. Everything was right with our world. She was warm and caring, looking after my every wish and need. We laughed together and talked nonsense and loved every moment of it. It's so different now. We don't even quarrel anymore. Hardly. We have become strangers to each other. No, not that really, but it seems we have grown afraid of each other. We used to be such good friends. And lovers. Now she's startled the rare times I touch her. Don't, please, don't . . . Now she calls me vulgar when I try to be funny, describing to her how my patients' penises look, so down and sad and defeated not only during the fifteen-minute operation but before and after. You know they really look so damn funny. Sometimes I laugh all by myself recalling what they look like in their various postures of fear, I mean, their penises, cold and boneless meat that had never had their prime.

45

As I have said earlier, Imelda's not only an excellent pedia-trician but an astute business woman. Her instincts—or hunches actually—never fail her in investments that count. And what investments don't count even in the best of times?

"What does she think of this project, I mean, the magazine? "

During the few times I met with the Board members and their wives, the ladies kept to themselves and every time they looked my way I said to myself, Goodbye, Mister Editor: fare-well, *Filipino*. They made me feel as if I were an evil influence on their husbands that threatened their security, their lives.

"Well," he began, pausing ominously.

I knew it! None of the wives were in favor of the project. I told Dr. Sotto about my feelings, my suspicions. What made it worse for me was the fact that I really needed the job and the wives must have thought I was simply out to serve my selfish interests at their expense. It made me feel like a parasite.

"You see," he continued, "all you need to do is convince me that it's an excellent idea and, more important, that you can do the job."

"I'm sure I can do the job as editor-in-chief," I said, won-dering whether the anxiety showed in my voice. "But I'm not sure what you mean by excellent. If by this you mean will it make money immediately, I doubt very much whether the returns will be of the magnitude some of you expect on your invest-ments during the first year or, say, the first six issues if we decide that it's going to be a monthly. Let's wait and see what our busi-ness consultants have to say."

"That's the trouble. Imelda thinks it's not a sure-fire invest-ment."

"I had the impression," I said, with still that funny feeling that I was trying too hard to hold on to what looked like a great job, "that all you were looking for was a chance to serve our countrymen here while at the same time finding another source of investments. I take it you have much more money than you know what to do with."

"Not exactly. But service, indeed, is paramount in our minds. Unfortunately, our wives look at it from another point of view. They are *pa seguro*, nothing chancy for them. But let's not talk about this now. We'll cross our bridges . . . how do you say it now?"

"Before they fall."

He laughed. "Yes, something like that."

46

Imelda was not exceptionally bright as a student in medical school. Just a bit above average in a group where a majority were honor students, valedictorians and salutatorians in high school. But she had the right personality. Her patients got well, the little angels, just looking at her, listening to her assuring voice. Her bedside manner was superb. She was born with it.

As usual, it was past midnight when the doctor walked to the door to say goodnight. There had been times when he would walk to the door in the act of leaving, then change his mind, come back to the room and resume his talk. He would not actually leave until an hour or so later. I didn't have the guts to ask him to go. After all . . .

"Good night, David. I enjoyed talking to you; I always do," he said as I held the door to close it after him. "You know," he continued, "sometimes, Imelda shows she still retains her old sense of humor. For instance, tonight, on my way down here, she said, 'If I didn't know you too well, I'd suspect you're in love with David.'"

He was still chuckling as I shut the door.

17

AS A COPY READER and sometimes desk man after a successful stint as provincial correspondent for the *Philippines Herald*, I used to go home past midnight when a special edition was due. A good-looking young man, an apprentice linotypist, often waited for me to take me home in his car. He said he lived not far from where I was staying. It was not until later that I found out that he lived in Caloocan, many kilometers away in the opposite end of town outside Manila. When I asked him about it, he said he didn't mind, but I began to feel uncomfortable. I recalled that he used to touch me when we talked, but I assumed it was just his way of expressing himself. It was much later that I realized he was a homosexual and wanted to make love to me. So I avoided him after that until one night when he cornered me in the men's room. He was not violent, but his face looked terrible and pitiful as he cried, "I mean you no harm, David. I love you, I just do. God, can I help it if I do?" He broke down sobbing the way

47

a man cries who has no other recourse but tears. I gave him some toilet paper to wipe his face with.

Since then I have been gifted with a built-in radar, my own dependable penis. It tells me when I am about to be propositioned by one of these sad men (why in heaven's name do they call themselves gay?). It goes in hiding. In serious onslaughts of intent it disappears for a long time, once for more than a week. I wanted to put out an ad in our paper under Lost and Found. "Lost: a penis belonging to a promising journalist. No questions asked. Address: DDT, Editorial Department, this paper."

So far I felt certain that Dr. Sotto was not one. If he were, the darn thing would definitely go in hiding again. And I might have to take an ad under personals in our projected magazine similar to the one I thought of earlier except that instead of "no questions asked," I would insert: "Only one question asked, no, two questions (to the tune of a recent song hit): "Oh, did you happen to see the most beautiful penis in the world and if you did, was it crying?"

18

REMINDERS FOR FUTURE REFERENCE

Clippings (an assortment):
* Filipino Blood Flows in Penance
* Impalements, Flogging Mark Holy Week (Manila, (UPI)
* Special Christmas Offer: Money Transfers to the Philippines Rate: P7 per $1.00
* We move money
* Filipino, Arabic: "The National Board of Education adopted yesterday the use of Pilipino as a medium of instruction starting this school year for Grade I and Arabic for schools or areas where its use is necessary." Lead paragraph to news item from Manila.
* A double spread ad from travel agencies in San Francisco captioned: HAVE YOU BEEN AWAY TOO LONG?

Cruel, I thought. Made me think of other ways of getting
rid of them: gas chambers, kicking 'em in the groin, bending their
backs . . . You see they've had too much backbone.
More.
Visit greenhouses, down the Sunset Area, also in the suburbs.
Am told they're lovely any time of the year. Should stop me from
gravitating too much and too often to the Tenderloin District
even if Little Manila is there, so what?
Heard a song with the words "In my little corner of the
world," and I've been moping all day.

19

FATHER BELARMINO didn't look too different without his
cassock. The Professor had told me he was his guest once in San
Jose, occupying the same bed in the guest room. So I knew he
was in San Francisco. Still I hardly recognized him. He was so
short I towered over him. This was not the way I remembered the
Father. We had always stood eye to eye. Could he be shrinking?
But he was not that old.

"Father Belarmino," I said, taking both his hands in mine,
wanting to hug him. I was so happy to meet someone at last
whom I knew in the old country. And, too, my favorite priest!

"You're David," he said. "What are you doing here?"

"Father, that's what I should ask you," I said, smiling.

"Frankly, I'm afraid I'm lost," he said shamefacedly. "Where
are we?"

"Mortal sin, Father?" I asked, beaming down on him.

We were in the Tenderloin District and the poor padre didn't
know where he was. He looked bewildered. I asked how his dona-
tion campaign was doing. Fine, he said. There were still quite
a few churches in San Francisco where he had permission to say
mass and make a plea for alms for his little parish in the Philippines. As we talked, it seemed surreal that we were right in the
middle of San Francisco's notorious area, surrounded by blinking

49

lights and neon signs that were beginning to show distinctly against the falling darkness.

A beautiful man in white flannel cutaway, his face ruddy with rouge and eyes dark with mascara, stood by the door of the House of Ecstasy and tried to usher us in.

"No, thanks, mister, no," Father Belarmino said, dodging the tempter's grasp.

As we walked on leisurely, the Father asked, "What's in there?"

"Naked bodies, Father, what else? Just read those signs."

His lips moved as in prayer: Cupid's Corner. The Tunnel of Love. House of Joy. The Powers Nude Encounter Parlor. Naked City. Den of Love.

He shook his head, biting his lips. "America, America," he said softly, sadly. "What's an encounter parlor?"

"All of them are encounters of some sort or other, Father." I tried to describe what I had heard went on inside those places. On Kearny, we found a Filipino restaurant and we went in.

We sat facing each other across a table so small, I could smell the sweat on his body and hear his heavy breathing. He was listening intently. I told him what I knew. If I had described in detail what went on inside those shops and parlors, I would have felt revolted myself. The rare occasions I had been tempted to see X-rated movies, I felt sorry for the men and women, actually very young boys and girls, who debased themselves for a fee, going through the simulated motions of the sex act, surrounded by a crew of camera men, directors, and that motley crowd that usually hung around such studios.

As I talked to Father about what I knew of these places, I dwelt on what I considered relatively less offensive, and without unnecessary details.

For instance, in some of those places, the customer engages a naked woman to talk to him from a glassed-in booth, mostly about sex or read to him from a dirty book. The name of the game is "no touch."

"Like Filipino custom," Father said.

"The customer could ask the woman to do practically anything except engage in sex and so long as he doesn't touch her."

"What does he get out of it?"

"That's his kind of kicks."

"Kicks?"

I was reluctant to resume the subject. Even if I knew that Father Belarmino wanted as much information as was possible under the circumstances, I was afraid to trespass the confidentiality beyond a point of no return. I respected him very much. Besides I didn't know too much of the subject myself except in a vague, street-wise way.

"That's all," I said, as the waiter brought in our food. Pancit canton. Beef steak Tagalog smothered with onions. Ampalaya with shrimps. "Looks good, doesn't it, Father?"

"It's terrible," he sighed and I knew he was not thinking of food.

What had I done? Did I talk too much? Father looked like he was going to cry. His curiosity, like a child's, was touching. Did he have capacity enough to understand and forgive? I felt like asking him to forgive me, too.

Somehow we couldn't just ignore the food. I felt ravenous. After a while, the Father started eating and saying something like, "This is good. Just like home, *hindi ba?*"

Our talk shifted to Father's alms campaign for his church in San Juan. His eyes shone when he revealed that the response everywhere was heartwarming. "Including Americans," he said. But he needed more money; he had to visit other parishes, talk to more people.

Father insisted on paying for the meal. I tried to settle for a dutch treat, considering the state of my finances, but he would not have it any other way. He had always been a generous person.

I had been walking all day except for a couple of hours I spent in the Public Library, which I had begun to visit frequently.

"Thank you, Father, and good night," I said softly as he went his way and I went mine—towards Diamond Heights.

He was gone so quickly in the crowded street. Under those garish lights, I doubted for a moment if, indeed, he had been there at all.

20

A YOUNG MAN who worked in the reference section of the public library told me he had seen a colored map of the United States, issued by the Bureau of Immigration of the Department of

Justice, indicating the population distribution of Filipino immigrants. Or maybe it was issued by the Census Bureau, the man was not sure, but he had definitely seen one and he would take time to look for it. He told me to return after the lunch break.

When I came back, he still hadn't located it, but he assured me he would have it ready for me the next day sometime in the evening before closing hour. I planned on having copies of the map made to the size of the magazine as a kind of fold-in supplement in one of the issues.

It was a beautiful evening, not too cold. I lingered at the library feeling at home, as I always did in libraries no matter how small or big. This one was huge with several floors, marble stairways and manned elevators. Some of those behind the counters and desks looked like Filipinos. I wanted to find out for sure if they were, but I couldn't see myself asking each of them, are you a Filipino? I would feel foolish. I believed I looked Filipino enough although I have been mistaken for something else, once for an Eskimo.

The library hardly had any books written by Filipinos, in translation or in English. A half shelf contained less than a dozen Philippine titles, most of them printed at the turn of the century. None of my favorite authors among Filipinos writing in English had their works on that tiny shelf. It appeared on this evidence that Philippine literature in English did not exist in America, hardly, anyway, judging from the token samples I had seen in other libraries in the United States. And here I was crazy enough to think that a Filipino magazine written in English would make it in this country.

I met an interesting lady librarian who was as Filipino as her looks and her accent. It wasn't long before we knew a lot about each other. I introduced myself as the editor of a Filipino magazine in English that would soon hit the newsstands of San Francisco. She was the daughter of an illustrious Filipino intellectual, a former President of the University of the Philippines. She showed me old photos to prove it, as though she had to. There was a resemblance between her and a nun whom I knew vaguely in Manila.

She apologized for the library's lack of contemporary books on the Philippines and by Filipinos. She knew quite a few Filipino writers in English who were now residing in the United States. Some of them passed through the city and stayed in this country. Many more, she said, were right now in the Philippines seeking immigration status in the United States.

"Martial law is making it quite difficult for some of them to immigrate, but the repressive regime in the Philippines is too much for those who can only write in an atmosphere of freedom. Some of those who stay on will have to learn how to deal with the restrictions on free expression."

"I must quote you, may I?" I said, opening my little notebook.

"How did you get out?" she asked.

I told her I beat martial law by about a year. I was interested in the Filipino writers in English in the States who could write for my magazine. I asked her if she knew their addresses. She promised to look.

But I never saw or heard from her again. The few times I visited the library I looked for her but I was told she was on an extended leave of absence.

One evening, I passed by a room on the second floor of the library where a group of adults sat listening to a woman explain what looked like lines of a poem on the blackboard. She looked younger than her audience, even if her hair was grey, a shade of blonde. She had lovely, tapering fingers which I watched entranced as she held a piece of chalk. She gestured as she talked about the poem in a heavy accent, calling attention to the soft and hard lines. I had never had a teacher as attractive. I sat down on a vacant seat close to the door and listened attentively, watching her unsmeared lips, her unmanicured fingers, her, what we call in Pilipino, "talking eyes." I think she saw me come in and take a seat. I was afraid she would send me out, but after that brief glance, she never turned in my direction again.

By then I knew what I had stumbled into, a poetry workshop which I had read about advertised in leaflets and posters in and around the building, a two-week session sponsored by the Poetry Center of San Francisco.

When it was over I waited for a chance to thank the teacher for allowing me to stay on even if I was not enrolled. It was a long wait. There were several women and a few men who surrounded her, eager to talk to her. Some had manuscripts which they wanted the instructor to criticize. I was worried she would criticize them right there and I would not have a chance to talk to her. Big deal, I said to myself. Besides, after thanking her, what else would I tell her? Ma'am, would you care to contribute

53

to my still unborn magazine? Who said there would be poems in my magazine? Oh, yes, it had crossed my mind. As fillers only.

Luckily for me, she collected her students' papers and walked towards the door, pursued by the babbling group of student-poets. Her glance fell on me and she smiled.

"You're a new student," she said in her rather mannish voice.

"No ma'am," I said, but she didn't hear me above the babel of her students. I made no attempt to wade into the group to reach her.

She made a swift gesture towards me that completely took me by surprise. "Come," she said as she extended her hand to take mine. Like old friends, we walked out the room hand in hand down the stairways, past the guards at the door of the building, and out into the chilly night. Her students, their voices trailing, faded away and we were alone.

"Do you have a car?" she asked.

"No," I answered.

"Get in," she said, gesturing towards a rundown Beattle. "I'll take you home."

"No, thanks," I said, "but you can't."

"Why not?" she asked imperiously, her accent heavier than usual. "Unless you don't want me to."

"No, it isn't that. I said you can't," I repeated as she fumbled for the lock on the driver's side of the car. The parking area was ill lighted. It felt more chilly in the dark. "My home is thousands of miles away, across the Pacific."

"I thought so. You look like an orphan. Let me take you home with me then."

"I guess your true home is also a thousand miles away."

"Yes, across the Atlantic. Farther away. Past the Mediterranean. My original home is a little town near Paris."

"I'm from the Philippines," I said, walking around the car to sit beside her. I sat on some books and sharp objects. "Ouch!" I exclaimed, jumping up. With one sweep of her hand, she cleared the seat, pushing everything on the floor.

The car didn't get heated up until we were almost at her place. We said very little on the way.

As we entered her apartment, she said, "Well, for tonight, we're home. The both of us."

Her apartment smelled like stale bread. It's the smell I notice first in any house I visit except for the obvious things

54

that grab the eyes. Cluttered ash trays turn me off as well as a woman who smells like one. There were no ash trays and she didn't smell like one. Always it's the smell that touches and embraces me, draws or repels me. I don't notice colors, curtains, draperies, furniture, except their absence. I gravitate towards paintings and books. There were books on the shelves and on the coffee table and aquariums of various sizes, all lighted up, in every corner. It seemed the fish which had not been moving when we got in started to swim about as soon as they felt the lady's presence.

She ran to each of the aquariums and purred as she put her face close to the glass, mumbling something, perhaps a poem the fish understood. She turned to me and asked, "Do you write poems?"

"When I was younger and foolish."

"In your language, I suppose."

"I don't write in my language. I have been speaking and writing in English ever since I learned to speak and write."

"You don't speak your language at all?"

"I speak it, but I don't write it."

"Very strange," she said, shaking her head, her grey hair tumbling in a cascade.

"I was born in a U.S. Naval Base in the Philippines."

"What were you doing there?"

"My mother was there. My father worked at the U.S. Naval Base."

"Hmmm."

"I can write letters in our language, but I'm not sure about my spelling. I can't write creatively in our national language. I have to use English."

"Really? I understand you have many dialects?"

"Lots of 'em. I speak a dialect different from our national language."

"Come," she said for the second time that night, leading me to her bedroom. It was a small room cluttered with odds and ends. The bed was unmade. The sheets were a dull brownish color with petal designs long faded. The dresser was littered with bottles of all sizes and shapes, medicines among the cosmetics. A huge mound that must have been the bed cover was piled high on a sofa, its ends spilling over on the floor partly covered by a rug of indeterminate origin, either Oriental or K-Mart. There were no pictures, neither photographs nor paintings. Against a wall by the side of the bed was a blackboard. I couldn't believe my eyes—a blackboard! An eraser and pieces of chalk lay on the edge. It had been cleanly wiped. Perhaps it had not been used for sometime now. What use could she have for a blackboard in her bedroom? Did she invite students to resume the class discussions here?

"Now, if you please," she said, handing me a piece of chalk, "write the names of the different Philippine dialects while I brew some coffee. You drink coffee, I hope."

"Yes, but . . . " I wanted to suggest, what about writing my name first? She had not asked me. Although I was in her bedroom I was still a nameless entity to her.

"Go ahead, don't be shy."

There was nothing to be shy about. I felt something was terribly wrong, but I couldn't tell what it was. But I knew it was there as sure as the presence of that blackboard on which I was now to write the names of Philippine dialects. How many of the nearly one hundred dialects could I name? And what the hell for? Although she was not a beauty, not even in a poetic sense, she didn't reek of cigarette butts, and that was definitely in her favor.

"Look," I said, following her to the kitchen, "I'd rather talk to you or you let me brew the coffee or . . . or something."

"Go back and do your assignment," she ordered, pushing me towards the bedroom. God, she was strong.

What the hell had I gotten into? Every time she said, "Come," I felt titillated. I wanted something else that sent a surge of life between my legs. She wanted Philippine dialects. How many did I really remember?

"Tagalog," I wrote reluctantly and broke the chalk in two unintentionally. I felt like a damn fool.

Disgusted I threw the chalk away and hurled myself on the bed. The springs creaked under my weight and I almost fell through to the floor. I jumped up, picked up the broken chalk and started writing down the dialects I could remember. I thought, why not humor her and let's see what happens.

"Keep going. Great going," she said with a note of urgency which I associated with passion, not dialects. Her voice sounded so close, I felt weak in the knees.

"Don't stop now. Please keep going." I remembered other bedroom scenes, same words, same urgency. I ran towards the kitchen, ready to pounce on her.

56

"Well, okey, come and get it," she smiled, offering a plate of sandwiches. Thinly sliced ham on white bread. Did I take ketchup or mustard? It was only then I realized how famished I was. The coffee was strong and good.

"Sorry, I can remember only a few of the dialects, the principal ones," I said after I had had my fill.

"That's not important. It's my fault."

"What is? "

"I've not been honest with you. You're not the first Filipino I've brought home. You see, I knew a Filipino once. He ñooked like you. I thought he had come back to me. Same smile. Same lost look in the eyes."

I thought of my father.

"Did he look a bit older than I?" I wanted to add, did he carry a toothbrusth wherever he went?

"No. As old as you. Perhaps even a bit younger."

"We Filipinos all look alike in some people's eyes."

"We can have more coffee in the bedroom," she said, "while you tell me about those dialects you have written on the board."

It was one of the dullest moments in my life. But not to her. We went on and on about dialects and I wondered how the night was going to end.

"Now I'm wiser than before we met," she said after some time. I took her statement to mean the class was dismissed.

I had never before or since run away from a woman's bedroom as fast as I did that night. She never asked for my name. She didn't give me her name or her old Filipino boy friend's.

What the hell was going on?

21

AS A VERY YOUNG MAN trying to write, I took a job as a part time correspondent for a Manila newspaper. I did fairly well contributing space fillers for the provincial section of the paper, news bits on conferences held in my province, the laying of cornerstones, commencement exercises, an occasional visit by a big shot from the central government whom I was often too frightened to interview and saw only from a distance. But I attended meetings of very important people who fielded questions from more competent and less insecure reporters than I. These I reported. I wrote as lengthily as I could, filling my reports with the minutest and usually irrelevant details because I got paid by the column inch. My Manila provincial editor seemed bent on starving me to death the way he slashed my reports into mere fragments of the original. He omitted the names I included or allowed only a few to be mentioned, inserting "and others" for what I had hoped would mean more column inches of text— and more money--for me. Some of my reports never saw print at all.

Thus I remained in absolute limbo. Anonymous was not just my middle name, it was my pen name as well. All my reports were datelined "Albay" and ended with "Contributed." Who cared about my name?

One day our provincial governor announced he would not collect taxes unless he got millions of pesos in public works funds which the province badly needed. Since he had become governor (he belonged to the minority party), the province received less and less in public works money. His announcement came at a bad time. The President of the Philippines had just announced the need to step up tax collection. Well known for his mercurial temper, the President lost no time in ordering our governor to show up at Malacañang Palace. In an unexpected show of courage, our governor refused and sent his regrets, feigning illness.

That's when my paper sent me a telegram, signed by God Almighty, the editor-in-chief himself (not the puny provincial editor). I was thrilled and frightened. The order was for me to interview the governor and file a report by wire on the state of his health. Unless he was really sick, the governor's act would mean insubordination, a rebellion of sorts. Big News.

When I arrived in the provincial building, there was the usual crowd of hangers on, job seekers, ward leaders, municipal mayors, who had come to express in person their one hundred per cent unstinted support of the governor's action; salesmen, sweepstakes vendors, and a few pretty girls with nothing on their minds, but I could have been wrong. I brought my credentials, a press card, just in case I was asked to show proof of my identity. But nobody asked me who I was. No one paid any attention to me. So I drifted on with the fluid crowd until I found myself inching through the door of the governor's office. For the first time I saw the man at close range.

He was big for a Filipino, taller than I, and ruddy like a foreigner, as some of his ancestors were known to be. There was persistent talk that among his forebears were Spanish friars. He looked like a Spanish priest himself. I imagined him in a soutane and there he stood, a Capuchin monk. But this one was far from priestly. He was shouting expletives and obscenities in Spanish, Filipino and English. Unless his demands were met, he wasn't going to be cowed into collecting taxes for Malacañang, so his tirade went, saliva splattering from his mouth.

He looked flushed; he could be running a temperature, unless he had already drunk a lot that early in the day, which was possible. He looked like a sick man, indeed. Every few minutes he walked over to a chamber pot on the floor back of his desk to urinate. Then he would shake his penis (I couldn't see this, but what the hell, I do it all the time), zip up his fly, turn to the crowd and resume his harangue.

The next day, my story was played up in my paper, but it didn't read anything like the piece I wired my editor. There was no mention of the governor's frequent visits to the chamber pot in his crowded office. I was not able to talk to him, but my story sounded like I had an exclusive interview with exclusive information: that the governor 'had an old kidney trouble which was acting up again and his personal physician had advised him not to make the long trip to Manila.

After my story came out, the governor sent for me. To this day I don't know how he found out that I was the author of the news item about him. It didn't have any by-line. I was helping my landlady dress a chicken for dinner when the governor's men came. They were burly men reeking of cigar and beer; a gun stuck out from under the belt of one of the potbellies. I threw the chicken into the cauldron of boiling water and hurried out to my unexpected guests. I barely had time to dress and put on my shoes. I was so scared during the ride in a limousine marked "For Official Use Only," I could hardly keep from urinating.

The governor turned out to be a nice gentleman, quite civil to a lowly taxpayer like me. I filed two more reports that got banner headlines—and this time, they carried my name! When the governor finally agreed to see the President, he took me with him, but I didn't see the President. Somehow I got stranded in the newspaper building. I saw the magnificent quarters of my paper and its sister publications, the loud and monstrous rotary presses, the cluttered desks and the men and occasional women behind them. I was filled with awe. I knew what I didn't want to be any longer: an anonymous, insignificant provincial correspondent, whose life was always a few column inches away from starvation and oblivion. I knew what I wanted to be: a big name like one of those men and women who run the paper behind their cluttered desks.

Maybe an editor.

Why the hell not?

22

NOTES:

Am I on the right track or have I been wasting my time, I keep asking myself, looking over my notes, some scribbled so badly I cannot decipher them. Most of them made sense when I wrote them down, something to remember.

If you can't decide where to place the material, don't bother. You may be right, it doesn't belong. A third column will prove not only ambitious but messy. (What am I talking about?)

What sells? To whom? How would I know?

Human interest stuff? Sensationalism? I want it factual and relevant. Damn it, there's that word again. Relevant. To whom? Meaningful is what I mean. Varied enough to include all types of readers of the magazine.

Filipinos are not known for good reading habits. The truth is, they'll do anything else but read. Look at their lavish, *moderne*, expensive homes. No libraries. If you find a library, it's usually a token shelf of books, mostly encyclopedias, or coffee table books acquired for status and purchased to blend with the furniture (and usually priced like furniture, too). Some of their libraries are fake like the fireplaces in the homes of millionaire Filipinos in Forbes Park in Makati, Manila.

So what will make potential readers buy the magazine?

Be sure that their names are spelled right and in bold types. Their titles, if any, including the lowly A.A. (Associate in Arts). And don't forget the smiling picture.

60

Sell stuff like dreams? Opiate? Blind mirrors but not too blind to lie that all is well, youth hasn't fled, beauty's intact.

Damn it, I wish I knew. I thought I did. But the more I looked around and got involved in the peculiar life in the city, the less certain I became about the nature of the magazine.

Maybe I should chuck the whole thing and do something else to stay on, if not in San Francisco, at least somewhere in this country. Or Canada, why not? Africa perhaps?

23

A TALL, TANNED WOMAN wearing flaring trousers which I thought were a balloon skirt, caught up with me near the Crocker Bank on Market Street. There weren't too many pedestrians that early in the morning on a week day. It was a little past eight; the city hadn't quite awakened yet. Bums curled up in sleep at doorways. On the pavements and street corners a low wind tossed about the night's refuse, newspapers, leaflets, empty boxes, beer cans. The stores were not yet open. Nothing seemed imbued with life except the all-night eateries, the 24-hour peep shows and adult bookstores.

It was one of those mornings when what I really wanted to do was play tennis, but I didn't know how to go about it. Where were the nearest courts and how would I find a partner willing to play me? So I decided to do some brisk walking. I had started quite early and by the time I found myself on Market I was a bit winded and hungry. I heard hurried steps behind me.

"Hello there," the girl said in a husky voice when she finally caught up with me.

"Oh, hello," I said, noting her tan and her health which radiated from her face, her clean, neutral scent. This abounding health oozed from her the way sex does from other girls. She was a bit taller than I on her flat sandals.

"I must talk to you," she said, her tone and her face serious, almost grim.

"What about?" I asked, looking around, fearing a trap of some sort. Surely, not that early in the morning.

"If you have an appointment, I don't want to delay you."

"I have no appointment. Nothing."

"I thought so. Could you use some coffee?"

We were standing not far from an all-night cafe which looked like it had not yet been swept or freshened up, but it was already full of customers, most of whom were not eating or drinking, just sitting as if they had been there all night and would stay all day. We found a table and the girl ordered coffee for two. She glanced towards me and I said, black. "Two black," she said to the waitress who came to wipe our table.

She looked Italian or Jewish, but how the hell could one tell by physical looks? She was a handsome girl, so healthy, she could be a star athlete. I wanted her to smile so I could see what her teeth looked like. If only she would smile—would her teeth be all there?

"Well," she began still unsmiling, "as I was saying, there's a lot more to this meeting than you think. A voice told me very early this morning, 'Get up and go, Thelma. Get off the American Savings Bank, cross Market, and you'll see him.' Which was what I did—and there you were. I knew it the moment I saw you."

"Now, wait a minute," I protested, trying to smile away my apprehension. "I don't understand. What's this voice or something that told you . . . "

"It's a long story."

The coffee came and she waited until the waitress was out of earshot. Then she resumed talking in a whisper, her elbows on the table and her face close to mine.

"By the way, what's your name?"

"You know so much already, do I have to tell you?"

She tapped me playfully on the arm. "If I knew I wouldn't have asked. Please?"

"David," I said, pronouncing it the American way. I didn't want to go into a hassle, as a I sometimes did, with new American acquaintances over so trivial a thing as the proper pronunciation of my name.

"You see, David, I have this peculiar gift of knowing things in advance."

"Clairvoyance," I said, interrupting her, but she ignored me.

"Perhaps it's a curse, this prescience, what you call, clairvoyance. I was standing near that joint when you passed by, walking slowly like a jogger out of wind after doing several miles.

62

As soon as I saw your face, I felt something, I felt drawn to you and I lost no time in pursuing you. Didn't you find it strange, me, coming to you that strong?"

"No," I answered truthfully, "just amazing."

"That's the word, amazing. You've got amazing vocabulary for an innocent abroad."

She looked so fresh and clean, as if she had just come from a hot, fulfilling bath. What could I say? After a cup of coffee, what could be better than a girl so fresh and clean?

"I knew you were coming into my life," she persisted. "And you knew this, didn't you? You knew I was coming into your life." She tugged at my arm as if to coax me to say, it's true, what you say is true.

"You see," she continued, "we know each other; we've met before."

"We have? Where? I don't remember. I've not been in San Francisco that long."

"Somewhere. Not here. Somewhere." She smiled, showing a perfect set of teeth. She seemed more wholesome when she smiled.

"Do you know what country I come from?" I asked.

"I've never seen a man look so unmistakably Filipino, and I've met many Filipinos all over the United States. You're a lovely people."

I felt warmed by her compliment, I wanted to give a toast to my ubiquitous countrymen. At least, a *mabuhay*, as I sipped my coffee.

"I'm not talking of cities or countries. I'm talking of an entirely different place, not this one," she said, smiling mysteriously. Her smile touched me like a child's.

She moved closer to me until our foreheads almost touched and I could feel her warm breath on my face. She put her hand on mine and pressed it hard. "Oh, David," she sighed. "You knew, didn't you? All the time you knew."

I was not sure what it was I was supposed to know all the time, but what the hell, this early in the day, I might as well play along, see where this amazing encounter would end.

She held on to me tightly as we walked to her place. She said she didn't live very far. It was a nippy season of the year. By the time we reached her place on Guerrero Street, it seemed we had walked for an hour no less. We walked arm in arm, her weight on my body as she said things I found difficult to follow.

63

I had been jogging and walking since daybreak and I was beginning to wear out.

Her apartment was on the third floor of a narrow, shoddy building that must have been constructed in the nineteenth century or earlier.

"Oh, David," she sighed clutching at me as I threw myself on the nearest couch, exhausted. She fell down on the couch with me and touched my face. "Have I made you wait too long?"

As a matter of fact, she had.

The naked woman standing before me had scars that looked like dried up centipedes all over her body, from the cleavage of her breasts to her stomach, her sides, her back, along one thigh, ending somewhere between her legs.

I tried not to look horrified, but I was. She took my hand and guided it all over her body, touching the scars which made me cringe. She was damp with sweat. All desire ebbed from me as my hand travelled down her flesh and she talked of numerous operations and sutures she had undergone to save her life. She must have been badly cut up.

"If I were a cat, I'd be living my ninth life by now," she said, trying to sound light.

"But you look so healthy," I said.

"I am," she replied, and she showed me. Everything she did was like magic. It was as if she had erased the scars from her body and they were no longer there for me to touch. What if she believed that we had known each other in another life? Perhaps I was David and she was Goliath's daughter. In another incarnation. We could have been gods. Or animals.

"Can you imagine," she asked, "what we must have said to each other then?"

"Moo," I said.

"Moo? Why moo?"

"Because I could have been a cow, both of us were cows."

"Mmmmmmmoooo," she lowed into my ear. "Oh, David, you're such a beautiful person. God, how I want you."

And she proceeded to show me.

64

24

THERE WAS A NOTE from Dr. Sotto waiting for me when I came in that night. It lay on a commode near my bed under a bottle of Black Label. It could have been scribbled in a hurry or perhaps that was how he wrote letters and prescriptions. I had difficulty deciphering the words. His signature was a mere scrawl.

Dear David,

How's everything? Fine, I hope. Will you be ready to meet the Board, say, at the end of the month? That will be on Sunday next week. I'll tell you where as soon as I know the venue. Give me a ring when you can.

P.S. Thought we'd kill this bottle together, Let's do that sometime soon.

When I rang him up, Imelda answered in what I thought was a sleepy voice.

"David here. Is the doctor in?"

"No, he's out. Where are you now?"

"Here in the basement. Hope I didn't wake you up. But I got a note from the doctor asking me to call him. Sorry, I didn't know it was this late."

"It's all right. So you've just arrived."

"Yes, ma'am."

"How's your work going?"

"Fine."

"Are you comfortable?"

"Yes, ma'am. And thank you, ma'am."

"You sound like a school boy. Do I sound like a school ma'am?"

"No, ma'am. I mean, no."

"That's better. I'll tell him you called."

"Thank you, doctora."

"Good night."

25

OBVIOUSLY WORRIED, Professor Jaime called from San Jose saying that Fr. Belarmino had not been heard from for nearly a month. Usually, he visited during week days to get his mail from the Philippines and from churches in the United States. Sundays the parish where he visited allowed him to say mass and ask for donations for his church. He chose to make his pitch at the masses attended by most of the Filipinos in the parish. After the mass, the Filipinos sponsored a brunch for everybody present during the services, including their American friends. Fr. Belarmino received additional pledges this way.

When word reached me that Fr. Belarmino was officiating at the 11 o'clock mass at St. Joseph's on Howard Street, I decided to attend. It would be like old times. When he became parish priest of the church of San Juan, he inherited a decaying church building from a long line of Dominican fathers that dated back to the late eighteenth century. The Dominicans had their indelible stamp on the church, on its ancient rites that followed life's cycle from birth to marriage to death. It cost money to get baptized, married, or buried. There was a big hassle over the choice of sponsors and godparents. A child's Catholic confirmation could cost more money and a long wait because it was dependent on the bishop's pastoral visits which were as capricious as his moods and various commitments, not to mention his arthritic joints and asthmatic condition.

When the Dominicans knew that their days were numbered, they seemed less inclined to visit the houses of the sick and the dying. Their masses appeared less fervent and sincere, more of an ordeal that had to be done with in a hurry.

When Fr. Belarmino came to our parish, he had to start from scratch. The parishioners had become quite indifferent. A coldness, a spiritual lassitude had overcome them like a contagion of the flesh. Only the diehard fanatic old women in black had remained faithful, willing to help out. During his first week in the parish, he had difficulty scouring the neighborhood for altar boys and such help as he needed to discharge his duties well. By the time I joined his parish he had already established a working schedule and had somehow rekindled the waning interest of his parishioners. Now there was a regular choir for high mass who attended rehearsals assiduously. There was a soloist in that choir whose heavenly voice made me turn my head in the direction of the balcony at the back of the church. I wanted to know who had such a voice, pure, clean, angelic. I was very young then and despite my shyness I would linger after mass around the rectory to look for the owner of the magic voice among the faces of the female choir members. As if I could tell by the face. I had fallen in love with a voice. But I never found out whose voice it was. I doubt if the Father himself would remember.

Fr. Belarmino's attempt to restore the faded luster of the church in his care was nothing short of pathetic. He took time away from the text of his sermons to plead for cooperation. He begged for his parishioners' understanding and love. Somehow, through the ensuing years, that love came through, but the church was too far gone. The popular belief was that one more typhoon as strong as the last one would raze the church to the ground. Although that never happened the church remained in terrible disrepair.

Now here was my old parish priest in San Francisco among friendly Catholics, mostly Americans. When he said mass I wondered what he would say in his sermons. He was a shy but very dignified man. How would he beg before complete strangers when he could not do the same well enough before his own parishioners? He appeared puny. The clean, well-scrubbed altar boys, still in their teens or younger (one was a brown boy thrown in, no doubt, at the last moment to add a Filipino flavor to the mass) towered over him. Much slower of foot—he must now be in his late sixties—he ambled about as if lost in the intricacies of a mass he was officiating a long way from home. God, I prayed, let him finish without mishap. Let him touch the hearts of the crowd. There were more Filipinos at mass than usual and I silently called out to them to pray hard for Fr. Belarmino, our countryman, our brother in this alien land, grown old and tired in the service of his faith. They should have sent a' much younger man.

After reading the gospel for the day, Father began his sermon quite tentatively, giving the impression that he felt out of place, a Daniel among the lions would not have been too far-fetched a comparison. His accent was pure Filipino, Visayan, the region of his birth, singsong, too sweet for the rough and tumble Anglo-Saxon language he was using. He did not apologize for his accent. Then he smiled and I loved him. I remembered he had not smiled all the time he was with me, lost in the jungle of the streets of

67

San Francisco. He told a joke which was uproariously funny. There are no suckers worse than Americans for a well turned out joke. And he kept them laughing. At first they only smiled and looked at one another as if to say, well, now, this old man has quite a sense of humor. And before they realized what he was saying, he was talking about his church in the Philippines. No exaggeration, only cold, hard facts, and sad. I wanted to stand up and shout, he's telling the truth. I know the church of San Juan. Just one more typhoon . . .

I had tears in my eyes when Father Belarmino was through. It grieved me that I could not give more. I was not even in a position to make a pledge. But I was sure he collected quite a sum that day.

At the brunch held in the rectory after mass, I complimented him on his sermon.

"I didn't know you were here," he said, embracing me. "I didn't see you at communion." Fortunately, someone took him aside and I didn't have to tell the truth, or worse, a lie.

That was the last time I saw him. Now where could he be? Professor Jaime was quite distraught. It wasn't like Father Belarmino not to call as he often did to inquire about his mail which had accumulated.

"I was hoping you would know where he is. You had dinner sometime ago in Chinatown."

"Yes. And I saw him again the other Sunday, at St. Joseph's. Maybe it was three weeks ago."

"Are you sure? But why has he not called for his mail? Some of them must be important. He used to call and I would read him the names of the senders."

I suggested that perhaps the Father was extremely busy. He must have gone somewhere out of town. Not to worry. I would be on the lookout for him. I moved around a lot myself. It was likely our paths would cross again.

"Look," the Professor said, changing the topic, "are you still interested in teaching at City College? Or would that be taking too much of your time?"

"Oh, no, not at all. I would have time. I would find time. I'm interested."

"You see, I've just been assigned counselor to Filipino students on campus, something I've been doing since I got tenured, but now it's official. I'm supposed to give up one of my subjects and I thought you might want to take it."

"Yes, sir, I do. Definitely," I said, thinking that even if the magazine came out, I could still find time to teach one subject.

The subject was Philippine Culture which was in the Humanities Department. I had to file a letter of application immediately and state my qualifications. The letter would be forwarded to the Professor and he would put in a good word for me.

"Write me down as one of your references," he said.

"You'll be my one and only reference," I said. If the magazine project fizzled out, I would have a stand-by job while I looked around for work. I was definitely not interested in returning to the Philippines under martial law.

In a few days I got a call from the Dean of the Humanities Department. It was a lady's voice, resonant, like a radio voice. She asked me to report for an interview in her office, preferably the next day. I took down the room number.

We met at her office at the appointed time. The Dean was tall and lovely. Looking at her, I thought, yes, black is beautiful, very beautiful. Her voice sounded even better and she appeared highly efficient, business-like.

"In a few minutes, I'll take you to the conference room where several faculty members and students are going to interview you," she said.

When it was time to go we walked the short distance between her office and the conference room. I had to walk faster than my usual pace to catch up with her. I noticed that she wore a scent that was none too subtle. "This is one campus in the city where the minority is in the majority. All our students live off campus. There are no tuition fees for those who qualify as city residents."

"Are there any Filipinos among the student body?" I asked, feeling silly for asking the question because I knew the answer.

"Quite a few," she said. "Professor Jaime should be able to tell you exactly how many. You will meet two of them in a few minutes. They're members of the class you're supposed to teach. They will ask you questions you better know the answers to." We paused in front of a closed door.

"I'm ready," I said, feeling sure of myself. With all due respects to my former professor, I knew I could handle the subject as well as he or anyone else for that matter.

As we entered the room with the Dean leading the way, I spotted the two Filipino boys immediately, seated next to each other. They looked shabby as everybody else did on the

69

campus, with the exception of the lady Dean. I knew right away the boys were Filipinos, including the taller one who had a light complexion. I had seen so many of the likes of them in the city.

Seated in one corner of the room was Professor Jaime himself and two other faculty members, both Americans. The dean introduced me briefly to each of them. The two boys shook my hand heartily. I noticed they were slow in rising as we came in. A trivial matter, I thought at the time.

The interview proceeded apace. Some of the initial questions seemed unnecessary. Each member of the panel held a xeroxed copy of my resume', but since I didn't want to sound impolite by referring to it, I answered each question nonetheless even if the information was on the sheets they were holding. Perhaps they just wanted to hear the timber of my voice.

What were my credentials?

"Well, I'm a Filipino," I began.

Only Professor Jaime smiled, the mere shadow of a smile. Oh, yes, in the Dean's lovely eyes, there, too, was the hint of a smile, encouraging.

Have I taught before? Indeed, I have, in the Philippines. I was editor of a magazine and a freelance writer: features, fiction, some poetry.

How will I teach the subject? How did they want me to teach it? Unless there was a cut-and-dried approach expected of me, I intended to teach it, considering the survey nature of the course, historically, chronologically, or topically, with emphasis on what I felt the class needed most as the course progressed.

"Have you had any experience with Filipino students in this country?" one of the Filipino boys asked without any trace of an accent. He was most likely the one born in this country who didn't speak the dialect his parents spoke. He was short and very dark. He had slanting eyes and looked as if he had not combed his hair for sometime. The other boy was much taller. He was a mestizo, son of a Philippine-American marriage. He had an American family name. Irish sounding.

"None whatsoever," I replied.

"Won't that be a disadvantage?" the other Filipino boy asked.

"I don't see how it could be a disadvantage unless there's a special knowledge needed to teach Filipinos in this country. Is there?"

70

"I think what Jim means . . ." Professor Jaime began, but the boy interrupted him.

"Let me explain what I mean," Jim said. "You're used to Filipino students in the Philippines, how they study and react to the teacher, but I'm afraid you'll find us different here."

"I expect to. If you thought I didn't think there would be a difference, you're wrong, but I could adjust. Give me a chance and I shall learn," I said, hating myself immediately because I detected a defensive ring in my voice. I sounded, to myself, at any rate, as if I were begging.

"Do you mean you'll be learning while you're supposed to be teaching us?" It was the other Filipino boy who spoke, whose name, I later found out, was Carlos. His mustache bristled as he talked.

"What's wrong with that? I learn as I teach."

"That's a new one," Carlos said, his voice dripping with sarcasm.

I was going to say something cutting and harsh. These boys were mere puppies and they were trying to show off, but they succeeded only in revealing their ignorance. I held my temper.

"That always happens," one of the faculty members said.

"Especially to the best teachers." It was the Dean who had spoken, her voice filling the room like a golden bell.

"Thank you," I said, bowing to her.

"Mr. Tolosa has a name in Philippine literary and education circles," Professor Jaime remarked, putting in the good word he must have waited this long to say.

"This is not the Philippines," Carlos said.

"Thank heavens for that," I answered quickly.

"What do you mean?" Carlos asked.

"Just that. Or let me put it this way, what do you think I mean?"

Carlos was quick to reply, "Ah, teach has begun teaching."

And just as quickly I said, "Might as well begin some place where it would do the most good."

Carlos smiled. Such a set of good white teeth. He had no business hiding them. The smile transformed his face. What a good-looking lad. Why did he have to be so hostile?

Jim and Carlos continued to alternate firing questions while the rest of the panel listened, putting in a word now and then.

At the tail end of the interview, I expressed one worry

71

that bothered me. "Do you think my students will understand me despite my accent?"

"We understand you all right," Carlos said. "Mom and Dad speak just like you do."

"What we aren't sure of is whether you'll understand us," Jim said.

"I understand you all right," I said, echoing Carlos' words.

The next day I learned that I could start immediately. I had not yet fully recovered from the impact of the interview. I thought it was ironic that there was more sympathy from the American faculty than from the Filipino students. I was told that my class was an all-Filipino group, at least, Oriental. I'll show 'em, I said to myself, determined to prepare as well as I could for the first meeting.

26

BUT FIRST THINGS FIRST. I had to tell Dr. Sotto that I had accepted to teach part time without his permission. He would understand when I told him that I wanted to play safe, and what could be better than a teaching job as a hedge against the magazine's falling through? Night after night I waited for further word from the doctor or Imelda, but in vain. There was no use talking to the help in the house. Once I asked them where the Sottos were, and all that the mother and son could say was they didn't know.

"Have they been at home at all, do you know?"

"Sorry, sir, I don't know."

"What do you know?"

"I don't know nothing, sir."

I tried sending a note to the couple through the servants, but there was no response either.

"On Sunday next week," Dr. Sotto had written in the note I received with the Black Label, but a few Sundays had come and gone and I had heard nothing from him. Not even an explanation. I was getting quite worried.

I tried calling some of the members of the Board whose names I remembered, but they were as much in the dark as I was. Even Dr. Tablizo, the friendliest in the group, had nothing to say.

"Do you think it's still on?" I asked with all the calmness I could muster because my heart was pounding. I sure was worried as hell. My bread and butter was fast melting in my hands. An awkward meraphor, I know, but I was in an even more awkward situation. I had gone deep into the project and saw day by day its possibilities growing brighter. I could make a success of it.

"Have you heard anything to the contrary?" was the usual reply or paraphrase of it in both English and Pilipino.

"Why haven't I heard from Dr. Sotto? Is he out of the country?"

"I thought you are staying at his place."

"That's right."

"Then you should know more than I. Be patient. We can be very busy, too, you know."

What the hell.

One night—it must have been past ten—I was occupied jotting down notes of what the day had been like in San Francisco when Dr. Sotto barged in simultaneously with his knocking loudly on my door.

"Hello, stranger, long time no see," he said, sitting down heavily on the nearest chair.

"Good evening, sir," I said, "but don't you think that's my line?"

He was quite high. He was redder in the face than I had ever seen him, and the veins on his temple showed plainly in the light.

"Let's kill that bottle," he said, looking around for it. "You don't think I have forgotten, have you?"

"Oh, no," I lied, getting the bottle out. I hoped there would be at least two clean glasses in my room. "But I've been kind of worried. You left me a note . . ."

"Oh, that. Something turned up, a lot of things, and I was not able to get in touch with you. Sorry." He watched me pour the whiskey over a few cubes of ice in his glass. "Enough!" he cried gesturing with his hand. I handed him the glass and I fixed a drink for myself, too.

"What shall we drink to now?" I asked.

"Let's drink to the Filipino," he said brightly, lifting his glass.

73

I lifted mine. "To the magazine or the person?"

"The magazine, of course," he said.

"To the magazine then," I said, as we took a sip of the whiskey.

Pointing to the papers on my table with his glass, he said, "Sorry, I must have come in at the wrong time."

"Of course not. I have been looking all over for you."

"Sorry about that."

"Even the other members of the Board didn't know where you were. Even the help. And I couldn't get . . . "

"Right, right. But we'll have that meeting yet. When will you be ready?"

"I've been ready for some time now. I couldn't be any readier."

"Of course. Silly of me."

He had never sounded this way before. Apologetic. He was forthright, almost brash, although there were times when he was gentle, too, but not apologetic.

"I'm ready with a few important facts and figures that I want to present to the Board. I've been doing sketches myself of the cover and the format for the Board's approval."

"Fantastic," he said as he took another gulp and wiped his mouth with his hand.

I handed him a paper napkin. This was getting nowhere.

"If I may suggest, will you invite the wives of the Board members to our meeting? I want them to hear what I'm going to present."

"Oh, yes, I intend to invite them. They will be there."

"Good. That's settled then. You see, I have the impression that it's the wives who will actually make the final decision. And they don't seem quite sold on the idea."

"How right you are, Mister Editor . . . er . . . I mean . . . David, you're damn right. How perceptive you are."

"It's so obvious. The Filipino woman doesn't dissemble too well. I also know that the Filipino husband usually yields to his wife's wishes. I may be wrong, but I think even in this country, it's the Filipino wife who holds the purse strings."

"Right, right!" Dr. Sotto agreed wholeheartedly, emptying his glass.

I filled it again and looked at mine. I had barely touched it after that first sip, and the ice cubes had about melted. I intended to nurse it all night.

74

"David," he said, stirring the liquid with his finger, "you say you're not married. Have you been married before?"

"Oh, no, sir."

"Engaged?"

"No."

"Will you, perhaps in the foreseeable future, get married?"

"I have thought of it. But why do you ask, you have no objection to a bachelor editor of the magazine, have you?"

"Oh, no. Sorry, I'm so sorry. But this has nothing to do with the magazine. Absolutely nothing. I'm just curious. You live all by yourself and you don't seem to be doing badly. You appear to be well adjusted to the single life."

"No big deal. Life is a continuous adjustment. No tribute to me. Frankly, I envy happily married people like you."

"But don't you see that we, those of us on the Board whom you've already met, might perhaps envy you your single-blessedness? "

"That's a laugh. This single blessed man is fighting for survival."

"Aren't we all?"

"I don't believe you. Look at this," I said, with a sweeping gesture that encompassed the entire Sotto mansion and the surrounding landscape on Diamond Heights.

He didn't say anything. He kept staring at the glass in his hand, turning it with a light motion of his palm as he shook his head.

"Not to mention the *doctora*, your beautiful, accomplished wife," I added.

"Yes, Imelda. She's a treasure," he said so softly I had to bend forward to catch his words. There was a sadness in his eyes as he looked up at me. "I can't see how she can put up with me all these years, especially lately."

Here we go again, confession time, I said to myself. I remembered Father Belarmino. The doctor needed someone like him at this hour. Not me. I wanted to change the subject, but the doctor didn't want to talk about anything else. The magazine was on my mind but it was the last thing on his.

I poured him another drink and got more ice cubes. He walked towards the window and drew the curtains aside. The city glittered beneath us. By now, the scene had become familiar to me from the window of the basement with a view of San

75

Francisco. The sight had alternately elated and depressed me on nights past depending on my mood. More often when I looked down at the city I was filled with remorse. What was I doing away from my native land at a time of turmoil, how long was I going to fool myself into believing that I was happier here because I felt free? Did I really want this kind of aimless freedom? Who wants to be alone among other lost souls? Oh, I had my share of wallowing in self-pity just drawing this curtain aside which opens to the blazing city below. To Dr. Sotto, it must mean something, too. I wondered what thoughts and feelings the scene below gave him when he looked out his windows on the top floor.

"Beautiful, isn't it?" he said as if in answer to my question. "Surely, we're all going to leave our hearts here when the time comes to move on. But for various reasons. What would your reason be, David?"

I didn't know what to say. I took a sip of my drink and it tasted stale, almost warm. I got more ice cubes.

"Sorry, doctor, I can't find the words for what I want to say. Maybe I haven't got a reason . . . yet."

"Let me tell you what mine is going to be. It's a long story, but I'll make it short. I want you to hear it from me and from no one else . . ."

He went back to his seat and I sat on the bed, my head against a pillow. He faced me as he talked, his back towards the city below. From where I sat I could see the skies over San Francisco.

"You can't hide too many things from Filipinos in this country. They seem to have a knack for discovering family secrets and skeletons in the closet, particularly back in the land we had left behind. They know everything. If not now, eventually they would. They make it their business to know including what didn't exist or had never happened but would be fascinating gossip. . ."

27

WHEN THE SOTTO COUPLE arrived in San Francisco, they tried to play it cool. They had persuaded themselves to believe that their life was no one else's business but their own. They were not too well known in the Visayan province where they came from. They were among thousands of other unknown but ambitious young professionals who wanted to make their fortunes in America. Their circle of acquaintances was made up of newly accredited medical doctors, new graduates from universities in Luzon and the Visayas. Their concerns were immediate like how soon they would be able to emigrate to the United States and make their fortune.

The Sottos got married soon after graduation. It would have been sooner because there was a child on the way, but waiting for graduation meant at most two months. There would not be, they hoped, any visible sign of pregnancy. Imelda was not too thin. It could easily have been mistaken for a slight gain in weight. But they were very much in love and they didn't really care.

When Imelda gave birth, they named the baby Estella. It didn't take any medical degree to notice that the child was not normal. She seemed afflicted with a combination of physical and mental illnesses. She looked like a freak who needed twenty-four-hour care.

Many nights while waiting for their travel papers to go through the U.S. embassy in Manila and the many government agencies of the Philippines, they discussed their problems. They prayed for guidance. Imelda wanted to take the infant with them, including the maid who took care of her. Dr. Sotto thought that would not be a wise move. True, he wanted their child with them, but they had to be practical. There were times during the long wait when both agreed to postpone their departure indefinitely, start practice in the Philippines and be with their child. They knew it wouldn't be easy in the United States to work and care for a baby, especially one in Estela's condition. They agreed the child had to be placed in an institution and as resident doctors, they would not be earning enough to afford this. Their parents, particularly Imelda's, were also against their taking the child to the States. They volunteered to take care of Estela while the couple were adjusting to the new life abroad. It seemed like a good decision, but not to Imelda.

"I can't leave my baby," she cried, "not the way she is. God will never forgive me. I'll never forgive myself."

By the time their travel papers had arrived, Imelda's parents had practically won her over to their way of thinking. It would be temporary, they consoled her.

Their first years in San Francisco were difficult. They lived in buildings close to the hospital where they worked, which were reserved for resident doctors and nurses. They had no social life. There were nights when Imelda was inconsolable. Guilt feelings assailed her, and she believed they had made the wrong decision.

They completed their hospital residencies almost simultaneously. They lived frugally, but spared no expense sending Estela toys in the hope of assuaging their sorrows, mostly their guilt.

Imelda made the first trip home. She wrote back that she wasn't returning to the United States. Her daughter needed her. Unless Dr. Sotto agreed that she take the child along, she would stay behind in the Philippines. The child was as helpless as ever. Her extremities had failed to grow with the rest of her body. She couldn't talk and made crying animal sounds. She clawed the air with her twisted fingers. Her eyes looked swollen and seemed to jump out of their sockets. She had palsy, too. Even in the States there seemed little hope her condition would improve.

But after a while Imelda returned to the United States. Alone. By then everybody in their limited circle of friends knew of the deformed child, and the whispering among them abated. Some came outright to offer their sympathy and suggest all sorts of solutions. None seemed practical. The couple went on frequent visits to the Philippines and the mansion on Diamond Heights took on a somber air. It scared them to have another child. The fear made a mess of their love life together.

But not their fortunes. Almost miraculously, they prospered through the years beyond their wildest dreams. Sometimes they convinced themselves that Estela was a gift that brought them prosperity. They continued to lavish her with gifts she had no use for, which now filled a room in Imelda's ancestral home in the Visayas.

Lately, Imelda began to resent her husband's heavy drinking, his staying away late at night, not knowing where he was. At the same time, the efficient Filipino rumor machine began grinding full time, spewing all kinds of stories linking her husband's name with one woman after another. When he came home Imelda would hound him with questions and accusations. Often she threatened to leave him so she could be with her child. He was ruining their careers, their lives.

The rumors were not without foundation, however. There was, indeed, just very recently, another woman, Joy Rowan, a nurse who hailed from Windsor, Colorado, taller than he and lithe and young, with a face like Imelda's. They could easily pass for sisters if not twins.

"I don't dare admit the truth, David. Imelda wouldn't understand. She'll never forgive me."

"Try her," I said.

Dr. Sotto shook his head. He had loosened his Sulka tie, a silky light blue lined with a deeper shade of blue that was almost black. It lay across his chest like a sling without the splintered arm. Now I noticed there were smudges of dirt on his white shirt damp with sweat. His eyes were bloodshot and quite unfocused.

"That's why I asked whether you've been married. But no matter. You look like a man who would understand. You're not as naive as you seem to be at times. You have been through a lot. I can tell. You have known love, haven't you? You've loved a woman?" He screamed the last sentence and I wanted to shout back, "Yes! And her name is also Imelda." I was a bit drunk myself. The glass I had intended to nurse all night had already been emptied twice or more, and refilled.

"Well, yes," I admitted timidly as if my credentials were not right.

"I knew it," he shouted in triumph, sipping his drink, but there was not a drop left. As I moved towards the nearly empty bottle to give him what was left, he shook his head. He held on to his empty glass and gazed into it as if expecting to see the solution to the riddle of his life in it. "You look the part. You've been through hell, too. Like where I am now."

He loved Imelda, never loved any other woman in the world. In their early years in America, they had to fight for whatever opportunity that came their way, and there were such opportunities, not only golden, but solid gold. They were closest during those beginning years. They were together as much as their work allowed and consoled each other over their crippled child in the Visayas. They prayed together.

Temptation from other women had always been there. In his profession, it was everywhere, patient, neighbor, co-worker, hospital personnel, young pretty American interns, nurses, especially nurses. Joy Rowan was not the first nurse to catch his attention. He knew he had a roving eye. He had admitted as much to Imelda. At night, he would tell her of moves that were meant to attract him, seduce him, most certainly, but he found them nothing more than passing distractions that fed his ego. Imelda would tell him, "I bet you like that," or "I doubt if it's what you think it is. You're so conceited you think every girl is chasing you."

"But the things they tell me, Imelda, not even you have ever said to me. I must be better looking now than I have ever been."

"Dear Don Juan, your swell head's making you forget how short you are by American standards, and even in the Philippines, you're the shortest man I've ever met, you know, outside of carnivals."

They laughed together. Sometimes they quarreled. Nothing serious. She continued buying him expensive clothes lately because they could now afford to. She would tell their friends, "He just doesn't have any taste for clothes. He would be the laughing stock everywhere if I let him buy his clothes."

That she had expensive taste didn't bother him now; it never did even in their impecunious days. She bought herself expensive jewelry. That was her weakness. And real estate. She had business acumen, he was fond of bragging to friends.

A religious woman, Imelda often dragged her husband to church, particularly after an unusually bad hangover. She was also very sure of herself. She knew he would do nothing seriously wrong because they loved each other very much.

It was not to be this way for long. He found himself more and more attracted to Joy. It could be that he was simply rationalizing, but he found her to be another Imelda, especially during times when he and Imelda seldom saw each other because of conflicting hours and the pressure of work. Joy was refreshing fun. She laughed at all his jokes, and he, at hers. They would meet at the hospital canteen and talk much more than eat or drink. As they parted, he would touch her arm and say, casually, "See ya." Always she turned around to wave him goodbye. He noticed that she sought his company. Once he drove her downtown to go shopping and when she said, "Will you wait for me? I won't be long," he gladly waited. When she was not around he missed her. And worse, he had stopped confiding in Imelda, passing off his growing closeness to Joy as inevitable but, at bottom, meaningless.

One day, Joy informed him that she was now living all by herself in a rented apartment. Up to this point in their relationship, he had never given her anything, not even a stick of chewing gum.

One thing led to another, gradually, imperceptibly. A snack together. A date at the movies. A dinner. A goodnight kiss. By now he wanted to tell Imelda, but he realized he had already gone beyond the point of no return. Wrong. He thought he would be able to stop there and no further. Now on hindsight he realized he had been acting like a teenager. At his age, for heaven's sake.

He didn't have to lie to Imelda because she didn't ask him. Not until the rumors began to spread in the Filipino community in San Francisco. He had not reckoned on how insidiously gossip worked among Filipinos in the area.

"Who's this Joy Roman who works at the hospital? " she asked him one night as soon as he arrived, even before he could remove his jacket. He was taken completely by surprise.

"Oh, she's a starry-eyed kid who thinks I'm super," he replied without much thought. How well he put it. How completely, it seemed, he had exonerated himself in Imelda's eyes with such a beautiful answer, unrehearsed.

"I thought so," Imelda said, already half asleep.

Yet as he cuddled her in his arms, he felt guilty for the first time and quite unhappy about it. This has got to end, he thought, as he pressed Imelda close to him. And what the hell was happening. Of course, he knew. What else, but the international Filipino pastime: *chismis.*

Then Joy didn't show up one day and the next. Before the week was over, he was calling her at her apartment every chance he got. One evening, he dropped by her place and knocked lightly and listened. There was nobody in. It embarrassed him to be seen standing by the door, waiting. He knocked louder. Still, there was no answer. He would ask personnel or one of the nurses whom he had seen often in her company. He didn't care what they would think of him.

Back in Diamond Heights, he was often restless and in need of a drink. Those were the times when he often went out. Imelda noticed he had become absent-minded. When she asked him if there was anything wrong, he said, "One of those things at the clinic. Nothing serious. The usual meddling. I'll get over it. Sorry, if it bothered you."

"Good. I thought perhaps you had found out you could not get too much joy out of that woman." She laughed at her own witticism.

It took him a while before he noticed the intended or unintended pun and was a bit late in joining her in her laughter. How he loved Imelda. Her sense of humor. Her wholesomeness. What was happening to him? Wake up, Pacifico! That's what his mother used to tell him. He should wake up. He promised himself he would. Quit acting silly, childish. But it was not that easy.

That Monday, he was sitting at his desk in the same hospital where Joy worked when she appeared before him.

"Dr. Sotto, did you miss me?" Joy asked.

She held a clipboard, looking lovely as ever in her white, crisp uniform. He sat there, staring at her, tongue-tied.

Joy went over to him and passed one hand in front of his face as if to determine if he had gone blind.

He snatched her hand to kiss it, but she pulled away.

"Did you hear me, Doctor?"

"What did you say?"

"I said, did you miss me?"

"And why should I miss you?"

"Because I missed you."

That evening he took her to an early supper and brought her to her apartment. He almost stayed the whole night.

Oh, the guilt ever since! He promised himself that it would not happen again, but it did—again and again. He told himself that Imelda was the only woman who truly mattered in his life, that Joy was just a passing flirtation and so forth, but the more he tried to convince himself, the deeper he got involved with Joy. They saw each other practically every day.

It was during this time that Imelda left for the Philippines to get Estela. "At least I would have someone who needs me and who can be with me while you indulge in your so-called flirtations," she told her husband.

Shortly after Imelda's departure, Joy confessed that she was with child by him. "I'm sure it would be cute and brown and sweet like you," she told him.

But he had doubts. The only way he would believe the child was his was for him to see. He had mixed feelings about the baby. Although it seemed unreasonable that he should doubt the unborn child's paternity, still he did, and it upset him that he did. He saw his future crumbling before him. What if the child were born abnormal, too? If it were not, the contrast would be shattering to him, the irony, the anguish! The Filipino community would be in an uproar. Wild rumors would spread, growing more poisonous and uglier.

But beyond and above all these frightening possibilities was what the event would do to Imelda. How would she take it?

28

WHILE WORKING on the syllabus of the course I was going to teach, I wondered where I could obtain the source materials I needed. I wanted to do well, to excel beyond everybody's expectations and I wanted to show those doubting Filipino boys who had interviewed me. So I devoted a lot of time to the syllabus. The more I thought of it, the more fascinating the subject became. I found much in it that would also be useful for the magazine. This somehow helped assuage the guilt feeling that occasionally disturbed me.

The pay was measly any way you looked at it: $14.00 an hour, 3 hours a week, M-W-F. But this was money I would be earning, not a handout like the allowance given me by the Board through Dr. Sotto. I suspected the Board didn't give me anything and whatever I got came from Dr. Sotto's personal funds, not to mention the free board and lodging on Diamond Heights. In due time I would be able to leave the comforts of my basement home and move into my own quarters. For some reason I didn't feel like staying on in the mansion, living off the generosity of the Sottos. They might wish to be alone with their problems, and with Estela around, they might not want me to see her.

Meanwhile, the syllabus.

The exact title of the course was: Special Study in the Humanities: the Philippines.

I had to have a keynote, a theme of sorts, an idea that would unify the loose ends in so wide a scope as the subject I was assigned to teach. Fortunately, in one of my visits to the library of the Philippine Consulate, I came across an article by Fr. Horacio de la Costa, S.J. I wrote down word for word some of his sensitizing ideas which I hoped would provoke a lively discussion in my class.

Philippine progress toward self-identity has had to adapt to roles conceived for the Filipino by a variety of colonial temperaments and occupation policies during nearly four centuries of suppression.

We must steel ourselves against the shock of finding somewhere in this vast area an Asian nation of Malay stock, socially structured on a basically Indonesian pattern, containing a large infusion of Chinese blood and attitudes, but with a cultural heritage in part Spanish, in part Anglo-Saxon.

Filipinos resent dependence on others for his cultural description.

The average American, if he thinks of the Filipino at all, is likely to picture him as someone rescued in 1898 from deprivation, and nourished sacrificially ever since, until he has become undistinguishable from the creditor whose goods he imports so lavishly.

In self-defense, and under the influence of postwar nationalism and racial assertions of identity, Filipinos have felt compelled to assert vehemently that they are not Americans. Hence they are accused of being anti-American.

I read the words over again. Super! With these ideas as touchstone to the course, how could I fail? And almost instantly, the answer came back. Oh, yes, you could. You don't know your students. What is their background? How interested would they be in the course? How receptive would they be from day to day to absorb what you intend to dish out to them?

More questions than I cared to answer. But I had to know. I prepared for my class with more than my usual zeal, going through the more humdrum aspects of the course in detail, hoping to discover in them something that would kindle interest, a spark of curiosity perhaps, a sense of wonder, among students who very often are interested only in passing. Just a passing grade, sir, that's all . . .

It was with this realization that I began to jot down ideas as they came to my mind or as they came to me in the course of my readings. It was not until much later while I was going over my notes that I began to see how I was doing a double take, shifting from one role to another: now, I was a college teacher

84

teaching a course on the Philippines; then, an editor of a magazine for Filipinos in America.

Items:
Review books, one or two per issue. Use these as reference texts should the class prove intelligent and willing enough to work hard. Possible titles:

Christ in the Philippine Context, by Douglas J. Elwood and Patricia L. Magdamo
The Sulu Archipelago and Its People, by Sixto Y. Orosa
The Oton Diggings, by Jose B. Tiongco
Philippine Institutions, by John J. Carroll
Philippine Mass Media in Perspective, by Gloria D. Feliciano and Crispulo Icban, Jr. (eds.)

Reprint or xeroxed excerpts for distribution in class:
Recipes of the Philippines, by Enriqueta David-Perez
Visayan Folk Dances (2 vols.), by Libertad V. Fajardo
Dictionary of Philippine Folk Beliefs and Customs (4 vols.) by Francisco Demetrio.

Check out audio-visual sources: films, film strips, video tapes on the Philippines (find out where you can get them on loan or for rent).

Review Philippine laws (forgotten, neglected, abused, controversial, the latest)

Formulate a statement of purpose for the magazine/class Goals (aims):

— to inform correctly and interestingly;
— to fill in gaps of knowledge Filipinos abroad desire to have for personal, social, or whatever reasons
— to chronicle lives of Filipinos abroad among the distinguished, the neglected and almost forgotten, their achievements, failures and problems
— to examine the new and growing life-style among Filipinos in the United States
— to dramatize human-interest stories of the new immigrants abroad, the wave after wave of Filipinos in the U.S.
— to catalogue and immortalize through the teaching process (the printed word) the Filipino dream—what is it?

— to stimulate awareness of the Filipinos' strengths and weaknesses.

— to keep in mind what our true identity is, the wealth of our culture, pride in our heritage.

29

FROM THE PUBLIC LIBRARY I would often walk all the way to the Post Office across the street from the Greyhound Bus Depot, hoping to get some mail. I had been doing this for a week now with no reward of even a single letter or card. During the first two or three days, the distance didn't seem that great as I walked leisurely, sometimes stopping by show windows, but when one week had passed and still I had no mail, I began to tire quickly, the Post Office seeming quite far away. It got to be embarrassing when I showed up at General Delivery every day, asking whether there was any mail for me. I would spell out my name at great pains and the fellow always came back from the rear room empty-handed. Now as soon as he saw me from afar he would shake his head and I would walk away quickly, afraid the guy would see the disappointment in my face. I vowed never to return but I often did.

I thought of changing my address, using the Sotto residence, quite certain the couple wouldn't mind, but how long could I keep using it? Some day soon I would have to stay elsewhere, so under these circumstances General Delivery was just right for a wanderer like me. And I kept visiting the post office.

On one such visit I saw a dark-haired woman in a long ill-fitting coat with its fur collar frayed at the edges. At first I thought she was a Filipino woman of Spanish ancestry, but on closer look, she appeared to be definitely Caucasian, tall, pale white and thin. It must have been the oversized coat that made her look quite frail and thin. She was accosting men, talking to them. I couldn't hear what she was saying as she leaned against the banister of the short flight of steps of a run-down building not far from the main entrance of the post office. Each time a man passed by, she would run to him, her palm extended. Later, she came close enough for me to hear her.

"Got a quarter, mister?" she was saying.

Most of the white men walked on without looking back, completely ignoring her, but a couple of blacks stopped to talk then walked on. An old man hobbling by with a cane gave her a dollar bill and she thanked him profusely, touching his hand that held the crook of the cane. He smiled at her, the flash of dentures brightening his face. Three other men gave her some coins. Some of the men looked Oriental but not Filipino. Somehow I could tell.

Now from where I stood I could see her back, and just when I had decided I could afford a quarter, she ran into the building and disappeared. There was no sign of her anywhere nearby. So I went inside the Bus Depot where I usually browsed around the magazine shelves where there was always a crowd, leaving quickly when the mean, obese woman who ran the place drove us away.

"This ain't no library," she growled, her tone as mean as her looks.

In the waiting room close by, I took a vacant seat and waited for nobody and nothing in particular. There were the usual Filipinos who looked so old and wasted, they looked unreal to me, as if they had left their true and healthy bodies somewhere for use only on rare and special occasions. They dragged their feet when they walked, shuffling from one phone booth to another, looking for coins in the slots. That look on their faces as they came away empty-handed one saw only on the faces of those who had just learned that they had lost everything in the world. Hell, my imagination was wearing me down, I felt like crying and wishing I were back home in the Philippines. What the hell was I doing in San Francisco? Then it dawned on me that I probably looked like them now, much younger but just as ragged and lost. Even the way I dressed. Yet it consoled me to think that with what I was wearing, I had somehow blended with the scene, become one of the faceless crowd. And what the hell did that mean?

Some of the old Pinoys in the waiting room stood behind the men and women who were watching the small TV sets attached to their seats. The Pinoys bent their bodies forward to better see and hear. When someone left with a portion of a quarter's worth of TV program still on, they rushed to the vacated seat, pushing one another for the chance to watch the show for free.

I have seen the likes of these Pinoy old timers in many other bus depots in California, New York, and Illinois. Often I thought

87

of myself as one of them, a bum, grown old and decrepit, aimlessly wandering in the United States. Would this happen to me if I stayed on? Did any of them know my father? Had he become one of them? How would I recognize him? The thought depressed me but it kept recurring.

It was perhaps for this reason that I postponed for as long as I could visiting the area around the 800 block on Kearny where there was a so-called Little Manila. In my visits to these places, wherever I looked there were Filipinos, old and young, subdued and infirm, brash and healthy; eateries and night clubs with Filipino names. An old building called the International Club housed many of the aging and destitute Filipinos. I had yet to visit those places. The material I was likely to find would not be fit for publication in the magazine I was supposed to get off the ground. But what the hell, I coudn't stay away forever.

The bus depot was bad enough but I was drawn there as I walked from the post office or the public library by a need to find someone, a familiar face from home, an old acquaintance, perhaps my father.

One late afternoon I was at the bus depot when again I saw the pale white girl in the ill-fitting coat. It was raining lightly but the low gusty winds made the rain seem like gentle slaps on the face and actually refreshing. She was dressed in the same shabby coat, the collar the shade of mud, the hem touching the ground and soaking wet. Strands of her hair clung wetly on her cheeks.

"Spare a quarter, mister?"

The question startled me because I thought that she hadn't seen me yet. Her voice had a down-home unaffectedness, humble, even as it begged, its burden clear and honest. She was gazing straight into my eyes as I looked at her, my heart pounding.

I dipped into my pocket, searching for change, and without bothering to count how much I had in my hand, I gave it all to her. As I did so, my fingers touched her palm wet from the rain and felt a current pass through my body. I walked away hurriedly, embarrassed that I should be so agitated, and bumped into a man carrying a huge suitcase as he pushed a glass door open.

"Sorry," I said, holding the door to let him through, but he didn't even glance at me. The rain was coming down hard. I went straight to the men's room and when I came out, there she was again, standing at the foot of the stairway across the rest rooms. She was waiting for me as I walked down to the waiting room.

88

"I want to thank you," she said, sidling close to me. She was nearly as tall as I and not as thin as I thought she was. Paler, yes, and dirty.

"That's okay," I said, moving on towards the exit. She walked in step with me.

"That's all I can give you, I'm sorry," I said, thinking she wanted more.

"You don't understand," she said.

I turned to her, trying to read her face. Then, as if it were the most natural thing to do, she took my arm and pressed it against her breast as we walked down Mission Street. For about a block we said nothing to each other. At an intersection, we had to stop and wait for the green light. It was one of those unexpected rains. There were very few pedestrians carrying umbrellas. It had been pouring and I had barely noticed.

"You're soaking wet," I said.

She tightened her grip on my arm.

When we resumed walking, the rain gradually abated. Quite a few walked bare-headed like us, unmindful of the rain. They must love rain in San Francisco. It's rain like it is nowhere else. It falls and touches you gently on the skin, soaking through whatever you're wearing that's not water repellent, not a thorough soaking but just enough to feel a tingling, a fresh cool dampness all over your body like a much needed cleansing.

We stopped by a restaurant where people sat without eating or drinking, filling almost all the tables. These were the cowards seeking refuge from the rain, strangers to its touch.

"Hi, Judy," the guy behind the counter greeted my companion. She seemed at home here. Ordering a half dozen sandwiches to go she paid with change, mostly quarters.

"Hey, what do you need all those sandwiches for? Saving them up for another rainy day? Look, the rain's stopped," I told her.

She smiled at me and ordered coffee, also to go, which she made me carry in a brown paper bag while she placed the sandwiches in a leather pouch slung across her shoulder. We walked on until we came to a building with a lot of ladders leading from fire exits. We went through a narrow broken-down door that smelled of garbage that had been pissed on. The building looked quite empty.

"This where you live?"

"Oh, God, yes," she said with a sigh as if, indeed, it was, and she was home at last.

Leading the way, she walked up the stairs ahead of me and lifted her long coat, revealing muddy sandals and legs, blotched with red and blue marks, but shapely. On the third floor we walked through a long dark corridor that led to a huge hall which looked like an abandoned hospital ward for indigents. Instead of beds, there was a scattering of mattresses and sleeping bags on the tiled floor. The air was heavy with the smell of fresh paint. It was stuffy and nearly as cold as it was outdoors, but there were no winds here and it was safe from the rains. I learned later that hot water was available only at certain designated hours, mostly at night and early in the morning.

Judy went straight to a corner which must have been hers the way she approached and occupied it like she had a long-term lease. She had a knapsack, a sleeping bag and a bundle in her corner. At the far end of the spacious floor area were human bodies. From a distance in the badly lighted place, they looked like crumpled heaps of rags, until they stirred or a sound came from one of them.

"Still raining out there, Judy?" The voice came from somewhere among the heaps of rags. A man's voice.

"No. It has slowed down quite a bit," she answered.

The nearest body, which I had not noticed immediately, sat on its haunches like someone meditating deeply. He had not even turned to look at us.

"What's with that guy?" I asked, motioning with my head towards him as Judy began removing the sandwiches from her pouch. "Is he stoned or something?"

"Nah! He's just unhappy. Must be missing his dog. Left it in Wichita."

The building was about to be condemned when a group of these transients—couples and singles who had drifted into the city from all over the country—found the place suitable for their temporary needs: a few hours' sleep at night, a shelter from the cold after a day of wandering. They petitioned the city government for permission to use it, promising to make it habitable. They had worked together to clean the mess, paint the walls, fix the plumbing. Thus it became a refuge for vagrants and transients. At night, the place sometimes got crowded. They came and went, others stayed on. Like Judy who seemed to know them all.

They were mostly young, their ragged clothes and unkempt bodies were a perfect disguise for whatever they were fleeing. Bury the past, forget the familiar places and faces that burden the memory, seek peace and ultimately, the truth, whatever it was. There was a name for these lost, confused young men and women, but it changed with the passing years; and their wanderings almost always brought them to the crowded cities where it was easier to get lost.

"Here," Judy said, offering a sandwich to the guy from Wichita. He took it with the least movement and laid it on the floor. His beard moved as some sort of sound emitted from his lips, perhaps he was saying thanks, then he reverted to his meditations.

Judy distributed the sandwiches and I helped with the coffee. Nobody stared at me. No one asked who I was. She didn't introduce me to anybody.

Later we went back to her corner, sat down close, facing each other, our bodies touching through our damp clothes. I had taken off my wind-breaker but left my sweater on. I helped her remove her coat. It smelled of mold. I noticed nobody touched the sandwiches or drank the coffee.

"Perhaps they aren't hungry and the coffee's cold," I observed.

"They haven't eaten the whole day," she said. "If you look into those coffee cups, they must be empty now."

They started coming around midnight, she said. No trouble, especially with those who were more or less "permanent," but with the transients it was something else. Some needed hospital care. Young girls in their teens, boys barely starting to grow a beard.

"And what are you doing here?"

"I belong here," she answered.

"Why don't you go home or wherever you came from?"

"This is home."

"But surely you must have a place better than this, a family to go back to."

"God, I didn't know you were a social worker. Are you? If you are, get lost. I was wrong about you. I thought . . ."

"You know damn well I'm no social worker."

"I thought so, but just now you sounded like one."

Quite a few times, she had noticed how I frequented the bus depot and the post office. She didn't know what to think of

91

me until I gave her all those coins. "It seemed that was all you had. And you were in a hurry to get rid of me."

"What did you take me for then?"

"What did you take me for?" she echoed back my words.

"Nothing in particular."

"Come on."

"I thought you had a weakness for quarters."

She laughed, swaying slightly, tapping me on the chest. She had moved even closer. Her smelly warmth felt good.

Although we spoke in low tones, I was worried everybody was listening. Yet nobody stirred. They must have all fallen asleep.

"What did you take me for?" I insisted on knowing.

"A kindred spirit. Someone I liked."

"You mean, lost and homeless, like everybody around here?"

"Hey, where did you learn your English?" She smiled and touched my arm. "You had that look in your eyes . . ."

"Suppose a guy gave you more than a quarter."

"That would be great."

"I mean, say, fifty dollars."

"I've had offers and I have been tempted."

"Saves you a lot of running around all day to buy coffee and sandwiches."

"I said I've been tempted. But, no, thanks. The guys I like are those whom my guts tell me I should like, that's all."

"Tell me about you."

"You *are* a social worker."

"You've been to college."

"Graduate school," she said, but must have quickly realized that she had said more than she wanted to reveal about herself. "Why don't you just shut up? " she screamed, more angry at herself, it seemed, than at me.

I looked around, embarrassed. No one had stirred. Nobody was looking our way, I hoped.

She sighed and placed her hand on my chest, looking up at me, her lips half-parted. I kissed her tentatively, at first, but she responded with such warmth, her soft lips clinging to mine with a hunger I found easy to match. After a while she didn't smell too unpleasantly any more.

"My name's David," I said, cuddling her in my arms.

"Hi, David," she said, closing her eyes and groping for my face. Soon she was breathing regularly as if she had fallen asleep.

They really started coming later that night. They were silent, like shadows, as though out there in the streets all day, they went through enough to render them speechless.

"They're pretty subdued," I said.

"It's cold outside, it isn't any better in here."

"They know their way around," I said, thinking how dimly lighted the place was. The street lights helped but little.

I had many questions to ask but I was afraid Judy would scream at me again. She was capable of driving me back into the streets where she had picked me up. Not the first time for me. Story of my life. But these circumstances were unusual. Would she open up a bit if I talked about myself? No, I didn't think that would work, especially if I told her about my father who deserted my mother when I was five and came to America; that occasionally I actually looked for him, hoping I would recognize him; that I walked the streets of San Francisco looking for human-interest material for the magazine I was supposed to edit. Why, she might even suspect I was using her.

Some time that night we moved to a room that must have been a closet, but it was no warmer there. It was quite stifling until I succeeded in pushing up a window glass pane that had been stuck so I could breathe easier. There was no view from up there. Alleys and half-blind light bulbs. Nothing more. It could have been anywhere else in the ghettos of Sulucan or Chicago.

While we lugged her sleeping bag, I noticed that the guy from Wichita was gone. The last time I looked his way, he hadn't touched his sandwich. "That guy hasn't touched his sandwich," I told Judy.

"Maybe he's keeping it for his dog."

"What dog?"

"The one he left in Wichita."

As I lay down beside her, she welcomed me warmly, adjusting her body to mine. "No. . . No. . . Yes. Now hold it," she whispered. "That's better. Okay. Are you okay?"

I was uneasy and still had difficulty breathing. The dampness and decay in the cramped corner were oppressive. There was no space for love beyond the usual words. At this odd moment, I wondered about Judy, her goodness, her caring enough to beg for these other orphans like her seeking shelter in this condemned building, her own secrets. Surely I must mean something to her more than just another puppy.

93

"Where did he go?" I asked eager for distraction.

"Who?"

"The guy from Wichita."

"Oh. Him? Must have gone back to Wichita for his dog, who knows? They come and go."

Finally, her body fitted mine, comfortably enough to make love if I dared. But there was no hurry. We had all the time.

"Tell me about that guy. He didn't even bid you goodbye."

"We never say goodbye here. We don't waste words."

"Waste words for me, Judy."

"We get used to things around here. When something goes wrong, we try to solve the problem. But some of us are too far gone. Like that guy."

I remember snatches from her story. On the whole it made sense, strange though it sounded. And sad.

*

The guy's sitting on the stoop of the steps of the Civic Center in Wichita with his dog napping at his feet. He calls to every passerby.

"Wanna dog?"

Nobody pays attention except an old man who drags his feet as he walks. Perhaps he doesn't want to listen, but he can't walk fast enough not to hear or to ignore what he hears.

"Wanna dog?"

"What? What dog?"

"This one."

"Are you kidding?"

"No kidding."

"What's he called?"

"It's a she. No name. She answers to any name. She's too dumb to know the difference. She'd stick to anyone who takes care of her. No problem."

"You got to get rid of her, eh?"

"That's right. Got to leave Wichita."

"Why don't you take her with you?"

"Not allowed on the bus."

"How long have you had her?"

"'bout a year. She stayed on when my wife left."

"Won't you miss her?"

94

"What's to miss?"

"Seems she knows you're giving her away."

"No way. I told you she's dumb."

The old man stoops down with great effort and strokes the dog, saying, "No name. Poor no name, he's giving you away to me. That awright with you?"

The guy steps down and the dog stirs.

"Sit down," he says and the dog obeys. "You stay here now and go with this man. He's gonna take care of you." And he walks away.

The dog makes a sound, whimpering like, but doesn't make any move to follow him.

The guy looks back and waves.

"Take care of her," he says but not loud enough for the old man to hear. The dog whimpers and wags her tail.

"Let's go, no name," the old man says, shuffling off. The dog, silent now, walks beside him.

"Wanna dog?" the old man hollers at the first person he meets.

*

Someone was snoring from somewhere on the floor. I heard footfalls going up and down the stairs.

"Whose room is this?" I asked Judy.

"It's ours now," she said as we huddled closer.

Now she smelled like the spices mother kept in the kitchen for the new man in her life after my father left for San Francisco. I never knew his name because he, too, deserted my mother not long afterwards. Besides, I did not care.

30

THERE WERE twenty-three students listed on the class roll, but only about half of them came on the first day of class. I arrived a few minutes late because I had difficulty locating the room where we were supposed to meet at 1:30 that Monday afternoon. Late as I was, there were not more than six students present who looked up briefly from whatever they were doing. I greeted them "Good afternoon," but they ignored me. I paused at the door before proceeding to sit down at the instructor's desk and asked, "Is this the Humanities course on the Philippines?"

"Right," a boy said, his mouth full.

Most of them were eating. This must be their lunch hour. They sat scattered in different parts of the room eating their lunch, chattering like island birds. My arrival did not stop them from continuing with their lunch. Nobody told me about this. What was I going to do? They didn't appear to mind my presence. They acted as if it was the most normal thing for them to be eating during a class period. Did they expect me to go ahead while they ate and chattered? They must be hungry and it seemed that had priority over the lesson.

A few more students arrived and sat down, opening immediately what looked like their lunch—potato chips, sandwiches wrapped in wax paper and drinks in paper cups.

They all looked like the Filipino students I used to teach in the Philippines, but with some differences. Much of this I learned in due time. These kids, including the girls, were shabby by Philippine standards. None of those I heard speaking had an accent. Their English was pure American. Of the twenty-three students, eight were girls, Chinese looking except one, a black girl who was the most beautiful in the group. Since her family name was Jimenez, I concluded her father was the Filipino and her mother, the black American. Two were white and didn't have anything Filipino in them except their family names. I recognized Carlos, the guy who had me answering all sorts of questions during my interview, but Jim was not around. I couldn't have missed him. One of the students named Wong, said he was pure Chinese. For one reason or another which I didn't bother to look into, Wong was interested in Philippine courses. A majority of the class were born of Filipino parents in California. Two or three were less than ten years old when their parents migrated to the United States. One girl, quite thin and timid and who looked older than most of the other members of the class, was not eating. She had nothing but books on her desk. She was attentive and followed my every move. She even smiled occasionally. When I managed to elicit a few words from her, she talked just like me, heavily accented and very Filipino. She had not been a year in the States, I learned later. She was a college student

96

in northern Luzon when her parents sent for her. I marked her name, saying to myself, bless your little heart, we're in this together. She had an unusual name for a girl, Patrocinio. Patrocinio Umali.

The noise in the room had not abated. Everybody kept moving about, talking loudly among themselves long after they were through eating. I noticed, however, that they did not litter the room. Nobody was listening to me with the exception of the new arrival from the Philippines.

I had xeroxed a two-page syllabus which I distributed to the class, explaining that a few of the reference materials were not yet available in the school library but would be by next week. I discussed what the course covered, but I felt no rapport with my students. A wall, almost palpable, lay between us like a transparent glass through which I coud see them, indifferent, noisy, inattentive, as if I were not there. I glanced at my watch; barely twenty minutes had elapsed. The way some of them sat, holding on to their bags, gave me the impression they were watching for the first opportunity to skip out, never to return. I was beginning to wish they would do just that. The thought flashed in my mind: was this worth 14 dollars by the hour? It was the longest hour in my experience as a teacher. I was tempted to dismiss the class, right on that first day. To me the first day was the most important. It was usually the time for getting to know each other, for laying out the rules. But with this kind of class, would rules be any help? What sort of extra effort did I need, what guile, what wisdom, to get the attention of the class? More important, how would I reach them, make them realize the relevance of the subject to their lives in America?

I had called the roll. But did I introduce myself? I had meant to. Yet there was something awfully wrong. Everything was wrong. The worst vibes ever. This was no class. I had stumbled onto an indoor picnic. I felt that nobody gave a damn about who I was, where I came from. So my name's David Dante Tolosa. They would ask, "How do you say that again?" perhaps to pretend some kind of interest. Of course, they would laugh. They were always laughing. I had a class of hyenas of the brown variety. Everything sounded funny to them. They heckled one another. They were not heckling me to my face, but from different parts of the room, I heard titters every time I opened my mouth. I looked at my watch again. The minute hand hadn't moved, it seemed. I placed it to my ear. It was ticking.

97

Then just when I was about to dismiss the class, vowing never to return, I realized I had been too damn serious. I glanced at the syllabus I had distributed. It was perfect, if I might say so myself. Professor Jaime would call it great. The beautiful department dean would nod her head in approval. I was everything my credentials promised. But what the hell, I was not getting anywhere. I was a miserable failure. Had I smiled? I thought I had. The truth was, I felt like crying. Why didn't I just stick to the magazine? What magazine? Suddenly I wanted to laugh, but I barely managed a smile.

The class was beaming, too. Humor, your old sense of humor, David. Where have you misplaced it?

"Look, you guys," I said, feeling a smile widen on my face, "you'll have to bear with me for a while. It's possible we'll be half through the course before you begin to understand what I've been talking about and by then you'd be pretty sure I've not been talking sense at all."

Everybody looked at me for a change, listening. Yes, they were paying attention!

"I'm sure my accent reminds you of your parents'."

"Grandparents," someone shouted and the class laughed.

"Touche," I said, laughing with them.

The next time I glanced at my watch, it was past the hour. We had not even heard the bell.

At our next meeting, the same picnic atmosphere prevailed but not for long. By the time I had gone through the class roll they were all finished with their lunch. One student raised his hand, wanting to know what I thought about Marcos.

"You mean. . . the . . . the dic. . . ruler . . . the guy who declared martial law?" I said in my best imitation of a confused stammering peasant.

The class was in an uproar.

"Yes, the dictator of the Philippines," someone said.

"I didn't know that," I said in a sad parody of Jack Benny.

"What do you know?" The class was in a jovial mood.

Easily, I warmed up to the subject closest to my heart—the freedom of the press, or rather, the absence of it back home. I was impassioned, a bit eloquent. To hell with my accent. I knew friends, writers who had been thrown into jail, still languishing there.

The class was listening in rapt attention as I shifted gears from humor to seriousness, putting on the brakes when the levity seemed to get out of control. Purely a matter of timing.

My students had much to contribute. What they said was often revealing.

Every time we discussed the so-called generation gap, the students seemed to have found at last a forum for their thinking on the matter. The growing alienation between Filipino children and their parents in the States was no laughing matter.

"My parents understand each other because they talk in the dialect, which we don't speak. They speak English, too, but it's as hard to follow as their dialect. I advised them to attend a speech clinic and they nearly threw me out of the house."

Even more distressing was their failure to communicate attitudes and concepts like morality and change.

"They're out of this world," one of the girls confided. "They're so strict it isn't funny. They don't approve of dating. They tell us, my sisters and me, that they never went out alone on a date. They were always chaperoned in those days. They want to impose the same rule on us. I suspect they want us all to grow up old maids."

Another girl said, "Every time I go out on a date, Mom waits till I return. She doesn't sleep. I'm told she says the rosary, gets on her knees in front of the Blessed Virgin while I'm out with my date. And after my date takes me home, she asks all sorts of crazy, personal questions. Why, she's sure one of these days I'm gonna get pregnant."

My students claimed they loved their parents, but they didn't know how to show their love for them. The parents insist on respect and obedience but the children "just wanted to be friends" with them, but that was not allowed.

"Dad says we can't be friends. He always reminds me he's my father and I'm his son," complained one young man.

One day I borrowed cassettes of Philippine songs. My students called the tunes "weepy" and the lyrics "corny." I tried to make them understand that Filipinos are a sentimental people. That's "backward," the class chorused, "old fashioned." My attempt to acquaint them with the Philippine National Anthem was even less successful. It just didn't mean anything to them.

Often I had to remind them that their understanding of Philippine culture would make them understand their parents and themselves, but all they wanted to know was, "Will this be asked in the finals?" After a while, I felt I was getting more from teaching the course than my students were. Now I seem to know better and appreciate my Philippine heritage more. Maybe I was being overpaid earning $14 an hour.

31

IMELDA WAS BACK from the Philippines with Estela but I had not yet seen either mother or child. It was Dr. Sotto who told me they had arrived, but he didn't say anything about the condition of the child. I hoped they didn't keep Estela home away from people. That would be tragic.

True to the doctor's word, the Board met the following Sunday at the Sotto residence. There were more than the usual members present and they all came with their wives. I liked that. The meeting was scheduled a little after noon to give allowance for those who had to attend the 11 o'clock mass. I heard mass early, jogged all the way and back. Quite refreshed and invigorated, I had a light breakfast of cold cereal with bananas and milk. I was ready.

From my room in the basement I could not tell how many of the guests had already arrived. The cars were parked on the other side of the hill. Dr. Sotto said he would just send for me. I cleaned the small table in the kitchen where I had just had my breakfast and pored over the papers I was going to submit to the Board. They included a rough sketch of the first cover of the magazine and two or three suggested logos for the word FILIPINO. I hoped there would be no hassle over the spelling. I was for the F instead of the P. I didn't think the National Language Academy or whatever body was responsible for the many variations in the spelling of Tagalog words would decree that F could not be used. It was hard enough arriving at a name for the magazine. The doctor and I had simply decided on it, taking advantage of the fact that the board members had no ideas of their own and, actually, didn't care. I had doubts whether they were really interested in the magazine, much less in listening to my presentation of the facts and figures which I had painstakingly researched.

I took more care than usual in getting dressed, deciding to wear a coat and tie because I felt the occasion called for some sort of formality. I knew the members (fat cats I called them in my mind) would be dressed in their usual natty best and their wives would be there. I knew the womenfolk had the deciding votes when it came to a showdown and I didn't want them to be prejudiced against an editor who looked like a bum out to help himself. Frankly, there were times when I felt that way. This was especially true during those days when I had not yet started to teach at City College. I remembered I had not yet informed Dr. Sotto about my part-time job. It might not be necessary, but I had to tell him. The worst he could say was give it up after the current quarter.

When he finally sent for me, I went upstairs to join the party, willing hard to appear composed and respectable.

The Board members had already started drinking; their wives were busy fingering the variety of choice meats, fruits, and the usual cucumbers, carrots, and celery cut up into thin sticks with a creamy dressing—party fare adapted from the Americans—and pickled eggs surely not centuries old in spite of what they were called. There were steaming dishes in silver trays over a low fire, fondues for dipping into various sauces. Food and drinks were the first order of the day.

Imelda had on a lacy off-white dress which went down below the knees, but neither the dress nor the bra she was wearing helped any in accentuating her rather small breasts. I was certain she had naturally wavy hair. Her curly locks clung on her nape becomingly.

"David," she said, turning to me. "Put down those folders and eat first. How have you been?"

"I'm okay, ma'am, doctora, I mean. I'm all right," I said, walking towards the piano on the far end of the room and putting the folders on the floor against the wall somewhere at the foot of the piano.

Dr. Sotto was talking to a group of men when he saw me. He waved, saying above the din, "Help yourself, there are drinks over there, then come and join us." The others smiled towards me, then resumed talking among themselves.

The waiters who served us wore white uniforms with the name of the catering firm embroidered on their breast pockets. Most of them were white Americans and looked professional,

101

smiling as they served us with drinks and appetizers. The old woman and her son were nowhere in sight. Perhaps they were with Estela. Will the couple allow the child to be seen by their guests? Soft music issued from the walls and ceiling as some of the guests started sampling the dishes. The men continued drinking and were now noisier than ever with their boisterous laughter, gesturing excessively and stomping their feet. When I joined Dr. Sotto's group I thought I heard a strange sound above the piped-in music and the loud talk. The women were the loudest; and as usual, they were separated from the men either by common consent or tradition, but definitely not by accident.

In spite of my resolve to appear comfortable, somehow I felt out of place. They talked about everything, it seemed, about new cars, a comparison of the merits of their respective accountants, who saved them big bucks in income tax returns. Trying not to look stupid, I smiled at their clever sallies, nodded when everyone else was nodding. I heard that eerie sound again. It couldn't have been my imagination. What could it be? The talk had reverted to cars with strange sounding names, mostly foreign, and expert income tax manipulators called accountants.

"What happened to that good-looking brother of yours who seemed to have taken over your Porsche?"

"Back in the Philippines."

"How come?"

"Got bored here. He couldn't get along particularly with the young American-born Filipinos his age. I don't know why."

"*Pasikat naman masiado*—he was quite a show-off, that's why maybe. Parading in his sports car."

"Not really. He was just bored. Couldn't stand it here. Without his *barkada* in the Philippines. Besides, *para daw siyang alila.* Thought we were treating him like a servant. But he could see all of us helped around the house."

"So you sent him back."

"No. He wanted to go home."

"And you gave him a Porsche?"

"Consolation prize. Besides, you know, I got a new one."

"Even then. It's like giving him a prize for not coping, for being a cop-out. I wouldn't have done that."

"*Mahina ka.* You're not using your head. My brother is not college material. But he's good looking. With a Porsche he'll look like a good catch and he could marry into a rich family, maybe a daughter of one of the martial law oligarchs."

102

Dr. Sotto had left the group. I didn't notice him leave. Perhaps I could also leave the group as inconspicuously.

Now they were bragging, yes, bragging about their gambling losses.

"The trouble with poker, sometimes it's like your manhood being challenged. I dropped one thou the other night."

"That's nothing, last month I lost five thou, and the missus nearly killed me."

Back to cars.

"What are you trying to do, own a fleet of luxury cars?"

"Not really. *Mabuti nga* I'm not buying a Rolls."

"Why not? You got everything else."

"Too complicated *ang pag order, eh.* Besides, I think that would be too conspicuous."

"As if you're not conspicuous already."

"Look who's talking. I got no airplane like you do."

"But nobody—okay, very few—only intimate friends know about my plane. Close friends *lang* like you and others whom I take fishing in Alaska."

Once, he related, he flew with a few other Filipino doctors, some of whom were at the party, in his six-seat plane to the Philippines. They had an audience with the First Couple. It was easy. They had a sizeable check with them from their association for one of the showy projects of the First Lady.

"What do they look like? I've never seen them except in pictures. Are they really. . .?"

"You're missing something, *chico.* I don't have the words to describe them . . . perhaps Mr. Editor here . . . Enchanting. *Talagang en grande. Parang* king and queen. *Luma ang* royalty *sa ibang* countries."

"You must have felt good. Did you declaim for everybody to hear, 'I Am a Filipino'?" Raucous laughter, laced with liquor.

Back to cars again.

"Is that right? Like you always have a new car outside your clinic every day? What do your patients say about it?"

It was my voice. I had spoken. They stared at me as if to say, the man can talk. Bravo. His question deserves an answer.

"What could they say? They own fine cars, too. Olds, Mercedes Benz, Cadillac . . . "

"Ah, you must have wealthy patients."

"Wealthy? Hell, no. My medical center is in Oakland. Many of my patients are on welfare. Some get unemployment benefits."

103

"That's a black neighborhood over there."

"So black, I suspect they think I'm a white man among them."

This time they laughed so loud I thought I was in a cockpit at a *Pintakasi* in the Philippines. I took advantage of the bedlam to get me some food. No more drinks for me until after the meeting if it was held at all.

Shortly before three in the afternoon, Dr. Sotto called attention to the reason for the luncheon.

"Let's go to the other room," he said.

The room looked like another dining room although nobody used the long table that could easily seat a party of twenty-four. It was, indeed, a dining table so elegant—it must have been a one-piece Philippine mahogany, each chair with a high back, lavishly carved. Against each wall stood similarly carved mahogany chests, and showing through the glass were neatly arranged china and silverware. A dining room fit for royalty. A portion of Malacañang Palace transported to San Francisco!

"This must be from the Philippines."

"It is. The workmanship is by the Bilibid prisoners in Manila."

"Is this table ever used?"

"Rarely. Like now."

"I mean for dinner."

"Not yet."

I was asked to sit at the head of the table. I had collected the folders from the foot of the piano and spilled the papers in front of me.

Imelda was the last one to come in and all the gentlemen stood up, some offering her a seat around the table. "No, thanks," she said. "I'll be in and out and I don't want to disturb the proceedings."

"Please, ma'am, doctora, I want you to listen in on this," I pleaded.

"Don't worry, I will," she answered, pulling a chair near the door.

Although thoroughly prepared, I was nervous just the same. I felt I knew everything that they might wish to know, but if they asked me questions for which I had no answers, I would say so.

"I shall begin from the beginning," I announced, looking around as calmly as I could. "And as I move from one item

104

to another, feel free to stop me if you have any question. I shall have to speak in general terms; the specifics can come later. I have here a prepared outline. It's likely that the question you raise in the course of my explanation would be covered before I am through with my talk. So if you can wait till I am finished, that would be better, but as I said, feel free to stop me any time you wish."

Nobody stopped me. They were all listening, the women's faces no less concerned and interested than the men's.

Briefly, but clearly, I hoped, I stressed what the magazine was to contain, the purpose of its being as I had gathered from conferences with Dr. Sotto and some members of the Board. It would be a specialized magazine in the sense only that it was for Filipino residents in America and other interested readers who didn't necessarily have to be Filipinos. It would neither be a high-brow magazine, nor a cheap one, perhaps a slick magazine, a monthly as I envisioned it, although the number of issues per year would be open to discussion. We would make it interesting for readers to want to read it regularly and attractive enough so we could solicit advertising without a guaranteed circulation to start with.

I suggested that an experienced advertising manager be hired regardless of nationality. I emphasized my role as editor-in-chief and the different departments that would be needed. I said I would prefer Filipino writers in my department. Distribution, marketing outlets, subscription campaigns and gimmicks would be under a well staffed department although a skeleton force to begin with would have to do.

I expressed my willingness to assume the main responsibility of getting the magazine started outside my editorial department. I discussed the content, its broad appeal, its variety. Each issue must enable us to put out better subsequent issues. This was not going to be a one-issue magazine. Many similar enterprises here and in the Philippines end up as one-shot publications. One issue comes out with all the fanfare, the hoopla of a political convention, and after that issue, nothing. Subscription money collected is not returned. Not a few Filipino residents in the States have been stung by these one-issue publications. I was thinking of a one-year twelve-issue magazine. The capital involved would be considerable. I could only make approximations in the absence of a study in this area. I understood that it would be a

105

business venture. We intended to make profits, but I doubted whether the magazine could show profit during the first year. It might be necessary to put in more capital the succeeding year, whatever start-up capital we decide to invest based on minimal needs.

At this point, there was a murmur, a restiveness in the group gathered around me. Whispers went around. Imelda stood up to leave. Dr. Sotto tried to hush the group.

"No, please, let them talk," I said. "Perhaps at this point you want to ask questions."

This evoked a rash of questions, most of them asked at the same time. In the confusion I had to request some questions to be repeated.

"Are you prepared to make an estimate of the start-up capital needed?"

I was not and didn't care to make an estimate without expert advice. "With your approval, I intend to consult an appropriate agency."

"Aren't you being unduly pessimistic in your assumption of initial losses?"

"I believe not. Just being realistic."

"But you have no figures on which to base your assumptions."

"No reliable figures. But I have some experience in this matter. For one, I know that printing costs have gone up considerably in the past few years. Data on this is available. And please remember, ladies and gentlemen, we have no printing press of our own."

"So what do you suggest?"

"About the press? I don't believe we can afford to buy one at this stage. It would be unwise. I suggest that we hire a consulting firm to make a study of our projected magazine."

"Why have you not done so in the first place?"

"It will cost us a pretty penny and I have not been given the authority."

Dr. Sotto took over and consulted the members and their wives. In spite of the initial confusion and maybe shock over my report, I felt we were getting somewhere. I realized that a majority of the Board didn't have any idea of the magnitude and the huge expense involved in the type of publication they wanted. Someone suggested that I be authorized to consult a competent firm.

106

"Better yet," I suggested, "why don't you appoint some among you to look for a consulting firm?"

They had no time. They would rather leave it to me.

"So perhaps we could now move on to other matters?" I said.

No, not yet, they protested. This is the most important matter and should not be thrust aside.

"I beg your pardon. I realize its importance and I'm not ignoring it. But could I go over the other items I want to discuss with you, then go back to the funding?" I was thinking it would be difficult, if not impossible, to meet again soon with everybody in attendance.

When they agreed with no little grumbling I enumerated some of the more important ideas I wanted to explore with them. First and foremost: how independent is the magazine going to be? Do we have to make a stand on vital issues that affect our wellbeing as Filipinos?

"Make that Filipinos in America."

"Right. But what would keep us from voicing our opinions on, say, what's currently happening in the Philippines?"

"But definitely. Otherwise what good would the magazine be? I don't want to have anything to do with a spineless magazine."

"You're talking about Marcos and martial law. The question is too disruptive. *Magulo.*"

"I don't mean for the magazine to be anti or pro-Marcos. Then we would be no different from the numerous Philippine publications in this country. I have stopped reading them, to tell you the truth." It was an older man talking, one of the few businessmen in the group.

"Can't we keep the magazine out of the martial law imbroglio? Most of us here are U.S. citizens."

"But still Filipinos. Being an American citizen doesn't or shouldn't change what we are essentially—Filipinos. The Philippines is still our country. Personally, I love the Philippines no less than before I became a U.S. citizen."

Now everybody wanted to say something. This last statement from one of the doctors elicited a quite audible reaction of approval, particularly from the women.

"Okay. We take sides. But which side?"

"It seems an obvious choice." I thought it was the guy with the six-seater plane who was talking. Didn't he present a check

107

to the First Couple? I could have been wrong. Maybe it was the guy with the good-looking brother in the Philippines trying to snare the daughter of one of the new oligarchs.

Someone was quick to respond. "Not really that obvious, come to think of it. We study both sides. Present the plus and minus signs of the New Society as objectively as the editorial staff is capable."

By the time snacks were served, it was almost evening and the talk was still on martial law in the Philippines.

"At the rate we're going," someone remarked, "we might have to stay here for dinner."

"You're welcome. Any time," Dr. Sotto was quick to answer as he was expected to, and started looking for Imelda.

She appeared at the doorway. Assisted by the old woman, she was pushing a wheelchair in which sat a pitiful looking girl dressed in a long silky gown, a plaid woolen blanket on her lap. Estela could not hold her head still, nor her arms and hands which twitched in various contortions as involuntary as they were awkward. She was dribbling at the mouth and making strange sounds.

A heavy silence fell upon the party. Some of the women gasped and looked away, their hands on their lips. Imelda was smiling down at her daughter. Dr. Sotto rushed towards them and tried to adjust the blanket around the child's legs although it needed no adjusting. Then Imelda spoke, her voice firm as if stating a principle she believed in against the world.

"This is Estela, our daughter, who accompanied me all the way from the Philippines. Estela, these are our friends."

Estela could have been a lovely child but for the wasting disease that racked her body and withered her extremities, making her look like a hag, old, far beyond her years.

"Say hello to our friends, Estela," Imelda continued to address her daughter and seemed she actually expected her to say hello to everybody.

She made some strange sounds in her throat, her head moving around as in a loose ball bearing. Her eyes were bloodshot and rheumy as they looked around the room. None of us had said a word. No one had moved or so it seemed to me. In that awkward silence I tried to rearrange my papers in their respective folders and stood up. Then one of the women said, as she approached the wheelchair, "Estela, welcome to America, your new home. We love you."

108

"Say, Estela, say, I love you, too," Dr. Sotto whispered, bending down close to the child's face.

Everybody was talking now. Imelda started to say something and paused to wait for the gradual silence that followed before proceeding.

"When we gave this luncheon, we decided it was as good an occasion as any for you to meet our beloved and only child. We were sure some of you knew she was around but you didn't know where. My mother didn't want her to make the trip. I know she would miss her. Estela would miss her too. But I was able to convince my mother that there are better doctors here, much better facilities. We're praying. We realize we're expecting nothing short of a miracle. Prayers help. We doctors really don't know much. We've never been happier than now with Estela with us." She looked at her husband, who nodded, his eyes misty. He walked towards his wife and put his arm around her waist and she took his hand and kissed it.

An applause seemed called for but there was no clapping of hands. The crowd trooped towards the couple and their child, saying many things at the same time, not quite sure what to do, whether to touch Estela, express sympathy, smile, laugh, cry?

After everybody had left, I went down to my basement room and tried to evaluate what had just happened. I was tired and needed a drink. Somehow I was happy I had met and talked with the Board and the Sottos had had their peace with their friends and themselves. In my own way, I prayed for a miracle, too. Not only for Estela, but for the magazine.

I was about to change into my pajamas when there was a knock on the door. It was the boy and he was carrying a basket of food. Dr. Sotto had a note for me: Be down in a minute. Wait. Enjoy.

I put the food in the refrigerator, stacking the freezer to its capacity and putting the rest in the refrigerator. The fruit went into the vegetable compartment.

The boy left the door ajar and before I was aware of his presence, the doctor was already inside my room.

"Thanks for the foodstuff. I have enough to last the entire season. You didn't have to. I still have plenty of provisions."

"What do you think?" he asked, ignoring my remark.

"What do *you* think?"

"I want your opinion first."

"Well, frankly, I'm not really sure. It could go one way or the other. Too bad I could not explain with more detail the other *musts* we need to do to start: the photo deparment for instance. We need a photo editor. The magazine could be more graphic than textual."

"I was not talking about the magazine," he said.

I was a bit confused, then I realized my mistake.

"I meant our child. Estela. Did we do right introducing her the way we did? And the timing, ha? Oh, David, we had worried so. We knew the rumors kept going behind our backs, insinuations, half-truths, so tell me . . ."

"It was the right thing to do, the only thing to do. I was so proud of you and your wife."

"We had agonized over it while preparing for the party. Together we prayed for guidance."

"From now on no more rumors."

"God, yes, I hope so." His voice trailed off, heavy with anxiety. His face showed it, too.

"Where's Joy now?"

"In Colorado. She left two weeks ago."

"Did she resign?"

"I don't know. I'm afraid to ask."

"Anyway, one problem at a time. Estela is a lovely girl."

"Could have been. You don't know how devoted Imelda is to her. Now she says we shouldn't have left her behind. As doctors, we know there's very little hope of her getting any better here or anywhere else."

"Even doctors can be wrong."

"I know. We've decided not to put her in an institution. We are asking advice from specialists. We'll never give up hope."

"Miracles still happen, doctor."

He didn't say anything as he sat pensively, his hands clasped in front of him. His tieless shirt was rumpled. He stood up abruptly and opened the door, listening.

"You don't hear anything from here, do you?" he asked.

"Not a thing. Not even that city blazing beneath us."

He shut the door and walked towards the window, pulling the curtains aside. San Francisco in all its jewelled splendor turned the skies above her deep red where no clouds hung. I could feel its warm breath but heard nothing—what did I expect? He drew the curtains back and turned to me.

110

"Come, I'll show you something. I hope she's still there."

On our way up, he explained how one night when they had just arrived and Estela was unusually restless, Imelda and the old woman had a hard time trying to quiet her down. She kept flailing her arms and swinging her legs as far as they would go as if she wanted to get rid of her wheel chair. Every time she got hold of the blanket she tried to rip it off violently. When Imelda tried to feel her brow for a sign of fever, she groaned and pushed her mother's hand away. They didn't know what to do. In desperation, Imelda drew the curtains in the room aside and for want of anything really sensible to do, she pointed to the city lights beneath, saying, "Look, Estela, look at all those lights. Pretty, pretty, aren't they?" Estela turned, swaying towards the window and the two women pushed her close enough to touch the glass. She stared down as much as her condition would allow and stopped moaning. Her contortions ceased. Slowly, she started to make sounds that were different, happy sounds, as if she was singing. She accompanied the beat of the sounds coming from her throat with the motions of her hands. Although it was not easy to tell, it seemed that she was smiling. She was clapping her hands or trying to. And she stayed on, looking down at the city below, making those sounds and those movements with her hands and her legs and her body as though beating to the rhythm of a melody the city was sending up to her, and she was responding. A great happiness suffused her whole being. Finally she got tired, her eyes closed, her head falling on her chest. They pushed her away from the window, drew the curtains back and wheeled her to bed where she slept soundly.

As we reached the top of the stairs, we saw that Estela was still there. I heard her before I actually saw her. The lights in the room had been dimmed so that the sparkling diamonds below showed even brighter.

It was a repeat of the scene Dr. Sotto had just described.

Before long they were pulling her away from the window. I touched Dr. Sotto's arm to tell him that I was returning to the basement. He nodded, pleased no doubt, that I had seen Estela's strange fascination for the city blazing up at us among the mists and the drifting clouds, the red skies and the ragged edges of darkness down and away.

111

32

THERE WERE MEETINGS scheduled among different Filipino organizations, sometimes three times a week. There was always one, at least, on Saturdays. I believe the involved Filipino in California attended such meetings as part of his lifestyle. He looked forward to seeing the old faces and an occasional new one. He loved to talk, to argue endlessly. Perhaps living alone much of the time made him seek the company of other Pinoys like him. Yet even in the Philippines where most Filipinos didn't lead solitary lives, they loved to attend meetings, to talk in front of a microphone. It was something to tell the other guys about, something to remember, the sound of their voice, its impact, actual or imagined, upon the audience. One recurring memory I hold of my younger days in the Philippines is the picture of Filipinos of both sexes, talking endlessly and vehemently in front of a microphone, their voices amplified many times, reaching out everywhere; how loath they were to give up their place to others awaiting their turn.

This one I attended was an organization of civic-minded and religiously inclined Filipino-Americans as they called themselves, which had been allocated a Federal grant for the purpose of helping out needy but deserving young Filipino college students.

The meeting was to decide what criteria the organization would enforce in choosing qualified scholars, and how the money would be apportioned among them. The basement of the St. Joseph's Catholic Church served as the "venue," as most Filipinos like to call their gathering places. A good number were in attendance, both young and old. The mass was over at 8 that Saturday night and the meeting was advertised to begin immediately, but by 9 o'clock, it hadn't started yet. As I looked around I couldn't decide who of those present was supposed to open the proceedings. The oldtimers talked among themselves, laughing out loud. They appeared self-conscious, important. The young ones were unusually quiet. Most of them smoked constantly. I could not see their faces clearly from where I sat, so thick was the smoke in the air.

"When do we begin? It's almost ten," a voice from among the younger group said, from the rear of the hall.

There was a collective movement to look at wrist watches.

112

"It's only nine," someone said.

"The meeting was scheduled at eight."

"Filipino time."

"Shit!"

"The chairman isn't here yet."

"Does he need a wheelchair?" again from the young people in the rear, followed by snickers.

When the chairman finally arrived, he seemed fit and robust, carrying folders under his arm and smoking a cigar. A few approached him as he sat down. They exchanged jokes, inanities, laughing and tapping each other on the arms, forgetting, it would seem, that there were others waiting for the meeting to begin.

"Do we need a mike?" somebody asked.

"I don't think so. The acoustics here is quite good."

A few more brown men and women who probably believed in Filipino time, drifted in later, packing the room. The chairman was taking a long time puffing his cigar and bantering with his friends.

When he finally called the meeting to order, after beating about the bush in English, a language he had not mastered too well, he announced that there was less money than they thought would be available for grants, but he assured the audience, *"okay lang."* There was still enough, everything was in order and they could now proceed to discuss the business at hand.

What criteria should be used to determine the needy and deserving? What courses should have priorities? What would be the cut-off age level? How poor should an applicant be in order to qualify? What proofs would be required to indicate level of need? Would full-time working students be qualified? Etcetera.

Every suggestion was preceded by a lengthy, rambling introduction. Surprisingly enough, even these boring speeches elicited some kind of applause. There was mild, good-natured heckling.

A middle-aged man with an unusually thick crop of hair introduced himself at first in English as a "humble member" of the association, and later launched into a flowery speech in Pilipino.

My God, he was fluent, poetic. Some of the oldtimers sat at the edge of their seats, eager to applaud. And applaud they did every time the speaker paused dramatically. A murmur rose from some sections of the room. "How sweet it is," or in Pilipino, *"ang sarap,"* or similar words that meant as much. Many of them

113

had not heard Pilipino spoken in all the years they had been away from home. Their eyes followed the speaker's gestures approvingly, mouthing softly some of the Pilipino expressions he used. How sweet it was, indeed, even in my own ears and I had not been away that long from the homeland.

As the man continued speaking, he began to sound—to me, anyway—excessively sentimental, banal, commonplace, more ornament than substance, but it was beautiful! I was entranced. What was he trying to say, anyway? It didn't matter; it sounded good. It was fun to watch the oldtimers as they took in the speaker's performance with such child-like enthusiasm. It was touching, the way their faces glowed with excitement; perhaps the speech took them back to their childhood in half-forgotten barrios and villages of long ago.

In spite of myself, I, too, was getting carried away by the speaker's eloquence. Then, from out of the crowd, a young Filipino dressed in dirty blue jeans and ragged army shirt, its olive-drab tails reaching down to his knees, started heckling the speaker. At first, the speaker ignored the heckler. Annoyed, the young man walked up front to confront the speaker, asking him to shut up.

"Wait a minute now," the young man said, an edge to his voice. "This has gone too far. We don't have all night, you know." He looked like he needed a shave badly, or was just starting to grow a beard; the stubble on his face made him look filthy. His English showed no accent. It was pure American. His long hair fell over his face and he kept brushing it off as he spoke, his tone loud and menacing. "Stop, please, will you? We're supposed to attend a meeting here, and I think it's time to begin. Time to stop all this crap. And please speak in a language we can all understand. What you're saying sounds worse than Greek to me and my companions out there." He pointed to the rear of the hall as he held his ground with no intention of getting back to his seat. The crowd in the rear, presumably all young Filipinos born in this country, stood up, clapping, and roared in approval.

"Who are you?" one of the oldtimers asked loud enough to be heard above the babel. Everybody was speaking in English now.

"Who's he? Do you know him?"

"What's he talking about? What does he want?"

"He has absolutely no respect. No manners."

"Who are you?" someone asked again, advancing towards the young man.

114

"What the hell for do I have to identify myself? Who are you? This meeting is open to all those interested in scholarship funding, right? Okay, let's get on with it and stop this meaningless blah blah."

"Young man, are you a Filipino?" an old, Chinese-looking man asked, as he limped towards the front, signalling the native speaker to move aside.

"You bet your bibby, I am. Can't you see? Look around you, old man."

There were quite a few of them—young boys and girls— seated in the back rows, all shabbily dressed with wild, unkempt hair. In the old man's eyes they must have looked more like the descendants of Genghis Khan and his warriors than the offspring of Filipino oldtimers.

Not daunted, the young man continued, "You bet we are Filipinos. Born here. Not in the steaming jungles where our ancestors are supposed to have come from, who speak that language that eats up so much precious time. Some of us live quite a ways. Now please go on with the meeting. We don't wanna hear any more speeches. We wanna know how we can qualify for the funds you got for college. See? We're good boys and girls. We wanna go to school. Get an education. So let's get on with it, okay?"

"What's your objection to one of our countrymen speaking in Pilipino?"

"Because it doesn't make sense to me, to us. Because we didn't come here to hear speeches in Pilipino. We wanna know how much and how we can get into this funding game, can't you see? It's so simple."

"I don't think you're no Filipino!" An ancient, sick-looking man who could hardly stand sputtered as he tried to hold on to his chair. Trembling with rage and pointing his cane at the brash young man, he tried to outshout him. "You don't belong here. If you're Filipino you should have been born dead," he cried.

"Drop dead yourself," the youth replied calmly, showing no sign of withdrawing from the fight.

The old man staggered, as though he would really drop dead. The group in the rear tittered and applauded, enjoying the scene. A voice said, "Bury the old man, he's lived too long."

There was no order now. The chairman was frantically babbling away. A few hot heads had rushed to the front to strike at the young man in any way they could, but he held his ground,

115

legs apart, arms akimbo, his eyes mean and unwavering, ready for combat. His companions had rushed into the melee.

"Take it easy, guys. Don't lose your cool!" the chairman was shouting, banging his hand on the table.

One of the girls pulled the young man back to the rear away from the flailing arms of angry men. There was no way I could see how the chairman could call the meeting back to order. The young Filipinos appeared ready to leave. Their curses filled the air with vulgar obscenities.

"Shit!"

Never did the English language sound so heart-warmingly picturesque until the old timers responded with their own version of English, especially now that they were mad. Pandemonium. The chairman was still trying to call the meeting to order. But he had completely lost control.

In the midst of the bedlam I sought the Filipino orator to ask him what he thought of the scene. When I finally located him, sitting alone in a corner, he looked quite confused and disoriented. He raised his eyes towards me and, for a flitting moment, I thought I saw my father's eyes. He had been crying, silently.

"How beautifully you talked," I said in Pilipino.

33

DR. SOTTO had requested me to prepare a detailed and complete report on the magazine which he would submit to a firm of consultants. It was not difficult to do. I had the data which they needed on which to base their estimates. I did most of the work in a section of the Public Library on the second floor where there was a lot of desk space and not too many people. What I didn't finish I brought home.

On the night I was supposed to hand in the papers, Dr. Sotto appeared early in my room. I found it odd that he didn't have a bottle with him this time. It was disconcerting to see his lack of interest in the papers I had given him in a neat black imitation leather folder. When I tried to call attention to the papers, he closed the folder, saying, "I'm sure everything is here. Be ready if and when you're needed by the firm."

"Which firm have you chosen?"

"I've asked Dr. Tablizo to suggest the firm which would give us an estimate of the over-all cost."

"Do you have any idea how much it's going to cost?"

"No," he said. "Do you?"

"More or less," I answered. "I've been making inquiries."

Oddly enough, he didn't ask how much. Instead, he said, "What do you think of Estela? I mean, her fondness for the view of the city from way up here?"

"It's incredible. Does she also like to see it in the daytime?"

"There's nothing to see in the daytime."

"On a clear day perhaps."

"It's the glitter, the lights, the colors she loves."

Then he went on to talk about Estela and about himself.

"Even the old woman has grown very fond of her."

I was about to say, "Because she's so helpless" when he continued as if reading my mind.

"Not really because she's helpless, but she's just really a lovable child. We don't pity her. We love her."

Estela seemed to have drawn the couple together. The troubles of the past seemed far away now. Joy had not returned and he couldn't care less whether she did or not. Imelda had reduced her work in the hospital. She was home earlier now. He himself could hardly wait to get home to see how the child was doing. Both parents tried to learn to communicate with Estela in sign language and to understand the noises she made, her gestures, and her moods. They were thinking of bringing the child to Boston where a world-renowned specialist had a clinic.

The Filipino community had stopped talking about the child. What else could their friends say now?

He looked at his watch.

"It's about this time when Estela's shown her favorite movie as we call it. Do you want to watch her?"

"Not tonight," I said. "I have some writing to do."

"Good night, then. Be seeing you soon," he said, taking the folder with him. At least, he had not forgotten it.

34

OFFICIAL HOLIDAYS usually fell on Mondays. No classes. Fourteen dollars gone. That's a lot of sandwiches, I thought, remembering Judy. She was in my thoughts more often than I wanted her to be. The rare times I visited her on the same floor in the condemned building, she was not around. The place looked cleaner. The paint no longer smelled and those who were there were mostly fast asleep or in deep meditation. I looked for her at the usual places near the Greyhound depot, but there was no sign of her. I knew that if I wanted to see her, the best time to visit would be at night, but I didn't feel like going out after dark.

One Monday, a holiday, I took the bus to the Golden Gate Park tennis courts. If I was lucky, I could rally with someone who, like me, had no partner. Usually I was not lucky and I had to be content with hitting the ball against a backboard or practising my service on a vacant court.

That day I found someone to play with who said he never showed up with "no pardner" but got to play more than he cared to sometimes. Everybody knew him, the Filipino who beat guys half his age or even younger. He was tiny, wiry, dark brown. Even on cool days he played without a shirt.

"My name's David," I said, "David Dante Tolosa."

"Cesar. did you ever play in Manila?"

"I lived there for a while."

"The Victoria Gardens?"

"What Victoria Gardens?"

"That's awright. You're too young."

He proceeded to drop names of well known Philippine tennis players some of whom I recognized, like Ampon, Ingayo, the Deyros. He talked of players and events before my time.

"I'm 72," he said as if announcing an award he was proud to have won.

How did one play with a 72-year-old man who, according to him, could still beat the best of those who had played him on these courts? He was popular among the regulars. As we talked while waiting for our turn, men and women in tennis togs called out his name as if it were royalty's.

"We need only two balls," he said when our turn to play came. "A third ball is unnecessary."

He talked with a clipped accent as if trying hard not to

sound like a Filipino. When I shifted to Pilipino, he would answer in English and continue to talk in English.

As we began exchanging balls, I said, "Let's just rally."

"No, we play. No fun without scores."

Before long I realized I was playing with a pro. His movements were fluid, his strokes had a zing to them, underspin, overspin. His overhead smashes were not too strong, but they were well placed, his volleys, firm and unerring. We practiced serving. He had terrific first balls, not hard, but curvy and like most players of his generation, he chopped the ball, forehand and backhand, beautifully.

It was going to be some game. I regretted I did not have much practice. He played every day, weather permitting. He was good but I was not bad myself and how long could he keep running all over the court?

All day, I soon found out, tiring before he did. We could not play more than a set, which I lost 7-5. No, I didn't give the game away. I wanted to win.

As we shook hands across the net, he said, "You're okay, perhaps a bit rusty. Wanna have lunch with me?"

I begged off, muttering a vague excuse, but he was not listening.

"You come," he insisted. "I don't live too far. We can walk. I always walk. I jog, too. Do you?"

I told him, I did.

He was inviting me to his place. At our first meeting! I was curious. He was the first Filipino in San Francisco who showed instant kindness, the well known hospitality, which is supposed to be our trademark as a people.

He lived in a hotel which looked shabby even from a distance when he pointed it out to me after what seemed an interminable walk from the tennis courts, and even worse, no better than the condemned building on Market where Judy stayed, on closer view. It was called ROYAL, the five-letter word in tarnished gothic over a shaded doorway. It was three avenues away from the Golden Gate Park beyond Lincoln, or was it Fulton or Irving, several blocks farther north in a seedy neighborhood. Who stayed in that kind of a hotel, I wondered. Maybe penniless transients and old-timers like him. What served as a lobby—two upholstered chairs, their arms ripped, the insides showing like battered dolls, and a sofa the color of green guavas—seemed like a second thought or an

119

irrelevant requirement, its area further narrowed and actually truncated by the counter behind which stood a Hispanic-looking old man in a green vest, also the color of guavas. Over his head in a half-curve was a stairway that ended in a mezzanine.

"How izzit going?" Cesar asked without pausing as he climbed the stairs with me in tow. The man didn't bother to reply.

'He's just substitute, won't be here tomorrow. Dizzy'd be back. My pal, he runs this hotel. I work for him."

Cesar's room was near a door marked Exit on the farthest end of the mezzanine facing the street. It was barely enough for one occupant. A well-made bed close to a glass window with a view of the fire escape. There was an old refrigerator in what served as kitchen and dining room. It was the only room in the hotel with kitchen privileges, according to him. No bath. The bathroom was a few doors away. There was enough space for a closet; this one was chocolate brown. It was amazing how colors in these surroundings impressed me who never noticed them too much before. What I was looking for was not there: the smell of old age, of decay, of death. It was a tidy room, pleasant in a reticent sort of way. He turned on a small black-and-white portable TV set as soon as we got in and turned it off immediately without explanation. Perhaps a daily ritual he observed or maybe he could not hear what I was saying. The noise from the street was bad enough.

I was also looking for something else that was not there: his tennis trophies. Where were they? I was sure he must have won a few in his lifetime. One of these days I was going to ask him. By then I knew I must see the man again, play with him, get to know him better. There were such persons you don't want to miss seeing again.

"Give a look at this," he said, opening his freezer. It was crammed full of food, mostly fish wrapped in cellophane now encrusted with ice, which he identified as crab meat, chicken parts, a few slices of beef, and tiny cans of orange juice concentrate. "No pork for me. I haven't tasted lechon for years. Funny, I don't miss it."

For lunch we had mackerel cooked in vinegar and ginger. Since he ate with his hands, I didn't think it would be polite to use the silver he had given me.

"I can't eat fish without using my hands," I said, "especially fish cooked the Filipino way, bones and all."

120

"It's the only way. To eat."

I noticed that he was watching me while I ate but it didn't bother me. I was too busy separating the bones from the meat.

"Good," he said, after a while. "You're a regular cowboy." It sounded like a compliment and helped me feel quite at home.

"You take care of yourself very well," I said.

"As my teacher in grade school used to say, 'God help those who helps themselves.' "

He claimed that staying outdoors most of the time made up for the crummy room he lived in. He considered exercise the menial tasks he had to do in the hotel in exchange for the free room. He worked hard, did a lot of bending and lifting. Now he weighed a mere 110 pounds.

"Never weighed more than 132," he said.

"A flyweight."

"Did you box? I did. As a kid in Sulucan, I had to. But that didn't last long. A glass jaw and a very sensitive nose. Every time it smelled my opponent's gloves, it bled like a goat."

On a subsequent visit, remembering the orange juice concentrate in the freezer, I brought him a bag of sunkist oranges on an impulse. When he saw them he smiled, saying, "I ain't sick."

I remembered. In the Philippines we usually brought sunkist oranges to hospital patients: the supreme offering.

By this time I felt we had grown more comfortable with each other. When it was raining and we couldn't play tennis, we went to the movies, but not the X-rated ones. He had seen a few but he could not bear to watch all that coupling, saying it looked so sad. He had seen one out of curiosity because everybody was talking about it. The movie, "Deep Throat," was still showing across from St. Anthony's Church. The hard core pornography was too much for him so he walked out, his eyes burning with something like tears of anger or sorrow, he wasn't sure. None of that ever again. How well I understood . . .

I told him about my work, the magazine, and the rich Filipino doctors and businessmen in the city who were backing it.

"Oh, so, you're a writer. For a writer you don't play tennis too badly."

"I'm out of practice."

He laughed. "You'll need plenty more sacks of rice before you can beat Cesar," he said without sounding offensive.

"Hey," I said, "you know my full name but I don't know yours."

121

"Cesar Pilapil."

I told him about my father.

"Why do you think he's still alive?" he asked.

"I feel he is. I hope he is."

"Let's see," he began, looking pensive. "No, no," he continued, shaking his head.

"Tolosa, that's not a common name. You remember it when you hear it," I insisted.

"I remember no Tolosa. Me don't remember no names."

He could speak good, though sometimes ungrammatical, English and sometimes he lapsed into illiterate English.

"For God's sake, why don't you remember names?"

"I just don't. And I don't care. I never ask. You gave me your name even I don't ask. I give you mine because you ask."

"Cesar is a good name, but I like Pilapil better."

"The hell you do."

"Honest."

"A peasant's name. Do you know what it means?"

"Who cares?"

"Well, I do."

We had great arguments. I felt tempted to invite him to my place on Diamond Heights, but he gave me the impression he would not be interested. He would not be comfortable in the presence of the rich, particularly Filipinos who were ostentatious and looked down on his kind.

"They're okay," I assured him. "Once you get to know them."

"They brag worse'n Texans. Have you heard Texans brag? It's all fun. Everybody laughs. But not these Filipino fat cats, some of whom ain't really that fat. And they were nobodies back home, true? And they don't play no tennis. They're sissies. They forget they're Filipinos."

"What's to forget?"

"You're joking. I see you with your notebook. I see you jotting down stuff. You never stop working, do you now? Relax. You'll never beat me unless you relax."

"Boy, you're something. You ask me to relax when I play you. And you take advantage. You give me love set. You love to do that, don't you? "

"Because I like you. You love to eat my fish. You buy me fresh fruit. You take me to the movies. And you learn fast. One of these days, you're gonna beat me."

122

Indeed, one day, I beat him. We usually played only one set whenever we met except when there were not too many players and there were vacant courts. It was set point in my favor I don't remember how many times and he wouldn't give up. When I finally won, I ran to the net to shake his hand, but he said, "We ain't finished yet. That was only the first set. This is a two-out-of-three match."

"Man, you're crazy," I protested. "You're tired."

"Let's see who's more tired." Of course, I was, but he surely looked beat after that long set.

"Quit stalling and let's begin."

"Don't you want to take a rest first? Maybe drink a little water?"

"You do that. Looks like you need it."

When I returned to the court, he was practicing his service and he had a new pair of balls.

"Those balls we used were old. They didn't bounce well."

"Ho, ho! An alibi."

"I'm not kidding. Shall we begin?"

I was actually more tired than I would admit. He was fresh as if he had just warmed up. He was all over the court. He ran after each ball like a teen-ager and I was the septuagenarian. He kept passing me every time I approached the net, which I had to do because he was too steady on the base line. He also killed me with his lobs. I ran back after a couple that fell right on the base line, but even when I got them back across the net, he put them away neatly. I hated it most when he seemd to smile at my futile attempts to save a point or when he said, "Good try."

I lost the second set 6-4. He wanted a deciding set, but I gave up. "I surrender," I said.

"Don't take it to heart," he consoled me. "You beat me one set. That's good enough. Be happy."

That night I took him to his favorite Chinese restaurant where they served *mongo*, not lentils. He insisted on having it cooked the way it was done back home. Ever since I heard him say that I was always jotting down stuff, I made it a point not to pull out my notebook and pen in his presence. I knew so much about him now and the more I did the more I felt compelled to tell him about myself.

"Sometimes I think I've seen you before," he told me once. When he repeated it, I wondered whether he had met my father.

123

"I never knew him really but my mother talked about him a lot, saying I had taken after him. He had good teeth. Just like mine. I suppose even now he would still have good teeth."

"Mine ain't too bad. They're good. See? After all, they're mine now, all paid for." His eyes twinkled mischievously.

"Tolosa, Tolosa," I kept repeating the name to refresh his memory.

"Names don't mean nothing to me. How many times do I have to tell you? I don't remember no names."

"Pilapil, that's a good name."

"A peasant's name, but it's Filipino, I tell you. Not like. . . like . . . what's the name now?"

"Tolosa."

"Sounds Spanish."

Cesar was a dropout, barely finishing first year high school. Both his parents were school teachers who learned English from American soldiers turned teachers during lulls in the sporadic fighting that went on long after American occupation of the Islands. He had three sisters and one brother who graduated vale-dictorian in high school and was set on becoming a lawyer, but died of pneumonia. His sisters were all married with grown-up children of their own who didn't carry the name anymore. His parents had long been dead. Pilapil was a dying name.

Unlike his brother and sisters, Cesar wasn't comfortable in school, as he put it. He couldn't remember the things he read but he tried hard to study because he wanted to be like the other members of the family, brilliant. When report cards were due and all the children brought theirs home for their parents' signature, Cesar would hide under the house in shame because of his failing grades. He listened to his parents upstairs praise their bright children. Then his youngest sister would go down and look for him, and lead him upstairs to meet the rest of the family. They didn't blame him for his low grades. They didn't have to, seeing how ashamed he was of himself. He just wasn't made for academic work. So he tried to excel in something else like carpentry and athletics. He was a long-distance runner. He was competitive, he had the heart and the endurance. When he discovered tennis, he knew he had found his calling. Although he never made it to foreign lands in open tournaments, he was popular locally. I knew I should know his name because I followed the sports even as a young man, but no matter how hard I tried, I could not remem-

124

ber a Cesar Pilapil. Perhaps I was too young. I didn't even know where the Victoria Gardens were in Manila.

"Are you sure you played under your real name?"

"Of course. I was proud of what I was doing. I beat some of the lesser guys, but a lot of younger players were getting on and I wasn't getting any younger. When I left for the States, that's the end."

"Cesar Pilapil," I murmured. How could I miss a name like that?

"In those days everybody called me *Tingting*. You know, the midrib of a broom, very thin."

"Tingting, Tingting," I repeated, then, "Tingting!" I shouted, excited by the discovery. We were resting after a meal of eggs scrambled with fish, chopped onions and sliced tomatoes. He was putting the dishes away when it dawned on me who he was. I rushed to him and embraced him, lifting him off his feet. "You're Tingting, the terrible Tingting! Why didn't you tell me?"

"What for?" he asked, visibly startled by my reaction, but pleased that I had recognized the name.

"Because I know Tingting. And I beat Tingting!" I was still shouting.

"One set," he reminded me, "and Tingting is already 72."

"I don't see any of your trophies here," I remarked.

"Left them all in the Philippines."

"With your sisters?"

"No. With a friend. A girl friend."

I assumed he loved my company and enjoyed my friendship otherwise he would not have confided in me. I didn't have to jot down his stories because he repeated them as though to assure himself that they had actually happened.

There were facts in his life that I would not have known had he not, on his own volition, told me about them because I wouldn't have asked. They were too personal. For my part, I must have divulged aspects of my past without his asking. It was the way of the exile, a never-ending quest for common roots, similar beginnings. Our nostalgia took on the same shape, the same boundaries, the same hues and smells, sensations, real or imagined deprivations, hurts and grudges, little victories we had not shared with anyone else, a continuing hope for the future in a faraway land.

"Tennis saved my life," he was fond of saying. It gave him the foothold he needed to go on living without having to make

125

excuses for not being an intellectual achiever like the other members of his family. It kept him healthy at an age when most of his contemporaries had long passed away or were suffering from all sorts of ailments, and were visibly infirm.

Prayers, too, helped, he said: You can invent your own prayers, but you may memorize those prayers that say it all. You can't just talk to God extemporaneously. Remember, He is God, You owe Him. You don't address Him the way you talk to your tennis partner. Better, if you're not prepared to talk to Him well, don't talk at all. Practice telling Him things without your saying anything, without your lips moving. Then you can commune with Him anywhere anytime.

You need not be alone too much, David. He is there when you truly need Him. This sounds trite, but He has saved my sanity, my life. He has given me good fortune. I don't care for any more than I have.

He lived on a little more than $200 a month from Welfare. In addition to cleaning the premises for his free room, he substituted for Dizzy when he wasn't around and there was nobody to replace him.

"You're a writer, David, you're always looking for story material. Work as a night clerk in a crummy hotel like Royal and you'll write bestsellers."

"Not me, Tingting. All I pray for is to be able to work on the magazine or get a better paying teaching job."

"Just keep at it, man."

"I wish I could be like you. You're so at peace with yourself. Have you always been that way?"

"Of course not." When Tingting had something to say that meant a lot to him, he would sidle up to me and whisper, his head close to mine. He was doing that now.

"Have you ever tried to find out the reason why Filipinos emigrate to the United States? You young ones arriving in the late sixties have your own reasons, and we who came much earlier, have ours. You all want better economic life for you and your family. Those doctors and businessmen you're working for never have it so good. They're all over the U.S.A. We old ones come here for something else. We want adventure. We want escape."

Escape from what, I wanted to know. They could likewise have tried to escape penury, too. The spirit of adventure had always imbued those who had heard of this land of opportunity,

126

dripping with milk and honey—and gold sown like stars, from an old Filipino song—remember? So what was the difference?

According to him, a vast limitless difference.

When he talked of escape he meant it literally like running away from something or someone, usually family, a woman, or a potential scandal.

"If you look at me now, you'll say to yourself, poor guy, who could love that monkey face, a no-account life, a loner and a bum. He's as good as castrated. Who would love him except for a price? You could be very wrong. Look again. I, too, have been young once. These lines haven't always been there. This face, this body, they have felt the touch of a woman's fingers, a woman's love. But the script was not always right, not for me anyway. I'm the long-distance runner, remember? So I run. I'm still running and there's no end to this, so help me God."

What a speech. Eloquent. Tingting a dropout? I wanted more. Details. Specifics. Where? When? Who? How? Why, and now, what? But I didn't dare break the spell he had cast.

"Have you heard of the Four Horsemen of the Apocalypse? Of course, you have. But there's one thing you don't know. One of them is a woman."

"In disguise?"

"Whatever."

I had unwittingly broken the spell with my stupid question. The whole day we were together he didn't say anything more until I left, cursing myself, fearing I had insulted him. He was so goddamned serious.

At subsequent matches, we continued to play even long after the days had become too cold for him to play naked above the waist, and I had to keep my sweatshirt on.

Sometimes we played chess in the cold months. He and Dizzy had an on-going contest. They kept scores, but I never found out who was ahead. I was a patsy in his hands. I was not really that bad, but I lacked practice and concentration. Besides, it took him too long to move, it irritated me, forcing me to make dumb moves. Also, it was too stifling indoors. He would not jog with me, saying he was conserving his energy, his legs.

Soon I tired of chess. It was too time-consuming. I had very little time for the kind of slow moving game he played. He himself

looked forward to being able to go fishing again. He would sometimes be out fishing all day without a single bite. He called himself
the true fisherman, more interested in fishing than in the fish.

Choosing a shady spot, he often dozed off while fishing. He
cast the line as far as it would go and attached the handle of the
rod to a tripod planted on the ground. How would he know when
he had a bite? Neighboring fishermen or kids roaming around
would wake him up with the noise they made. It was fun, he insisted. Not for me, I said.

He also went crabbing. There was a season for it. Days not
too cool, with a lot of sunshine. There were times when that kind
of weather lingered on in San Francisco. The seasons were all
mixed up in the city unlike other regions in the United States.

Most of the crabbers he knew were Filipinos of all ages. The
old seemed to enjoy it more. The old Pinoy in California had ways
to break the monotony of his humdrum existence. Outside of the
usual vices that emptied his pocketbook and filled him with
remorse and guilt, he found other diversions. Crabbing was one of
them.

On warm sunny days, from early dawn to sundown, oldtimers like him flocked to the beaches to crab. They looked like
peasants from the old country, sunburned, almost black, bare to
the waist, their loose shorts reaching up to their knees. Some made
their own crab nets. They gave away their catch or sold it, sometimes in exchange for a few pounds of meat. Tingting kept his
catch in the freezer, but he ate so much of it, he always needed
more.

Long after the crabbing season some of the hardier ones, for
want of something better to do, continued to go to the beaches.
They stopped going only when it got extremely cold. Their old
bones ached too much by then. Yet the hardy ones kept going for
the feel of the water as their feet sank in the sand, and they didn't
even mind the pinch of the crabs' claws. On their way home, they
would compare wounds.

"I let 'em. Bother me none. Mean nothing to me."

"Still it hurts."

"So. Won't kill you, will it?"

"It's the female crabs, they pinch like hell, but they're fatter,
they taste more better."

"They sure do."

"Now if only I got me a freezer big enough..."

"Boil all of 'em then shred 'em. Throw away the shells, and freeze the meat don't take too much space."

There seemed to be a camaraderie among the Filipino crabbers, a kind of brotherhood. The group could tell who was absent. They looked around, each with a silent roll call. No one had to tell them. In their simple hearts they prayed that the absence would only be temporary. An indisposition perhaps, nothing serious. Everybody hoped there would be many more seasons of crabbing. They wondered how many more. Maybe next year would be the last. Or this year, who knows?

"Only God knows," one guy said, laughing, his black gums and decaying teeth showing. "Maybe this gonna be my last season."

"What you gonna do with your trap, looks good for many more years."

"You think the Salvation Army ain't gonna have it? Maybe I leave it to you, but what for do you need another?"

"Besides, who knows who's gonna go first?"

"You shut up, guys. You're gonna catch none talking about next time."

There were two fat guys, actually obese, like Sumo wrestlers, who could have been brothers or just friends, who dug far from where most of the other Filipinos gathered. They used their hands, sometimes tin cans to dig a huge gaping hole which they filled again before dusk. They wouldn't listen to the other Filipinos who told them they wouldn't catch anything on that spot.

The others came around to watch the two fat guys, naked to the waist, dig a hole, jabbering away in a kind of pidgin English which they seemed to understand quite well. They explained they were not really trying to catch crabs, they were just digging a hole. What for? For fun, what else, and they looked at each other and laughed. They seemed to have a secret that they shared between them. Some watchers were not too kind, especially the younger ones and they called the two *whackos, locos.* The two guys paid no heed to these insults and went on digging and laughing as if they knew something the others didn't. They had sandwiches and soft drinks which they kept in a portable cooler. They were the last to leave, waddling away in the sunset. These two had not come back for some time now.

129

Most of these oldtimers didn't know where the others lived or who they were. The seashore in summer time was the only place they met and talked. Those who talked. The silent ones kept to themselves and didn't say a word when addressed. They couldn't have been dumb, perhaps hard of hearing, or late in their lives, they had taken a vow of silence like the Carthusians. They went on with their work, feeling for the crabs quietly, just in case the trap's got something. Their eyes said everything about hope and disappointment. Anticipation must have been all they wanted, the thrill of not knowing what to expect as they felt with their fingers under the watery sand. When the long summery day was over, they walked away as silently as they had come, disappearing in the darkness that gradually shrouded the shoreline.

35

I LIKE TO THINK of myself as a shy person by the most conservative standards. That's why I called my encounters with women, those which ended as all such encounters should end, quickly and without regrets, amazing lays.

Right from the start I knew there was no place in the magazine for these amazing lays, but I felt I had to write them down. I didn't want to take a chance of missing something I should have recorded, whether useful ultimately or not. In my case I never knew what I could use or not until I could see it in black and white. The truth could have been something else. Maybe back of my mind I was thinking of writing another *Fanny Hill* to make money on since most of the bestsellers I knew had either sex or violence or both. In any case, these incidents were very much a part of my sojourn in San Francisco. Sitting alone in some crowded or near-empty restaurant or in my room up there on the Heights, in Tingting's closet of a room at the *Royal*, in San Jose, in that building marked for demolition on Market Street or even on campus at City College, I pondered on what a turn my life had taken since I had decided to migrate to the United States.

My motives. None or too many to mention. If I had to have one or two, reasons, as Tingting would call them, I found out that they changed every time I tried to put them into words so by now

I was tired of coming up with reasons. But I started to say something about encounters.

I must admit, however, that these accounts could be quite boring and certainly not all of them deserved the painstaking details I have taken to relate them. One or perhaps two stood out in my mind.

And what was so amazing about them? That is, outside of the element of surprise, the coincidence that seemed to characterize all of them? They were a surprise and, to me, amazing. There's no other word. All in all, they were congenial collisions, even those that were not predetermined by the stars or the seasons.

This one named Tamara went straight to the refrigerator looking for ripe tomatoes, the little ones sold in tiny baskets called cherry tomatoes. She ate them like grapes. As they burst in her mouth, a glint shone in her eyes and she clawed at me. Kiss me, kiss me, she moaned. At first I hated it. It was repugnant, the taste of those ripe tomatoes in my mouth, the mess as the wet seeds dribbled down my neck and chest, sometimes even farther down; and the way she behaved, like one possessed. The more I resisted, the more passionate she became. This was no ordinary turn on. It was wild, perverse. After a while she swept me along with her strange passion, as she devoured the little ripe tomatoes. She didn't need a dinner afterwards, not even a drink. A cheap date. Just made for me.

The next time we went to a supermarket we bought half a dozen baskets of cherry tomatoes before anything else; and we brought them to bed. We had a vegetarian sexual orgy, how else shall I call it? She crushed the tomatoes with her fingers and sprayed them all over my body, then baring her teeth like fangs, she practically ate me up. She was grateful afterwards because I let her. I didn't mind it like the others did. Were all Filipinos like me? The most terrible question to answer! I pretended fatigue.

"Now you tell them what they're missing, the bastards!"

But I couldn't go on with it, the steady diet of cherry tomatoes. There must be an easier way to make love. I tried to make light of it. Once, while we were in the shower together, I said, "Perhaps we should try ketchup next time, what do you think? Have your choice of flavor and trade mark—Heinz, Libby's or Del Monte, low calorie or regular, I'm not particular."

Obviously she didn't appreciate my joke because there was no next time. She said I had humiliated her. I was not as under-

131

standing as she thought I was. She hoped not all Filipinos were like me. I was a selfish, self-centered pig.

"Please don't call me peeeeg!" I cried.

To my surprise she burst out laughing. She didn't forget to dry my back, which most of them did. But there was no next time.

Why is Judy not among these amazing lays?

Well, Judy is different. It's almost as if she isn't really there. A ghost that leaves behind her a wake of old perfumes, sweetness of over-ripe fruits, wilting flowers, spices turned rancid after many secret years. She could be physically attractive, almost compelling with a beauty that imposes on you like a command: hey, look here, look beyond these sores and these blemishes. And you wonder as you pass your fingers over her naked body and stumble on unevenness, moles, warts, open sores, never quite bleeding but always on the verge, so livid, so awake to your touch. And you dare not say except think in your own simple faith, that these could be cured, there's a remedy, a salve, an unguent, a quack doctor's saliva, a miracle of faith for what ails this body that could be so beautiful, because deep in your heart you know there is no cure, neither science nor quackery nor miracle would help. Your fingers linger on spots now sticky with ooze and you wait for a cry of pain or her hand brushing yours aside, but nothing happens. It could be these sore spots are self-renewing like the seasons in this bewildering city.

Even her love-making is different. She waits more than she pursues. She seems to say, enjoy, the hour is late, you need me more than I need you. And you take her with an urgency that is without passion, almost in anger because she is right. You need her. God, how you need her.

36

MORE THAN TWO WEEKS had passed since Dr. Sotto was supposed to have hired a consultant firm, and still no word from him. The last time we talked on the phone he said that the committee he had assigned had not yet decided what firm to hire. I wanted to find out how much the consultation would cost be-

132

cause I suspected that was at the bottom of all this delay. If they wanted something accurate, reliable, and professional, they had better pay up. The Board's attitude towards initial expenses was what bothered me most. I was afraid they had no idea of the huge expense involved in the project. Most of them thought of it as a tax-deductible item in their income tax returns. Some were sure that it would be a profit-making venture right off. They had planned on hiring an editor who, single-handedly or with minimum extra help, would be able to put out the magazine. After my presentation they must be having second thoughts. I knew they were wealthy, but if they were getting into something they didn't know anything about, what was to become of it? Up to this point it was only Dr. Sotto who appeared to be carrying the burden. He was the only one who was truly interested in the magazine, but not the others including their wives — Imelda, too, I was afraid.

Once when I called upstairs it was Imelda who answered.

"Yes, David, is everything all right?"

Since I had not expected her to answer, I found myself at a loss for the proper things to say. I had never been at ease talking to her. I began to stammer like a damn fool, addressing her ma'am, making silly excuses for calling instead of coming out with the truth: that I wanted to know the status of the magazine, what firm was working on the estimates, that sort of straightforward confrontation. Instead I blabbered like a delirious patient with a high fever.

"Okay then, shall I tell him when he comes that you want to talk to him?"

"No, he might be too tired. I'll call again."

Some time later in the week, when I called, Dr. Sotto was out again, but this time Imelda told me that they had not yet decided which firm to hire for the estimates. Yes, the firms they had contacted were charging quite a stiff fee.

"They must be good, well worth the expenditure."

"Even then," she started to say, then changed the subject. "Well, I'm sure he will get in touch with you."

"Thanks . . ." I said and quickly added, "How's Estela?" But she had already hung up.

There was something awfully wrong somewhere. Me, who else? Whenever it was Imelda I was dealing with I lost my bearings, my cool. I acted . . . it's cruel to say this . . . but I acted no better than Estela, not in control, confused and confusing, a pathetic

133

figure. What was this power she had over me? No, it was not she, I told myself. It's the other Imelda, the name and the memories that refused to die no matter how often I had thought how well and safely I had buried them.

Back to my notes. My feverish jottings . . .

37

GET LOST, David, get lost. Learn to know the city like the bruises that still hurt. At least that section of this so-called golden city by the bay that was still open to you.

Back to my notes.

Soon my term at City College would be over. I wished I didn't have to teach another class like the one I had. I was terribly disappointed with my students. They just didn't have any feeling for the Philippines. They continued to complain and ridicule their parents, especially their grandparents. Why did the older people's presence have to be inflicted upon the young? How did they get to live that long and not know a damn thing? They couldn't say even one, just one, correct sentence or pronounce the words, even the simplest English words, as they should be pronounced. They always seemed angry. Nothing that my students (their grand-children) did was ever right in their eyes. How could they be related? They seemed worlds apart. They talked of the Philippines as if it were the greatest country in the world. If they loved it that much, what were they doing here where they despised prac-tically everything American, or more to the point, and closer to the truth, everything not Filipino? And yes, oh, yes, you won't believe this, they're so damned patriotic they sing the Philippine National Anthem in English or what sounded to them, no doubt, like English, while they took their showers.

Several times I tried to see Professor Jaime to seek his advice, but he was always out, no one in his office knew where. Later I learned that he had missed a few classes. What could be the matter? I got so worried I tried to call him up every day hoping that I would catch him. When I finally reached him, he said he was all right. "You sound different," I told him, doubting his words.

"Just a little family trouble," he said.

"Can I come over to see you?" I asked.

134

"Sure, when can you come?"

"What about this weekend? I'll see you at your office."

He agreed. Now he sounded like his old self.

He appeared to have aged and more careless with his appearance. I wondered why he wore a suit and tie all the time. They made him look shabbier, much older. Only the ancients in the faculty wore coats and ties, and Professor Jaime was not that old. Why couldn't he wear what I wore to school—jeans and short-sleeved shirts on warmer days, and for cool or rainy weather, a short London Fog jacket and a cap to match, both water repellent? Comfortable and neat and inconspicuous. Suits had to be well pressed all the time, the shirts that needed ironing had to be ironed otherwise they would be a mess. The Professor looked like a mess, messier than usual.

First we talked about my class. So it's rough going, eh? Sorry to hear about that. Would I be interested in another try? Same subject, but this time a different bunch. With good luck a more tractable bunch. There were many diligent Filipino students on campus. He knew all of them. They respected and trusted him. They came to him with their problems.

I updated him on the magazine. It was not really going too well, I confided. The backers didn't have any idea how much start-up capital they had to invest. I talked about the Board's reaction to my prediction that we would not make any profits for the first year, the shock that followed my revelation. I was not even sure if the Board would want to go ahead and spend a couple of thousand dollars for consultation fee only to be told it would cost a pretty sum to publish a magazine.

"That's too bad," the Professor said. He saw how bleak the magazine's prospects looked. "But if they're really interested, they will put up the money, unless they want a magazine no better than the fly-by-night tabloids that die after the first issue. I'm sorry about the whole thing. What about Dr. Sotto? He's the prime mover, isn't he?"

"Also the principal backer. He's such a fine man. He has supported me enough, but I don't want to stay any longer than I should in his mansion and continue to depend on him for petty cash."

The Professor agreed, but he was optimistic.

"Then, too, their wives don't seem to like the idea of having to invest so much," I continued.

"Ah, that's bad. That's bad news."

Considering the uncertainty of the magazine's future, I asked the Professor if he could help me get more subjects to teach at City College. This would enable me to stay in San Francisco while I waited for better opportunities. I knew there was nothing much left for me in the city outside of the magazine, which was right now in limbo. I had no intention of returning to the Philippines after all the difficulties I went through securing immigrant status in the States. Then there was martial law. How long was the damn thing going to last? The Professor had no idea.

"It could be permanent," he said in all seriousness.

"Then it would be San Francisco for me forever."

"It need not be. There are other cities."

"I tried other cities before settling down in San Francisco," I said, telling him where I had been before. I didn't tell him I had travelled around expecting to find my father.

"San Francisco is not the only city in the world for young men of talent like you. There are many others including those cities where you have been."

"But I like San Francisco best. It's exciting. It keeps me alive. If I can't go back to the Philippines—and I really don't want to under martial law—this is where I want to live."

"Ah!" he exclaimed but didn't go any further.

There was good news about Father Belarmino.

"He's back. He's doing very well," the Professor said. All the time we were looking for him, Father was visiting outlying cities in California—Delano, San Luis, Obispo. He even went to Seattle. He was given permission to say mass at these places and earn the funds needed for his church. Now he was scheduled for more masses in several churches in the diocese. He was looking for an architect, preferably a Catholic Filipino who wouldn't charge him very much to rebuild his old church.

"Some of the best ones are in the Philippines," I said, "unless they've since fled the country."

The Jaime house on Quentin Street had a fresh coat of paint, off white, the color of magnolia flowers. The two boys had taken time out of their chores to do the painting. Bob seemed to have lost interest in his painting and now wanted to save enough money to travel, if his mother would allow him to take time off from his work at the resident house. Art Junior was as pious as ever and got along very well with Father Belarmino. Their married sister

136

was doing quite well but the husband was no nearer his graduate degree than the first time I heard about them.

And the two teen-aged girls—Lila and Donna? Fely seemed more subdued than usual. There was something different in the atmosphere in the house. A clean smell pervaded it. The silence felt soothing for a change, I felt good, and yet, something about the atmosphere seemed brittle, as though it could break any moment. I wondered how long this seeming peace would last. I looked around, expecting the girls to come barging in, their faces lit up with a nameless ecstasy that was almost like agony to behold.

It was not until over breakfast the following morning that the couple told me why the girls were not around. It happened a month ago. But long before that, the girls had become increasingly insufferable particularly when their boy friends were around. Fely and Art spent long hours on their knees before going to bed praying for guidance. Their policy of leaving the girls alone, of completely ignoring their mischiefs, was not working. They had become openly obnoxious even in the presence of their parents.

Since the couple moved to their house, they had observed a daily ritual of praying before the image of the Sacred Heart at the foot of the stairs before going out for the day. They used to ask Lila and Donna to pray with them or by themselves before leaving the house for school. The couple had long given that up. What they were not prepared for was what happened one morning. That was soon after my last visit.

As the couple knelt before the Sacred Heart, they were startled by some noise from the living room. The girls had just come home from an all-night party and were either drunk or stoned. Before the couple knew what was happening, the girls were throwing pillows and rugs at the Sacred Heart, giggling hysterically as one pillow knocked over the image.

Art turned livid. He rushed to the girls and slapped one, then the other, with such force that they reeled back and fell on the floor. They began to cry. Their mother ran to them trying to shield them from their father's fury. No word had been exchanged. Art pushed Fely aside and resumed slapping the girls until blood dribbled from their mouths.

Fely pushed herself between her husband and her daughters. "Stop it!" she cried. "Art, please, you're hurting them."

For the first time Art found words to say. His mouth frothed, "I'm going to kill you! You're not our daughters, you

137

belong to the devil, I'll kill you first before . . ."

Fely flung her arms around him, sobbing, "Art, please, that's enough!"

Art's voice trembled, "Why are you this way? Your mother and I have tried everything to help you. What kind of creatures have you become? God, what have we done to deserve you? You're animals, that's what you are—animals!" He was shouting again, "Go! get out of my house, animals. I don't ever want to see you again!"

"No, no, Art, please, listen to me. Let me talk to them. Give them a chance, they're our daughters. All they need . . ."

"No, Fely, we've been too lenient. Every time we scold them they threaten to run away. Now let them run away. I don't ever want to see them again." He turned to the girls. "Do you hear me? Get out of this house!"

The girls had stopped crying, their faces rigid, sullen. Art disappeared upstairs to nurse his anger and grief. Fely turned to her daughters. Why couldn't they be reasonable? They had all the freedom they wanted, all the privileges they said they were entitled to just like their peers. They came and went with their boyfriends any time of the day or night. What more did they want? They made a mess of the house. They skipped classes, they had been reported smoking grass, they didn't do their housework, not even their laundry, and yet they got their allowance regularly.

"What more do you want?" Fely asked.

"Just leave us alone."

"But we've left you alone. We've tried to overlook your sinful ways. We pray for you . . ."

"Pray, pray, pray . . ." Lila said with sarcasm.

"Your father was angry, he didn't mean to drive you away."

Art had come back. He was standing in the middle of the stairway, glaring down at them. "I meant every word I said. Get the hell out of my house. Go to hell!"

Fely collapsed on a chair and cried. The girls got up and without bothering to pick up their clothes, walked out of the house, slamming the door after them.

The rest of the Jaime family came to help cool things down, but their father was firm. He would not change his mind. To him the girls were as good as dead.

"Children die, some earlier than others," he reasoned. "Those two just happened to die, that's all."

Junior suggested that they seek the advice of Father Belarmino. "He would know what would be the best for us to do."

Bob spoke very little. In a crisis like this, he felt helpless; he didn't know how to console his parents. The oldest daughter promised to visit more often.

Later they learned that Lila and Donna moved in with their boyfriends, but even that didn't work out. Both girls were pregnant and soon they were thrown out by their boyfriends' families. In a sense, the boys were also outcasts, unwelcome in their own homes.

Fely suggested that the girls be allowed to stay in one of their resident homes. She would look after them, just like the other residents. But Art was adamant. No, he would not have them staying in any of his houses. During this time, he missed a few classes. Even after he resumed teaching, he was surly, impatient, absent-minded.

When the girls got too big, the oldest daughter took them in until she found the proper government agency to take care of them. Fely wanted to take them back, but the girls refused. They didn't want to return to San Jose. They talked of having an abortion. Fely was horrified. "No," she begged them, "you would be murderers. Even I would turn against you."

"They're the crosses we carry," Fely later told her husband.

That day I learned about all this I could not concentrate on anything. What would happen now? This was only the beginning. How much good was prayer in this situation? How changed would the girls be after they had become mothers? What sort of babies would they have? What could be their future?

38

TO PREPARE for my class, I often visited the Philippine Consulate General Library where I found very scant material on Philippine culture. The consulate library could not really be called a library in the true sense of the word, but a glass case of books under lock and key.

The librarian and the minor members of the consulate staff were an odd group in this foreign office, but otherwise, a happy group. They hated to be asked questions they could not answer. They passed the time talking and laughing, mostly laughing.

I don't think the librarian knew anything about books or library science. She looked like a mother, that is, a nursing mother. Her breasts seemed swollen, ready to ooze milk at any moment and indeed, at certain hours of the day, she would run to the rest room. "Milking time, milking time!" the women staffers would chant in unison.

I never found out her name. When I identified myself, she didn't give me her name and I didn't ask. After unlocking the shelves to get the reference books I needed, she would tell me, "Be careful with these books, we don't have extra copies." Then she would return to her desk and marvel at her long painted nails, pressing her padded breasts now and then.

As I went over the books on Philippine culture, I realized how little I knew, how much I had taken for granted. "Go abroad and learn about your country," sounded closer to the truth than I had previously thought.

I missed the works of some of the better known writers in the Philippines so I asked the librarian if they had any of these in their collection.

"I don't know those books," she said, shaking her head. "If they're not there, we don't have them because we don't lend out books."

"But these are important Philippine writers."

"I'm sorry. I'm not responsible for choosing books. I just work here."

"How did you select these books?"

"Hey, Serena," she called out to somebody inside the partition that separated the library area from the rest of the offices. "Can you tell this gentleman how we selected these books?"

"Why does he want to know?" the woman named Serena called back.

"Ewan ko ba. I don't know."

I didn't realize that such a harmless question would lead to further questions. Pretty soon there was a mild uproar as other heads shot up from the numerous desks, and the employees began talking at the same time, mostly vice consuls or clerks and secretaries since everybody from consul on up had his own private office.

"Tell him those are all we have," an elderly man said loud enough for me to hear.

140

If I persisted with my questions, I was afraid I would be barred from the library which was adequate enough for my needs. I had asked simply out of curiosity.

"Thank you," I said to nobody in particular and returned to my seat.

I could always tell when the consul general himself had arrived, usually about noon. A silence fell on the scene. It didn't last long because the consul usually had luncheon engagements and since his staff remained noisy in the afternoon, I assumed the boss didn't come back. Maybe he worked overtime at night.

Much as I wanted to, I never got to meet him, although sometimes I caught a glimpse of him signing papers or handing documents to his subalterns.

It was hard to determine what each one of the consulate personnel was assigned to perform. They were mostly visiting among themselves or talking lengthily on the phone in Pilipino. They mut talk a lot with their families or friends. Not official business, I was sure.

Sometimes I wondered if anyone in the consulate would show some interest in me, ask me why I frequently visited their library. That never happened. They seemed wary of something; the way they moved and talked, they seemed suspicious of strangers, especially Filipinos, who visited and asked questions. Did they think I was a bum or a mendicant? Were they afraid I'd ask them for money? For personal favors? Perhaps they had their share of visitors like that. But if I were someone important and they recognized me, I was sure they'd give me special treatment, offer me food and drinks perhaps, maybe the consul might even invite me to one of his many luncheon engagements.

That's what they had plenty of. Food. They ate in the consulate at their respective desks. At lunch break, which they usually anticipated with an elaborate routine of preparations as if for a big feast, the atmosphere changed into a festive mood. They opened whatever they brought for lunch and walked about comparing and tasting what the others had. The air smelled of native cooking. It reminded me of Divisoria market where I used to buy and eat my lunch during my younger days. They had fish and rice, with sliced red tomatoes, meat cooked with vegetables, Philippine style. Some brought *bagoong* which smelled, of course. It was the right smell for a Philippine consular office, a touch of local color. They even joked about the smell. They joked and laughed a lot

141

while they ate. One of them recounted how the *bagoong* she was carrying was starting to smell up the bus she was riding.

"What did you do?" they asked her.

"I pretended that the smell bothered me, too; I held my nose and looked around as if wondering what the smell was, where it came from."

Lunch break was also off-color-jokes hour. To my surprise, the women told the more brazen, dirtier jokes. They were Filipino jokes which could only be appreciated best if told in Pilipino with the right gestures and voice intonation. In English, they fell flat, lost their flavor. The best raconteur was the elderly man who told jokes with a straight face. Even my nursing mother-librarian had some ribald jokes to contribute. This was her joke:

An American woman got the shock of her life when she asked her neighbor, an old Filipino lady, what Filipino husbands do in the Philippines. Replied the Filipino lady: "Most Filipino husbands, especially those who live in the barrios, wake up very early in the morning and go out and play with their cocks."

From the elderly man:

A Filipino lover boy told his young and pretty American girlfriend that she should stop smoking.

"What for?" she asked.

"It would improve your teeths," he said.

So she stopped smoking and after several months, she accosted her Filipino lover, saying, "For some time now I've not been smoking and . . ."

"So I've noticed," he interrupted her. "Now look at your gleaming teeths. Keep smiling."

"Hell," she exclaimed, I thought you said it would improve my tits."

Most of the other jokes were of the tired, old variety, so old they had whiskers, and were stale and quite vulgar. Yet they helped pass away the time and, who knows, cement Philippine-American relationship, a basic Philippine foreign policy.

The one-hour lunch break dragged on far beyond the alloted hour for the simple reason that the bosses themselves were out in expensive restaurants with their cronies, or, as was sometimes the case, with visiting dignitaries from the New Society for whom they performed chores above and beyond the call of consular duties.

The consulate was the last place I wanted to be in, but it gave me an educational experience—for free.

142

With all the reading I was doing, I went to my class more self-assured than my fourteen dollars an hour would warrant. I hoped the class would notice that I had mastered the subject, that I was fired up with knowledge I wanted to impart to them. But I was disappointed. In the middle of what I thought was an inspired monologue, a cute girl got up and asked: "Will you ask that in the final exam?"

For the class, that was the crux of all my lectures and class discussions: would it be included in the exams? I was so disgusted with their attitude that near the close of the term, I always prefaced my talk with: "Everything that I say today will be asked in the final examination."

I thought that would work, but not quite. The same cute girl with the teasing tone asked, "Are you sure, teach?"

"Of course, I'm sure. I make the exams, don't I?" Sign of defeat in the diminishing instructor.

"Oh, but why will you do that?"

"Because what I say from here on is very important!"

"Word for word?"

"Not really." Ah, the weakening instructor.

"Don't be hard on us, sir."

"I don't see why I shouldn't."

"Until now this was a fun course."

"It is a fun course."

"Oh, come on, teach."

"Now, may I resume?"

"Resume what?"

For me the course couldn't have ended too soon. It could have ended then. There was no use. These were damp souls. No amount of eloquence and mastery could ignite them.

Did I really want to teach another quarter?

39

PROFESSOR JAIME drove me back to San Francisco straight to City College. I was almost late but there were no students yet in the room when I arrived. Wong came in shortly, smiling his winsome Chinese smile.

"Where are the rest?" I asked.

He shrugged his shoulders. The rest drifted in later, one by one or in pairs and groups, most of them lugging their lunch with their books and notebooks. A few greeted me or nodded in my direction.

I managed to keep calm for one whose feelings were offended by the way my students trooped in late and ate their lunch without much concern about proceeding with the day's lesson. I had learned to ignore their unconventional ways.

My visit in San Jose was still on my mind. Professor Jaime had unburdened himself as we drove to school.

"Perhaps it's largely my fault. I hated those boys with whom they hung around. They were a bad influence on the girls. They had no respect for us or our home. They looked like bandits to me and I often wondered what my girls saw in them. Many times I had to drive them away. It was then that the girls threatened to run away. It scared Fely. I was mad but I kept my temper. I kept my anger inside me until I was ready to explode anytime. I should have unburdened my feelings to Fely or to my other children. They would have counseled me, and we could have headed off the crisis. But it's too late now."

I didn't think so. The Professor had calmed down considerably. In his own way, he loved his daughters and worried about them. He hated their boyfriends and their illiterate families, as he called them. It was they who had corrupted his daughters. He was relenting; he sounded willing to take back the girls, help raise their kids.

"It would make Fely very happy," he said, more to himself than to me.

What a mess, I was thinking, how could this happen to such nice people?

"Suggestion, sir," someone in my class cut short my reverie. He raised his voice above the din in the classroom. I nodded towards him, feeling a crushing sense of defeat. I was a failure, the worst teacher ever.

The student stood up and tried to hush the class. There were a few hecklers, but the young man glared at them and the class quieted down a bit. If those freaks were my daughters, I was thinking . . .

"Suppose, sir," the student began, and after a pause, added, "instead of our class on Friday—it's our last class, anyway, before the finals—suppose we hold a program? There's a hall across the

144

way which we can reserve for the occasion. Call it our final exercises. What do you think?"

"What kind of program will it be?"

"Leave that to us, sir. We'll form committees."

"What do you think, class?"

The class was unanimous in favor of the suggestion.

"What would you want me to do?"

"We'll tell you."

"When?"

"At our next meeting."

"But what kind of program will it be?"

"A cultural program."

I couldn't believe my ears. What cultural program?

"A program depicting Philippine culture."

"You're joking."

They were serious. They were going to show me what they had learned in class. I knew it, they were going to dance the *tinikling* and sing a *kundiman.* Go ahead. Let them.

"Well, if you need any help . . ."

"No, thanks. Teach, this is strictly a student production."

The spokesman returned to his seat. Much of the talking came from the other students. They were so noisy they could hardly hear one another. So the spokesman stood up again and the class listened. I tried to recall the boy's name, but I had to admit I didn't know it. Some time long before midterm, I had lost hope in the class ever learning anything from me. At one point I told them that perhaps what the class needed was something like martial law in the Philippines. Instead of feeling insulted, they burst out laughing. They thought it was funny, I was a funny man. Yet I continued to be conscientious. I did my homework, visited the Philippine Consulate Library and learned, in addition to Philippine culture, more dirty jokes. Ah, perhaps that was part of Philippine culture, too. What do the scholars say about it? I tried to find out but found nothing on dirty jokes as they relate to our people's culture.

"Looks like you need more time than you have for the program," I reminded my class.

"No, sir. The truth, sir, is we've been preparing."

I looked at them in surprise. Preparing? That delighted them and they started laughing at my expense. They had succeeded in keeping a secret from me. They had fooled the teacher!

When I realized that they had already taken more time than they should, I told them.

"Please, sir," the spokesman said. Ah, his name was Wilfred, but I didn't know his last name. Out of nowhere the name suddenly came to me. That had happened to me before. "This is our last meeting. We have to talk. We may not finish within the class hour. Then you can just leave us, sir. Yes?"

"Well," I began, but a girl in a shrill voice from the back of the room, interrupted me.

"If you like the program, sir, could we all be exempted from finals?"

I was so taken aback, I didn't know what to say.

The class took advantage of my confusion.

"Say yes. Yes?"

"No, of course not," I said with a force I did not actually feel.

One guy, obviously the class clown, stood up before the class and in a not bad imitation of me, repeated my own words: "No, of course not."

I smiled in spite of myself and the class roared with laughter. Teach has a sense of humor! He can laugh at jokes at his expense. Perhaps I had been wrong about these kids. Too engrossed with my personal problems, had I prejudged them too quickly?

They were still at it when I left. The class hour was over. As I was leaving, a girl shouted, "What about finals, sir?"

"What about it?" I paused just outside the door.

"Come on, teach, be a good sport, you know what we mean."

"Well," I said on my way out, "I'll think about it."

This was greeted with a standing ovation.

When I arrived in my room on Diamond Heights it was already evening. I had, as usual, made a detour towards that part of Market Street that was gradually turning into a shabby section of the city. By the time I had alighted from the bus, it was already dark and the lights in that area near the base of the Heights didn't help too much but it was better than groping.

A note from Dr. Sotto was waiting for me.

Dear David,

I have submitted the papers on the magazine to this firm (see attached sheet with the name and address) which has been highly recommended by a good businessman friend not

146

connected with the firm. Make an appointment with Mr. Marvin Segal because he wants to confer with you. You have been to Berkeley before and I assume you can find the place.

We've taken Estela to a specialist. Won't be back until some time next week. Be seeing you then.

Yours,
PS

The enclosed check should help until next time. Tell me if you need more.

40

AS THE DAYS PASSED and the day of decision became inevitably closer, I wondered what the Board would do. I sensed a wavering among the men, and the women, right from the start, looked with disfavor on the magazine.

It occurred to me that the magnitude of my responsibilities towards a non-existent magazine was beginning to wear me down. I could not do everything myself, and yet it seemed that I was expected to. Sometimes it crossed my mind that I might actually be grateful if the Board decided not to push through the magazine, then I would feel a great sense of relief from all these responsibilities that weighed heavily on my mind. But would I really feel good if that happened? I had gathered enough material to keep the magazine going. What would I do with all of them? Throw them from the Golden Gate Bridge and watch them sail off wherever the winds swept them away?

In my restlessness, I sought the company of those who had taken me in without question in the manner the Sotto couple did, or better yet, those who didn't expect anything from me in return. Like Tingting and, in an altogether different fashion, Judy, whose selflessness seemed unreal. But lately Judy was never around when I needed her and Tingting was always there, seemingly grateful for my intrusion into his day like a father welcoming his son. Sometimes in my hopeless, desultory search, I began to believe that I had found my father at last.

It was Tingting whom I was often tempted to invite to my basement room on Diamond Heights. I promised myself I would

147

never take anyone to my place without the Sottos' permission. But with Tingting, I had been tempted. He had cooked for me, fed me all the fish I could eat, called me up when I failed to see him for sometime. He never pried into my life but he listened to whatever I told him. Much older than I and having lived alone so much, he was glad to have me around, someone to talk to. We played tennis and I was now beating him occasionally. He was slowly wearing down. His legs were not as good as they used to be. Besides, now I knew his game. He never gave up. He had a fighting heart. We truly enjoyed playing together.

I took him to restaurants that he liked and other eating places which he had not tried yet. We would have done this more often, but I could not afford it. It seemed un-Filipino if we went dutch treat.

Not to be outdone he started inviting me out, too. This would not do. I would not allow it. I knew the mere pittance he was receiving and the care with which he handled his income. He liked to talk of his death, but always in a light mood. "I can die any time now and I know I would have a decent burial. I don't know how many people would come but I don't care about that. A decent, clean, and respectable burial is all I need."

"Oh, you're sentimental," I would tell him. "Why talk of dying?"

"Better to talk about it than think about it all the time like what the other o.t.'s do."

These o.t.'s read the daily obituaries, scanning the death columns for a familiar name. They didn't buy the papers, they didn't have to. They simply waited for someone to leave entire sections of the dailies intact on benches in the park or jutting out of trash cans, at depots and most waiting rooms. As they grew older, and their eyes failed them even with their glasses on, they asked others to read to them, and often they would realize that they were the last ones left. All the names had become strange. The more destitute ones consoled themselves, saying, "We don't feel so alone. We're not the last ones. Maybe one of us dies every day, who knows when our turn will come? Nobody knows us but that is never mind. We're the unknown civilians. Perhaps most of us anyhow will never make it to the death columns. We got no money for that. But okay *lang.*"

Tingting did. He had saved for that. He knew he would be there, his name in print again at long last. If he had his way, he would want his name printed thus: Cesar (Tingting) Pilapil.

"A simple burial, quiet, and slow, real slow."

"What do you mean?"

"Can't you understand English? Real slow. No hurry."

"Why, of course. Whoever thought . . ."

"You're wrong, mister. Have you heard of Dino?"

"The barber? Of course, I know him."

Dino owned and ran the barbershop that bore his name on Kearney close to Mabuhay Restaurant. The first time I met him was in the rest room at the Mabuhay where he went to relieve himself; the barbershop didn't have any. I didn't know there was someone ahead of me. I was about to back out when the man turned to me. "I'm finished, *paisano*," he said.

He was wearing a barber's white gown and looked like some oldtimers, forever in their fifties although they could have been in their seventies. As I took his place at the urinal, he looked at me closely. "I haven't seen you before. Are you with the artists' troupe from the Philippines?"

No, I said, but he was right, I was new in San Francisco. He waited for me outside the rest room and as we walked side by side in the cramped premises, he handed me his card, saying, "That's the one next door."

The card said Dino was not only a barber but also a travel agent.

The barbershop was air-conditioned. He had left a customer waiting. It was evident Dino had already started on the man when he felt like going to the rest room. He was in no hurry as if he had all the time in the world.

Two Filipino oldtimers were playing checkers in a corner. They barely looked up when we entered. Dino kept talking to me even as he resumed trimming the hair of his customer. It was idle talk, but sometimes he would face me holding the scissors and comb suspended in the air, or he would move about with gestures that seemed unnecessary. I felt like pushing him towards the guy in the barber's chair who didn't appear to mind the delay. He must have been asleep with his eyes open. That late in the afternoon, the floor was spotlessly clean. Were there no customers all day, or did Dino or someone in his employ, perhaps one of the o.t. regulars, sweep the floor immaculately clean after every customer was through?

It didn't look like a barbershop except for the sign and the red, blue and white symbol twirling by the door. Of course, it had

149

a barber's chair and the barber himself in his gown big as life. Dino was bigger-built than most Filipinos.

Calendars of all sizes hung on one wall, each bearing the day of the week from Sunday through Saturday, seven separate calendars in all. A sign above the cash register read, "Your credit is good but we need cash. No personal checks accepted." A row of broken-down chairs sat against the wall facing the mirrors. A corner shelf contained old magazines and newspapers: local Filipino papers, the *San Francisco Examiner, Popular Mechanics, Travel* and *Holiday* Magazines. No girlies. "These old stiffs would be in rigor mortis with all those nudes," Dino said, smirking.

"Don't underestimate the o.t.'s," I reminded him.

"Just look at them," he said, pointing outside.

Three of them were sitting in the sun.

"They move as the sun moves," he said. "And look at their eyes."

They were unseeing eyes, bleary, rheumy, fixed, dull.

"The eyes tell everything," he added, stealing a glance involuntarily in the mirror to look at his own.

"Those are extreme cases," I argued, tempted to say, look at yourself, but didn't. He might really be still in his fifties and that would be insulting him.

"It figures. You're still new in this country. Give yourself time, boy."

He could be, indeed, in his seventies.

"They flock to your barbershop."

"Where else will they go? Have you seen where most of them live? Have you been to the International Hotel?"

"Not yet, but one of these days, I intend to."

"By the way, what do you sell? You don't look like anything, I mean, with anything to sell."

"I don't sell anything, but soon, I will, maybe."

I told him about the magazine. He listened as he trimmed his customer's hair. The man looked like a retired Pinoy. When I was through with my explanation, Dino was also through with the man's hair.

"Man, those are loaded guys you working with," Dino said. "Some of them come here but very seldom. They know me. Ask them. But I don't give 'em no extra favors. They tip real well, though. They leave Dino's Barbershop completely satisfied."

"I can see that," I said, watching the guy unlimber before the mirror, eyeing himself from side to side.

Weekends the barbershop was full. The oldtimers came to play the musical instruments they brought with them. The barbershop became alive: loud talk, laughter, musical instruments being tuned, a smattering of sounds, jarring. When everything was ready, a full blown orchestra played a repertoire of haunting melodies from the old country. Pinoy bystanders sang the lyrics. Now and then someone from a group of newly arrived tourists attracted to the barbershop by the native airs, would give an impromptu solo. Sentimental Filipino listeners hearing the native songs sung and played wiped their tears and joined in. A regular festival, with a nostalgic air that turned eyes misty.

Dino was proud of them all. He loved their music. He didn't care even if he didn't have too many customers on these crowded weekends. "Lots of 'em got no more hair anyhow. But they're good musicians. They enjoy. Gifted. Come over. Yes, I'm here Sundays, too. We're closed Wednesdays."

There was a picture of Jose Rizal on a wall in the barbershop. It showed the Philippine hero about to pick up his hat that the wind had blown to the ground, on his way to meet the firing squad. Underneath the picture was the *Ultimo Adios* in Spanish. Nobody noticed the picture. No one talked about it. But it struck me and I remembered it afterwards when I thought of the barbershop.

Dino said these oldtimers often roamed around the city, lingering at the post office and the bus depot or wherever they found phone booths. They would stick their fingers into the slots hoping to get dimes and quarters from the phone machine. Once one of them came back to the shop, his pockets full of quarters and dimes, nearly ten dollars. It was the greatest moment in his life since Las Vegas when he was still a young man, and that was ages ago.

I turned to Tingting. "Is Dino dead?"

"So what's new? We're all gonna die. I was trying to tell you how he was buried. In a big hurry. I don't mean immediately after he died, the next day or whenever, but on the way to the cemetery. There was quite a long procession of cars—Cadillacs and the others—they were running at much more than cruising speed. Some claimed over the speed limit.

Two motorcycle cops with their lights on led the procession and they went real fast, faster than 65.

"I don't want that to happen to me. I want it real slow, sad like."

151

Mr. Marvin Segal was as forthright as I expected him to be. We were starting, from less than scratch, from nothing, he said. This was a new venture. It wasn't like we were buying into a magazine with a printing press and a working staff. We had nothing.

"Does your Board realize this?"

I pointed to my report. "It's all there," I said, "and they've read and discussed that report among themselves."

There was really not much point in our conference. I merely confirmed what he suspected. The Board was interested in making profits right off. A magazine starting from zero, as it were, would hardly be the project to make instant money.

"Please be as candid as you can. You have all the figures you need," I said, knowing that if he did so, it would be like saying goodbye to the hopes I had built up all this time.

"We have not yet agreed on the fee we'll charge them."

"We might not go beyond that," I said with a laugh, trying to suppress the bitterness.

Mr. Segal had expressive eyes and he had a small build like most Filipinos. As he sat behind a big desk, I wondered if he was even a bit shorter than he looked.

"Maybe you'd want to consider making estimates on alternate plans, say, a quarterly, if a monthly is too prohibitive."

"With the same number of pages?"

"Not less than 64, I suppose. But perhaps you can consider a lower quality of paper and printing."

He jotted all that down and thanked me for coming. He was very friendly and it made me feel better. I was impressed with his competence. He was going to make a candid report. I knew what that meant to my hopes, but I didn't want it any other way.

I played tennis more often than usual and Tingting had a merry time beating the hell out of me.

"You lack concentration," he said.

"You're just too good for me, but I'll take care of you, old man."

41

THE LEAST of my worries but just as bothersome was my failure to inform Dr. Sotto of the part-time job I had at City College. I had intended to tell him but it skipped my mind every time we met to talk about the magazine. He had stopped confiding in me his personal problems. Perhaps that was a good sign. Maybe there weren't any personal problems pressing enough to confide anymore.

My sin of omission weighed heavily on my mind. Had I subconsciously avoided telling Dr. Sotto for fear that he would have no compunction about giving up the magazine if he knew that I was, anyhow, employed, and his negative decision wouldn't affect me very much? Maybe if it took only that much or that little to sway his decision one way or the other, it would be to my advantage to keep my teaching a secret from him.

How absurd that I should thus rationalize, making much of an issue that actually was of no importance at all. The magazine did not take too much of my time; in fact, my readings gave me material and ideas for the magazine. And the term was nearly over. So what was I so anxious about?

All this boiled down to the truth which I hated to admit. I wanted the magazine because I needed the job to continue living in San Francisco. I wanted Dr. Sotto to do his utmost to see the magazine through because my future hinged on it. That was it! I wanted him to pity me. Shame on me. Hell, to what depths had I fallen?

One night as I was preparing to go to bed, Dr. Sotto showed up.

"I noticed there was a light in your room," he explained after I had admitted him. "Writing a letter? I hope I'm not disturbing you, but we have not seen each other for quite a while now. Did you see the guy at Berkeley?"

"Oh, yes, I did," I said, giving him a chair. I was writing some notes which I always did after the day's experiences. There were nights when there was nothing to write down or nothing that important, like tonight. I arranged the sheets on my table. "Just notes," I mumbled when Dr. Sotto glanced in their direction.

"And what did he say?" he asked.

I told him. In detail. My observation about Mr. Segal, how impressed I was with his knowledge of publication costs.

"He teaches at Berkeley. Did you get a chance to see the campus?"

"Oh, yes. It's so huge and so cluttered. I'd get lost on a campus so thickly populated and complex like that. City College in San Francisco seems small compared . . ."

"No comparison," he interrupted me with a wave of his hand. "And its faculty in most departments is tops in the world."

This was the opportunity I needed to tell him about my teaching. "Oh, incidentally, Dr. Sotto, I had meant to tell you this long ago. I'm teaching one subject on Philippine Culture at City College. We meet three times a week, one hour each, and I get $14 an hour. There's not much to prepare. I know the subject rather well, at least better than any of my students most of whom are Filipinos born in this country."

There, that was out at last. Why did I have to tell how much I got paid? Was I trying to stress the fact that I got very little? I felt embarrassed.

"Good, good," was all Dr. Sotto said.

I watched his face. What did he mean, good? His face showed no expression, no hint of what he was thinking. He looked pretty solemn. Was he just tired at that late hour?

"Imelda and I have just arrived. We have had a trying day," he said as if he had read my mind.

"Is it Estela?"

"No. Estela is fine. It's Dr. Tablizo. He's on the Board. Of course, you know him."

I knew him better than I did the others. I knew all the names and the faces but not which name matched which face and vice versa. This might seem odd considering that I prided myself in remembering faces and names. I had students from way back whom I met years later and immediately, almost instantaneously, I could identify their names. This always flattered them and delighted me. But I just couldn't place the members of the Board. There was a sameness about them, an unreality of sorts. They were voices and gestures and smells; their wives, varying complexions and sizes, shapes, and manners of dressing and scents, heavy and cloying as if underneath lay a sinister secret that they had to hide. Perhaps that they were the backers of the magazine made me wary of them lest I unwittingly became submissive or worse, act or talk as if I were fawning. When I told them at our first meeting that I needed the job, it was supposed to confuse them, even if

154

I knew myself that it was, indeed, the truth. Hence, I kept my distance from them with the exception of Dr. Sotto whom I had learned to trust like a true friend. The others remained shadowy figures in my mind through no fault of theirs.

Oh, yes, there was another exception: Dr. Tablizo, whom I also knew quite well.

Long after Dr. Sotto had said good night, I lay awake in bed thinking of Dr. Tablizo, what Dr. Sotto had told me about him. When I realized that I could not sleep, I got up and walked to my desk. I pulled out the blank pages I was trying to fill with notes earlier when Dr. Sotto interrupted me and sat down and wrote well into dawn.

42

WHEN HE THOUGHT ABOUT IT as he often did, Dr. Tablizo believed that he had a much easier time getting the necessary papers for himself and his wife and newlyborn daughter to immigrate to the United States than he had persuading his father to join them soon after they were all established and doing well in San Francisco. He was convinced this was the case, even if one considered the time element alone. It took the old man nearly five years to change his mind. If fate or God had not intervened, it would have taken longer. The old Mr. Tablizo hated the idea of leaving home, and home to him was the Philippines, in a little town in Luzon named Alcala where he was born, where his own parents were born, and where Noy, as everybody called the doctor, was born and grew up until he went to attend medical school in Manila.

Although he never went beyond high school, Mr. Augusto Tablizo, Sr. was for a long time an elementary school supervisor until he was retired at age 65, and that was more than a decade ago. He was already a teacher before he finished the seventh grade. Everybody in Alcala knew him as "the maestro." It seemed everybody who ever went to school in his teaching days had been in his class at one time or another. His wife, Pepang, Dr. Tablizo's mother, had been his student.

The Tablizos lived in an old house which had belonged to

155

their grandfather, an industrious farmer who, although he never spoke a word of English or Spanish, had been a barrio captain, resourceful, kind and well loved. It was in this house that Noy was born. He was an exceptional student who excelled in all subjects, but he was better known for his talent in history. Everybody thought and hoped he would be a lawyer, become the town mayor of Alcala, and later governor of the province. But nobody was surprised or disappointed when he became a medical doctor.

Soon after taking the government board examination and long before the results were known, Noy married his campus sweetheart, Dolores Siao, a registered nurse. She came from a Chinese-Filipino family from Virac, Catanduanes, and looked more like a Chinese than a Filipino. Their only daughter, twelve-year-old Karen, had taken after her, including the way she talked—fast, swallowing most of her syllables.

As soon as he had established a prosperous practice and acquired a beautiful home not far from Daly City—which took years of hard work—Dr. Tablizo asked his parents to move to the United States and live with them. His mother didn't care one way or another. To her it didn't matter where she was, on this side of the globe or the other (that's the way she put it), so long as she was with her husband. Her devotion to him was absolute. It was the old man who did not want to emigrate.

This is how Dr. Tablizo tells his father's story:

Mother lived for my father. She would not eat without him. Sometimes I would come home hungry and gobble up most of the food, not knowing that it was food my mother had saved for my father. Instead of chiding me, all she said was, Oh, you growing boys, you eat like sharks, and she would cook again. There was not much usually, but it was always enough, usually more than enough.

Mother looked healthy and kept busy all day around the house, in the truck garden where she grew vegetables to supplement our food supply. It was father who was sickly. At least, he was always complaining of pains. When I was still in medical school, he used to consult me on symptoms he felt which were as varied as they were imaginary. I soon became an expert on Father's pains, or what he thought ailed him. I knew that much of it was in his mind, but, of course, I did not tell him. He craved attention, my mother's attention, and she gave this to him unflaggingly.

156

When Mother died after a brief, devastating illness, I went home to help Father through the funeral and whatever else that needed to be done. It was then that I urged him again to come live with us in the States. But he was adamant. He said he could take care of himself. Mother would continue to look after him, so he believed, even in death.

I tried to humor him. "Well, she could continue looking after you even when you're with us," I assured him. "And she would be happy knowing we're all together and you will not be lonely."

"How can I be lonely? I have friends here. I have no friends over there."

"But where are your friends here? Most of them have already gone ahead of you. You're alone here now."

After Mother was buried and all our relatives and friends had left, I looked around the old, ancestral home and felt the emptiness. It was so quiet, even at noon on a sunny day. Shadows were everywhere and Father among them, himself an old, beaten shadow.

"What do you say, Pa? Your papers are ready. They've been ready for a long time. Please, come with me."

Still he refused to go. When I was back in the States, I wrote him regularly, pressing him to come. I sent him money through the mails and stopped only when the money orders and checks got lost enroute. Father wrote me, saying he was fine, no problem. It was his friends, much younger than he, who were sick most of the time. He wrote in detail about their various symptoms and asked me for medical advice. He was acting as their doctor through me. That kept him busy for a while, but soon he tired of playing doctor. One day he wrote he was coming. "Just to visit. I want to see my granddaughter."

The old man had difficulty adjusting to San Francisco. He found the weather too damp for him. His bones ached. At night he would wake up shivering. Dr. Tablizo had a special heater installed in his bedroom, which was ornately furnished, complete with an adjoining bathroom. He slept in a queen-size bed, the mattress firm and comfortable, the pillows downy. He had an easy chair where he could recline if he wished while watching TV, which he enjoyed doing. He refused to walk for exercise as Dr. Tablizo suggested.

"Walking will do you good, Pa."

"Do you know how much walking I have done all my life,

157

Noy? You have no idea. And you still want me to walk. You should walk, all of you. You ride cars all the time."

If he was impressed by his son's luxurious home, he made no mention of it. Once he told his granddaughter, "Karen, you must be very rich."

Those were rare moments when there was instant communication between the old man and the young girl. Many times he had to repeat what he was trying to say and this somehow annoyed him. It annoyed Karen, too.

"I can't understand Lolo," she complained. "He has such a funny way of talking. Where did he learn his English, anyway?"

The couple tried to shush her. "We don't speak too well either," the mother said.

"But I can understand you more often than I can't."

"Give him time."

That was all the old man seemed to have. Time. Plenty of it. Sometimes he appeared dazed not knowing what to do. Not a sociable man from way back, he suffered silently the frequent parties on weekends. When there were no parties, the family took him for long drives to the canyons where they went for picnics or sight-seeing. The cold air bothered the old man, he said the high altitude made him woozy, and he would come home complaining of a chill.

Dr. Tablizo had an enlarged, beautifully framed picture of his mother placed on the dresser at the foot of his father's bed. The old man spent time wiping the gold-laminated frame more than was necessary. Once, Karen caught him talking to his wife's picture.

"Why does he do that?" she asked her parents.

"What's wrong with that?" her father chided her. "I used to talk to that picture myself."

"You did that?" she asked, incredulous, laughing as if it was the funniest thing.

"One day when you're grown up, you'll also be talking to pictures," Dolores said.

"Why would I do that? I'm not bananas."

"You don't understand now, but you will later," the doctor said.

The old man quite often fell asleep watching television. Sometimes long after midnight Karen, whose room adjoined his, would be awakened by the static from her grandfather's TV set and she would scream, "The TV's on and I can't sleep!"

One of the things Dr. Tablizo found most difficult to do was to tell his father without hurting his feelings to tone down the volume of his set. He knew his father's hearing wasn't too good anymore, but just the same, the noise bothered them, especially at night when they were trying to get some sleep. Once the doctor tried closing the old man's bedroom door as quietly as he could when his father had fallen asleep with the TV on. The old man woke up with a start.

"Do I disturb you?" he asked.

"Not really," the son lied, "but Karen might be studying in her room."

"Sorry," his father said, walking towards the set to turn it off.

The old man always forgot the remote control. Dr. Tablizo had told him many times that he didn't have to walk back and forth from his chair to the set to turn it on or off or change the channels. Just push a button. He had shown his father how to do it. "You don't have to turn it off now. Go ahead and watch it for as long as you want, just turn it off when you're ready to go to bed," Dr. Tablizo said, sensing that he might have hurt his father's sensitive feelings.

"But I might disturb Karen."

"No you won't, I'll show you."

Dr. Tablizo turned the set on again, then showed his father how to adjust the volume. "Keep pressing this until you have the right volume. Or turn this dial on the set. So, no problem. And you can close the door."

The problem was the old man's hypersensitivity. At odd moments he would say more to himself than to anyone in particular, "I want to go home already." It was evident he didn't feel at home in his son's household. He felt like a guest, an intruder.

"No, you're not, Pa. This is your home," his son protested. It hurt him to hear his father say that. If the old man only knew! Why, he wanted him to be around so that he could lavish on him the love he felt, the gratitude that overwhelmed him. Everything he was and everything he had, he owed to his parents and he wanted his father to know this. Thank you, thank you, he felt like telling him again and again, I would not be where I am without you. He wanted his mother to know, too, but now that she was gone, he wanted to show his father what he truly felt for him.

159

Dr. Tablizo tried to talk to Dolores and Karen and begged them to be patient and understanding. Karen would laugh, "Gosh, what's wrong with telling him?"

How could the doctor explain that his father was very sensitive?

"He's old, he can't remember many things," he would tell his daughter.

"And, of course, I am too young so I got to wait to understand," she would reply sarcastically.

What could he say beyond mildly rebuking her, "Now don't you get too smart, young lady."

It was clear to the doctor that much of these happenings were not lost on his father. He was not that old. He tried to remember the instructions about the TV, but he couldn't help falling asleep. As for the volume control, well, he did turn the volume down but—he hated to admit it—he couldn't hear, his hearing had deteriorated. When the doctor suggested that his father wear a hearing aid, he tried one, but he couldn't get adjusted to it. "It screams at me," he complained. It made more sounds than he wanted or needed to hear. It confused him. He would rather hear nothing.

Dr. Tablizo was sure his father was well aware of these things —and more. For instance, he knew without being told to his face, that they hated the smell of his cigars. They stank up the house, but if he stopped smoking what else was there left for him to enjoy in this world? He also knew that every time he woke up in the middle of the night to relieve himself, which was quite often, he couldn't help making a lot of noise that woke up the household. He hoped the family would eventually get used to these nocturnal sounds, but they never did. Dolores herself suggested that it would be better if the old man didn't flush the toilet at night. The doctor had a better idea: a chamber pot. To which the old man agreed. Why had he not thought of that? That's what he and Pepang had back in Alcala. None of this new-fangled plumbing that made a lot of noise. He remembered that in those days the couple never got the chamber pot filled anyhow and they enjoyed taking turns throwing the urine out of the window into their garden. It made the plants very happy, especially the bougainvilleas which bloomed more lavishly than the neighbours'.

The chamber pot was expensive looking, and it was. But it was too heavy for the old man to carry even when empty. Perhaps the anxiety, that he would not be able to throw the urine into the john himself even if he didn't fill it up, made him forget to use it. He continued to go to the bathroom at night, flushed the john without thinking, and woke up the entire household.

These were irritants that worried Dr. Tablizo no end. Dolores tried to bear everything, but Karen was a problem. "But, Dad, I can't just ignore these things and sulk. You've taught me to be honest and tell you everything," she reasoned.

The doctor had no answer to that. One other thing worried him. His father had a chronic throat ailment which he had long ago diagnosed as pharyngitis. The old man would suddenly wake up nights in a fit of violent coughing, regurgitating phlegm and saliva which sounded obscene and offensive, to say the least. He had not rid himself of the habit as it was more of a habit now than a serious ailment. Even more disgusting was when they heard him swallow the phlegm instead of spitting it out. Dr. Tablizo had supplied him with a small cup which opened and closed automatically, and asked him to spit into it. When he used it around the family, especially at mealtime, Dolores would walk away, disgusted.

"He must be sick, Dad, don't you think?" Karen would say.

Before the first month was over, Dolores confided to her close friends, "I think it was a mistake bringing him over."

"But," her friends told her, "the old man doesn't want to stay here anyway, does he? Then why don't you let him go? You can pay someone to take care of him in the Philippines. He'll surely be happier there than here where you're keeping him against his will, and much to your discomfort."

"August won't allow it. He wants him here," Dolores told them.

They had various theories about why the doctor insisted on having his father stay, the most common one being, August was sentimental, he was a romantic. "He has his own set of ideas about what true love for parents is. It means being close to them, looking after them. It's very Filipino," said someone.

"No, it isn't. I am a Filipino but I'm not like that," Dolores said.

"If it isn't Filipino, I don't know what it is."

"It's just Augusto Tablizo, Jr., M.D. It must be in the Tablizo line. Or perhaps that's what Alcala, that little town where they come from, is all about."

161

This sort of talk got to the doctor and he was angry with his wife. They had a big quarrel. It was terrible because they had to do it all in whispers. They could not scream at each other even if they wanted to.

As the days passed, Dolores became more vocal about her complaints against the old man. She made these known to her husband and her friends. It made things very difficult around the house, and as a result, there was a lot of distortion, sarcasm, exaggeration.

"I try to cook the food he's supposed to like, but he doesn't like my cooking. He eats very little."

"Most old people eat very little."

"But he eats a lot when August cooks for him."

"Then let him do the cooking."

"But he's so tired when he comes home. I can't do that."

"Ignore everything then."

How could she, she asked. Why, even Karen is all confused, poor child.

"Why do you want to eat with your hands, Lolo?" she once asked her grandpa.

"Because God gave me these hands. They're mine. Besides they're clean. I always wash my hands before eating, do you?"

"You see how he talks. He confuses the poor child," Dolores said. "Then there's his bathroom. He has not learned how to use it. It smells of urine and something worse. He says the exhaust fan gives him constipation. Have you ever heard anything like that?"

When the doctor learned about this, he told Dolores not to bother about his father's bathroom. "I'm going to clean it myself," he said, and he did, often going down on all fours to clean the tiles free of every smudge and odor.

But it wasn't always like this in the household. There were some fine moments during the old man's stay. Karen learned to be fond of her grandfather in spite of the initial lack of communication between them. When her parents decided to move the old man to the basement, they were in a quandary over how to tell him without hurting his feelings. Karen saved them the trouble.

"If you're moving him because of me, forget it, I don't mind the noise now, not anymore. I'm used to it. I can sleep through whatever racket he makes."

"Are you sure?"

"Of course, I'm sure. Why would I be telling a lie?"

162

Dr. Tablizo was touched by Karen's gesture. He was relieved. He had not felt good in a long time.

"He loves you," he told his daughter. "He agreed to come and stay with us because of you."

Karen was usually the first one to arrive home in the afternoon and she would find her grandfather alone, eager to talk. She had a few things herself she wanted to unburden to someone, about school, her friends, how her day went. The old man was always there to listen to her. He knew exactly when the school bus stopped in the neighborhood to drop Karen off. He would watch behind the venetian blinds, and the moment he saw her alight, shouting and waving goodbye to her classmates, he would go to the door and open it before she even touched the knob.

"By golly, I don't even have to say 'open sesame,' " she would say, giving the old man a peck on the cheek. She was almost as tall as he, but then he had long suspected that he had begun to shrink.

Mostly Karen wanted to talk to him about school.

"Our chem teacher is a whiz."

"Say that again, please. Slowly only."

And she would repeat with exaggerated slowness. These repetitions on either side became rarer as they got used to each other's speech rhythm.

"Oh, that's good, Karen. You'll learn a lot from . . .   how do you say it . . . a . . . *w h i z* ?"

"But I'm a whiz, too, Lolo."

"In chem . . . chemistry?"

"That's what my teach said. I was the only one in class who could understand the lesson."

"I'm proud of you."

"Math's a breeze, too, for me, Lolo."

She had to explain that one, also, and more and more she enjoyed "teaching" the old man the language. Even if he never went to college, he seemed well read and in his generation of teachers, he was among the best. He could talk and write well. But not the English spoken in America, especially by the young ones like Karen. It sounded like an altogether different language and he was certain his English sounded as strange to her ears.

"You talk like Dad and Mom. I've asked them to enroll in a speech clinic, but they think it's a crazy idea. Do you think it's a crazy idea, Lolo?"

163

"Of course not, but I'm afraid they have no time."

"You have the time. What do you say? You wanna go? Do you good, we'll understand each other better."

"We understand each other already. Besides, I don't think there's anything in the speech clinic that I can't learn from you."

"You mean I'll teach you?"

"You don't have to. Just talk to me."

"How was Dad in school?"

"Better than average. Very studious."

"Was he good in chem or math or what?"

"He was a declaimer. Won medals and prizes."

"He really talks well even if he sounds different. You know what I mean."

"You talk like an American."

"But I talk too fast like Mom."

"What do you want to be when you grow up?"

"Haven't decided yet. Too early for that."

"Maybe a doctor like your dad or a nurse like your Mom."

"I really don't know. Well, do you really want to know?"

"Sure."

"I haven't told this to anyone. I really want to be a teacher."

"Like me!" There was joy in his voice. It sounded young for a change. "You'll be a whiz of a teacher."

"You learn fast, Lolo. Say, what's the Philippines like?"

"You mean Alcala."

"No, the Philippines.'

"I can only tell you about Alcala."

"Okay. Tell me."

"It's the most beautiful place in the world. I think there's only one car in town, it's owned by a gambler. The town's so small everybody walks. There are passenger jeepneys if we want to go to the other towns. It's a sleepy town. Many sleep at noon including the dogs. It's hot, never cold. Rains, too, practically all year. People are mostly farmers. We used to own lands . . ."

"I know. Dad said you had cattle, too, but not anymore, because you had to sell everything to see Dad through medical school. I remember he visited you when Lola was still alive and he wanted to buy back the land for you at any price, he said, but nobody was selling. He was very sad, Lolo."

"He's a good son."

"But why did you have to do that, sell all your property so he could go to school?"

164

"It's the right thing to do, Karen. Parents live for their children."

"I wouldn't want Mom and Dad to do that for me."

"You can say that because they don't have to. I'm sure you're well taken care of, your education, I mean."

"You better believe it. I hate it sometimes. They keep telling me, this is for your education, this is for your future. I feel like telling them I can take care of myself when the time comes, but it might hurt them."

"I'm glad you don't want to hurt them."

"I'd really want to take care of myself. I'm going to work my way through college until I become a teacher."

"A whiz of a teacher. Thanks for teaching me that expression. You'll make an excellent teacher."

"Like you, Lolo."

"Better. Remember I never went beyond high school."

"You didn't have to, I guess."

"You won't make money being a teacher."

"That's another thing I hate. Money. I mean we all need it, but why should it be our main goal? Look at Dad . . ."

"He's thinking of you, your future."

"There you go again . . . I bet you miss Alcala."

"Alcala . . . a as in . . . well, you've heard doctors say, 'ahhhh!' That's 'ah' for Alcala."

"Ah-lcala."

"That's better. Yes, I do miss Alcala."

"Because of Lola?"

"That, too. But mainly because I love the place. My roots are there. That's where I want to die. Believe me, Karen, I want to go home already."

"But Dad says you're gonna be alone there."

"How could I be alone there? That's where I belong."

"You mean it's wrong for Dad and Mom, all of us, to be here for the same reason?"

"Your case is different. You're better off here."

"And you'd be better off there?"

"Sure."

"You won't miss this place, Lolo? Everything around here? You won't miss any of these?"

"I'll miss you. And your Dad. And your Mom."

"I'd hate to see you go, Lolo. I love you, you know."

One thing the old man never tired of doing was to remind his son every time he had a chance, "Send me back to Alcala, Noy. That's where I belong. I want to go home already."

One morning the old man failed to wake up. He had died in his sleep. Just like that. There was nothing wrong with him.

The couple's circle of close friends, among them the Sottos, were deeply affected by the old man's death. They were disturbed by the way he died—it seemed, for no reason.

As if I were the wiser one, I told Dr. Sotto, "The old man died of a broken heart, doctor."

"Nobody dies of a broken heart."

"Filipinos do."

43

O.T.: Waiting's the name of the game.

The Jaimes: But why? Why?

A Board Member: *Ano ba ang* exchange now?

The Sottos: Look, Estela, look!

Student: Will that be asked in the test?

Judy: Can you spare a quarter, mister?

Tingting: I don't remember no names.

David: Did you know my father?

Father Belarmino: The Lord be with you.

Karen: I love you, you know.

Mr. Augusto Tablizo, Sr.: I want to go home already.

Voices: What the hell for . . .?

166

44

EACH DAY became a constant struggle against a failing faith in the prospects of the magazine. To begin with there had been truly no bright moments. Now it seemed that my earlier optimism was baseless. In the early days, what fed my hopes was my own personal need for the magazine to come through. As time passed I found myself more and more dependent upon the magazine's existence, as if my own were a part of it. It became my anchor for survival in America; its realization meant all the difference in the world to me between success and failure.

Lately, however, the lights that led my way into the city of my salvation had gone out and I felt as if I had been plunged in total darkness. So badly did I feel at times that the load of papers I carried with me wherever I went became heavier in my heart than in my hands. Of what use, I thought, were all these words, these ideas, these random notes that were supposed to be the life of the magazine? What a fool I was to keep on jotting them down. Sometimes I felt like dumping them into the nearest trash can, or, unseen in the dead of night, and for dramatic effect, litter the streets of San Francisco with them. Goodbye to these testaments of what I felt was vital and human. Goodbye, San Francisco. Oh, let me leave with my heart intact and in the right place.

But I stayed on.

Write your heart out, David, and get lost, as the doctor said, get lost in the streets of the golden city. Remember your father, you came here to find him, did you not? Admit it, do not deny your heart. Find him then. It won't be easy, but it will give purpose to your life. He could be closer to you than you think.

But where, where do I find him?

I had to have method in my search. I spent long hours in the reference section of the public library where old telephone directories were kept and looked for my father's name: Pastor Tolosa. There weren't too many Tolosas and the few I called, on a hunch, were mostly Hispanics. Some of the women who answered were unintelligible, old voices cracked with age. In several instances I didn't even get to ask my question. The few who were intelligible were usually in a hurry to hang up. Fear of strangers, no doubt. One was a husky female voice, although it could have been a man's. To my question, the voice answered in heavily accented English, "I am from Mejico," it said.

To which I replied in one of the very few Spanish words I knew, "Gracias," wanting to add, "Señora," but I wasn't sure, I could be talking to a "señor."

Quickly the voice answered, "You betcha!"

Well, perhaps my father never had a telephone anyhow.

The city department in charge of death records yielded nothing—to my relief—no Pastor Tolosa among them. However, it crossed my mind that my father could have died outside San Francisco, in some heavily populated Filipino community in California or the mid-West, in New York or perhaps, even a small town. Father, father, where are you?

Of the men I knew in San Francisco, the only one who could help me in my search was Tingting. He had lived the longest here. He might know. The few times he told me, "Your face is familiar, are you sure you've not been here before?" I held my breath in anticipation, perhaps he did remember. But nothing. Mostly he showed indifference, even resentment that I should waste time looking for a lost father.

"Don't you have children of your own, a son maybe?" I asked him once in the hope that he would understand my need to find my father.

"Maybe yes, maybe no," he answered, poker-faced.

"You mean you just sowed wild oats?"

"What do you mean?"

"I mean, did you just fuck around?"

"Hey, that's good, sowing wild oats. I like that . . . but I think I'd stick to fucking around."

"At your age?"

"Hey . . . wait a minute . . ."

That's how Tingting discouraged me. But the more he did, the more I wanted to talk to him about my father. I sensed an evasiveness on his part—or was I becoming paranoid?

Once he said, "If your father had played tennis, I couldn't have missed him."

"True," I agreed, happy that for once he showed some interest in my search.

"That is, if he played like you," he added.

"What's wrong with my game?"

"Nothing. I didn't say nothing."

"You're a swell-head, you know."

"Of course. Cesar *yata.*"

And so it went.

45

WHOEVER MASTERMINDED the program my students in Philippine Culture put up as their end of the quarter project deserved the highest grade in organization skill. When I heard that they had sent invitations to all school officials and the faculty, I became apprehensive. I had been made to understand that it was going to be a simple program, with only me and my class as audience. Not this big happening. All over the campus were hand-printed posters announcing the program and inviting everybody to come and learn what Philippine Culture was all about. This alarmed me. I tried to ask some of my students what was going on, but they were tight-lipped, as if some secret involving national security were at stake.

I tried to contact Professor Jaime but he was not available. His secretary said his appointments were fully booked. I could not get him on the phone. "If it's about the Philippine Culture program, don't worry," she said. "We'll all be there." That was what worried me.

When the big day came, I was so nervous I completely blotted out of my mind the fears that hounded me the last few days over the fate of the magazine, so concerned was I over the impending disaster at the school.

My students had secured permission to hold the program in the main auditorium that could seat at least a thousand. They had gone crazy! The auditorium would look empty no matter what my students did to encourage attendance. Someone told me he had heard the program announced over the radio. "Are you sure it's not on television?" I wanted to ask with sarcasm.

My understanding was that the program would be held at the same hour the class met so I was quite upset when I learned that it was going to be held at five o'clock that afternoon. I read a circular from the Dean of Humanities enjoining the other departments to encourage their students and faculty to attend. Since it was the last day of classes, the Vice-President for Academic Affairs had given permission for classes meeting at that hour to go to the main auditorium, if they so desired, "to witness a revelation in ethnic culture through music and illustrated talks."

Everybody seemed to know more about it than I did. How did I miss out on what my students were up to? It occurred to me that I seldom showed up on campus except on Monday, Wednes-

169

day, and Friday when I taught the class, and I had not developed any personal rapport with my students. I felt no bond between us. I had marked them out for what they were: just passing through. Perhaps in the same way, they had marked me out, too, for what I was: just passing through.

I arrived at the main auditorium at a quarter to five. The hallway was decked with buntings like in the Philippine barrios during fiesta time. I spied some of my students. The boys were in *Barong Tagalog,* the girls in *Balintawak* dress. Nothing too fancy about the *barongs* which the boys wore over black pants with matching black shoes. The girls' dresses were a riot of colors. I hardly recognized them in their costumes, and with their make-up, it was even more difficult to identify them. They smiled at me as I self-consciously walked in, feeling very shabby in my Levi's and end-of-the-week white shirt. My hand went involuntarily to my rumpled hair, but what could I do at that late hour?

To my surprise, the auditorium was filling up with students and faculty, and outsiders, Filipinos and Americans. One of the girls, dressed in *patadyong* with a folded scarf neatly pinned to her shoulder, ushered me to a seat in the front row near the lovely Dean of Humanities and Professor Jaime in a three-piece suit. He rose to greet me, asking me to sit down between him and the Dean. I felt even shabbier hemmed in by both of them.

As Wong, the master of ceremonies, began to speak, the audience quieted down. He had a good speaking voice and no accent. In our class, I was the only one with an accent; and, oh, yes, Patrocinio, the new arrival from the Philippines.

"Ladies and gentlemen," Wong began, "welcome to a program on Philippine Culture sponsored by the class under Professor David Dante Tolosa . . . " And he pointed in my direction. There was a desultory clapping of hands as I shrank deeper into my seat terribly embarrassed.

"We are giving you this evening a glimpse into the beauty and charm, character and mystery of the Philippines and its people, the only Christian nation in the Southeast, and aptly called 'the Pearl of the Orient Seas.' All the singers, dancers and performers belong to the class of Professor Tolosa. They are in no way paying members of the Actors and Dancers Guild of California, but they mean no harm. They are here to entertain you and I hope you will be entertained. They are here to show many things Philippine, and I hope you will see not only with your eyes, but with your mind

170

and heart as well. We ask you not to love us, although we would welcome that, but to know and understand us as a people, different and unique, but like all of you here, human."

The audience clapped quite spontaneously. Had they been rehearsed? I was suspicious. They seemed to be enjoying themselves as if they were part of the show. When the clapping subsided, Wong resumed his introduction. He was at ease now, more confident, his voice louder than I had ever heard him speak. He turned towards the curtains which gradually opened, revealing a small nipa hut built on the center of the stage. On the low bamboo stairs sat a brown maiden in a peasant's blouse. In front of her, one rung lower down the steps, sat a smaller girl. A Philippine melody played in the background, loud at first, then slowly faded.

"Ladies and gentlemen, a Philippine barrio scene: mother and daughter engaged in a popular pastime. Popular because it's free."

Wong exited as the lights dimmed and a single spotlight beamed on the stage.

The mother is intent on her work, scouring her daughter's hair for lice. She checks the girl's head, left side, then right side, front and back, repeats, until the hair is a rumpled mop.

"I told you, Ma, I got no more lice," the daughter protests, a whimper in her voice.

"Sit still or I'll spank you," the mother threatens.

"I have no more lice, I said."

"Why do you keep scratching your head then?"

"But that was last week. You got them all already."

"What?" The mother sits up, horrified. "You mean I have them now?" Her hands fly to her hair. Her face turns to a grimace as she scratches her head. She screams.

Mother and daughter exit. Music fades in and the curtain drops.

Voice over: "That, ladies and gentlemen, is a humble example of motherly love in the Philippines."

Thunderous applause. Laughter.

I could not help smiling myself, even as I worried that the scene might be misunderstood.

"That was so cute," the Dean said, smiling.

Professor Jaime was laughing as he nudged me playfully. "That was so real," he commented, "I'm homesick already, really, I am."

Songs and dances followed. They were well rehearsed. The songs elicited encores; so did the dances. The best applauded was

171

the dance called *"Pandanggo sa Ilaw."* The auditorium was darkened, lights were turned off except for a few dim ones on the walls and under the seats, to lend an air of suspense and drama to the dance, as graceful maidens swayed to the music, balancing candle-lit glasses on their heads and hands. The music was languid at first, then became fast, and the audience held their breath waiting for the flickering candlelight to die, or the glasses to fall, but nothing of the sort happened. These were professional dancers; these couldn't have been my students.

The *tinikling* bamboo dance also got enthusiastic applause, chiefly because here, too, was drama, excitement. As the tempo of the music increased and the clap-clapping of the bamboo poles became more frenzied, the audience watched breathlessly as shapely brown ankles dipped in and out, eluding the bamboo snares. It was only when it was all over and there were no bruised ankles that everyone relaxed and marvelled at the dancers' agility.

The skits and dialogues provoked the loudest and most prolonged laughter. They were most informative, often caustic, filled with the irony of the clash of cultures, not only among different ethnic groups in the United States, but also among Filipinos here and abroad.

Sample:

Two young Filipinos, one a long-time resident in the United States, the other, newly arrived from the Philippines, meet on the stage, which could be anywhere in the streets of San Francisco, a section of the campus, or in someone's home. They are dressed casually in blue jeans and T-shirt. They talk.

"Hey you, Pinoy, you must be new around here."

"That's right, I'm new around here. But I'm no Pinoy."

"Aw, come on, we're all Pinoys here in this country."

"You may be a Pinoy, but I'm not."

"What makes you think you're different? "

"My brother's a doctor."

"Funny guy. Better get wise, brod. We don't want you bragging around here like you own the place, showing off your designer jeans. Sasson. Jordache. Sergio Valiente. They don't mean nothing here, see?"

"Go away, I never bothered you."

"But you bother me."

"Can't we be friends?"

"I'm only friend to Pinoys like me."

The curtain drops.

172

Another skit is introduced as a class in Philippine culture. The professor is described as a disciplinarian who insists on a hundred percent attendance. He appears on the stage, in a parody of me, dressed the way I've always dressed in class—casually, in battered jeans, moccasins, and short-sleeved pastel shirts. He stands beside a blackboard on which is written a big capital letter "K." In one hand, he holds a class attendance record book close to his chest and in the other, a piece of chalk which he swings around wildly as he lectures. He addresses the audience.

"Class, you're absent again! I mean, most of you are absent again. Why can't you have a perfect attendance? Aren't you through with lunch yet? What? You're not through? When will you be through? Not till dinnertime? What did you say? Will this lecture be included in the next exam? Of course! Everything I say here today is very important, or should be, to you! "

As he talks, he keeps the attendance book pressed to his heart, moving around constantly to write on the board important words he wants to stress. He doesn't erase anything he has written and before long, the blackboard is covered with words, some of which overlap.

Guiltily, I realized how often I had done that. Without doubt I was being caricatured, and the boy was doing a good job of it. Even his "lecture" was lifted straight out of my mouth, although he exaggerated the accent, the gestures, the imperious mien.

"Listen to this truth, this *Katotohanan:* from birth to death the Filipino is governed by K's. K's rule our lives, permeate our existence. There's no escaping the letter K. I did not include this in the syllabus I gave you because it's merely a theory, a personal opinion which isn't backed by statistics or research. But let me mention everyday Filipino terms that begin with the letter K. Let me start with history."

As he mentions a word that begins with K, he writes this on the board and proceeds from there, mentioning other words. He starts with the famous K K K of the days of Bonifacio and the Philippine revolution. He explains the meaning of *Katipunan* and its synonym *Kapisanan;* then the words *Kataas-taasan* and *Karangalan,* the Highest and Honor, respectively. He dwells on Honor, one of the virtues which all true-blooded Filipinos believe in and, if need be, fight to the death for. The other virtues he enumerates are: Freedom or *Kalayaan;* Wisdom or *Karunungan.* We are a brown race called *Kayumanggi* or better yet, *Kayumangging Ka-*

173

ligatan. Movements are *Kilusan;* brotherhood is *Kapatiran;* Wealth, *Kayamanan.*

For the first time, the lecturer breaks into a smile, his face softens. "We are a tactile people. We believe in touching or body contact . . . in sex." He explains the meaning of *Kurot* or pinching, a form of affection or punishment depending on who does it and to whom—and how. *Kiliti* is to tickle; *kilitiin* is ticklish. There, too, is a K in *halik* which means kiss.

I thought of some K words that were downright obscene if not actually gross which I deliberately withheld from the class. Perhaps some of the older Filipinos in the audience were thinking about them now, suppressing a smile at the recollection.

Still in a lighter vein, the lecturer talks of *kuto* or lice reminding the audience of the opening scene. *Kangkong* is a nutritious vegetable, a common fare among the poor. *Kalamay* and *Kutsinta* are sweet delicacies, but not too sweet, that is, not so sweet sounding is a plant named *Kantutay.*

The lecturer stops here, still smiling. By now the blackboard is covered with words. He has proved his point.

"I have omitted some important words both the sublime and ridiculous, but in my next lecture I shall make up for my omissions," he says with a mischievous twinkle in his eyes. "And you can be sure that this will all be included in the next test."

Here the monologue is broken by a song and dance number, lively and engaging. It dawned on me as I watched with increasing wonder and admiration for my students that I had after all planted the seed of interest and love for Philippine culture among them. I was wrong to think they were inattentive, that they didn't care.

The girl who appeared more often than the others, playing various roles as singer, dancer and actress was Kathy Jimenez whose mother was black and whose father was Filipino with Spanish origins. Her eyes were coal black and large. They shone like black diamonds and her smile was pure temptation. Her long black hair, straight and gleaming, adorned her heart-shaped face. She was taller than even some of the boys in the class. I remembered her saying that prejudice existed and just as badly among Filipinos as among the Whites, in their attitude towards Blacks.

"My father who was homesick for his fellow Filipinos once took my mother to a Rizal Day dance, and it turned out to be the last they ever attended."

The Filipinos who he thought were his friends snubbed him and his black wife. The couple tried to ignore the blatant preju-

174

dice, pretending it didn't exist. They danced most of the pieces as if they enjoyed them as much as everybody else.

Gradually, though, they found themselves alone. Everybody seemed to shy away from them. They could discern that the others were whispering about the black wife. During refreshments, the Filipinos stood apart and kept the couple at a distance. Finally, one oldtimer approached them and offered his apologies, calling those in the dance hall "unChristian and illiterate." He offered to take the microphone and condemn the crowd in the name of the Philippine national hero, Jose Rizal, whom they were honoring.

Kathy admitted to the class that she herself had not been sure how she would be treated by her classmates. "You see," she explained, "I suffer from what you might call double jeopardy." She paused and smiled, "But why am I telling you all this now? I've found you all just great. I love you all."

The class chanted, "We love Kathy, we love Kathy." Then they broke into a refrain: "Black is beautiful. Brown is beautiful. Black and brown is the most beautiful."

It was this beautiful person who stood out this evening on center stage. Although the numbers were varied, one thing remained constant on the stage: the Philippine nipa hut. From the center on the opening scene, it was moved to the side or behind during the songs and dances, but it remained the predominant backdrop for the evening's show. The boy who parodied me reappeared and resumed his lecture.

"Well, class, here we are again for our next topic: our peculiarities as a people. Remember, this will be in the next exam! We are so naive as a people, child-like, at times childish. We don't mind revealing to the most casual acquaintance very personal matters like family sources of income and what you call 'skeletons in the closet.' When we ask our American friends, 'How much do you make?' or 'How much did you pay for your house?' or 'How much did your dress cost?' we don't think we're prying because we don't keep these things secret. These are things we like to share, especially when the items in question cost a lot of money and become on occasion for bragging which we like to do. We're so child-like we ask those whom we consider close to us to give us gifts—for Christmas, birthdays, weddings, whatever occasion. Sometimes we don't hesitate to name what we want—money, a dress, a pair of shoes, perfume. We don't wait to be given; we ask. For us, it's a way of life. And yet, on other matters, we are a very shy people; we think Americans are very frank, brutally open. We can also be very generous. We would, when the occasion demands, give the shirt off our back so when we fancy your shirt, why can't we ask for it?"

The audience lapped it up. Some nodded as if to say: "So . . . so . . . " And the applause was deafening, heart-warming to me who must have inspired some of this. The entire program took about two hours, but it was well-paced, with little time wasted. Now I was sure my students were proud to be Filipinos. How badly I had underestimated them.

For the last number the entire cast—at last my class had a hundred per cent attendance—trooped to the stage to take their final bow. Kathy asked the audience to join the cast in singing *Bayan Ko,* or "My Country."

"Please stand," she said softly, raising her arms to lead the singing. Printed copies of the song had been distributed to the audience earlier, but I didn't need one. I sang from memory, from the heart and soul, damn it! I had sung the same lyrics with other homesick Filipinos many times when we met together to celebrate a holiday—in the mid-West, in New York, in San Francisco. The year was 1975, three years after martial law had been declared in my country. Always I sang the song with my heart in my throat, thinking, how long, God, how long martial law would keep me here wandering in exile. Was I really that much better off in San Francisco on top of Diamond Heights with a view of a blazing city, while my fellow writers back home rotted in windowless jails behind barbed wires? Was I luckier indeed than those writers free from torture and prison only to suffer a worse fate —— death of the spirit and the will to write, a silence and acquiescence that made a regime of injustice, greed and corruption prevail?

An overwhelming sense of self-pity and sadness filled me. Before the song was finished, I was choking on the words, unable to continue. I wiped my tears, turning to the Dean beside me. "Sorry, Ma'am, I can^t help it, you see, we're a naive, sentimental people. We cry easily."

Professor Jaime himself was wiping his eyes with a colored hankerchief.

"It's all right, David," the Dean said, calling me for the first time by my first name as she put her arm around my shoulder.

I didn't realize till then she was that much taller than I.

176

46

WHEN DR. SOTTO sent for me to see him upstairs, I was so eager to hear what he had to say, I arrived ahead of the boy he had sent to fetch me.

The doctor was adjusting a huge telescope I had not seen before, fixing it as close to the window as he could, peering through one end while trying to focus it.

I stood by for a while, watching him, wondering why he had the telescope. To have a clearer and closer view of San Francisco? But what for? What was there to see, at closer range, of a city bound in fog, or on a good evening when the breeze cleared away the mist, a city blazing, always blazing with lights?

"Hi!" he said when he noticed me. "Don't you think this is the best position?"

I agreed. I wanted him to be done with it and talk to me about the magazine.

"Want to have a look? I think I got it properly focused now."

"What is it like?" I asked, to be polite, as I tried to see for myself what there was to see. The telescope was manageable in spite of its ponderous size. It could be moved to any level, turned whichever direction on a stool or a table, with the observer sitting or standing.

The city was there down below all right, glittering as always. However, the telescope made it look as if the city had suddenly closed in, more vivid in details and outline, almost frightening in its nearness as if the lights could burn you to death or entangle you among endless wires and vapor lamps. The traffic moved in a steady flow but in close-up, something was lost along with the distance: the enchantment, the air of mystery of a city alive but unreal, almost like a dream. I tried the skies. That was better. The stars at closer view were even more resplendent. I imagined their actual size and peopled them with creatures of my own imaginings. Vainly I waited for something to flash into view, a rocket in orbit, a falling star crashing down on the winking city.

"Great," I said, not knowing what else to say. He must have gone into a lot of expense to buy the instrument, so why should I make him unhappy?

"Isn't it though?" he was saying as I heard a rustling from one of the nearby rooms. "Imelda and I thought Estela would

177

enjoy watching her favorite show with this telescope."

"Has she tried it already? "

"It has just arrived. I've had quite a time assembling it."

Imelda appeared, pushing the wheel chair on which Estela sat in a long light-blue flannel gown, her head moving around, her arms twisting about as if fighting phantoms only she could see while her fingers clawed at the air. She looked no different from when I saw her last. I couldn't remember when, but now she seemed to recognize the people around her, including me perhaps. From her throat came those sounds which by now must carry particular meanings to the couple, like set patterns of speech that children have and which their parents figure out.

"David is here, Estela," Imelda said, bending down towards the child. "Say good evening, David."

The eyes she cast on me were baleful, but there was a mellowness in the tone of her gurgling.

"Daddy bought you a toy," Imelda continued, addressing her daughter, barely looking at me. She was as attractive as ever, but looked a bit harried.

Dr. Sotto rushed to the child, adjusting her limbs, wiping off the saliva that constantly dribbled like impure honey down her chin.

"Look what we got for you. Peep through this end like this and I'll hold on to it for you. You'll love what you'll see. Look Estela, look!"

The child was curious, hesitant at first, but not frightened by the new object. She allowed herself to be positioned so that she could without effort peer through the telescope turned towards the city below. Estela peered for a few seconds, then she reared backwards with a violence that caught us all by surprise, it gave me goose pimples. She pushed the end of the telescope furiously away from her, nearly toppling down the tripod on which it stood. Dr. Sotto and his wife could not understand why Estela would react violently against the gift they had just given her. They were —perhaps because I was around—embarrassed, and, maybe, also frightened, as they tried to calm her down, stroking her hair, patting her hand, whispering meaningless blabber. After a while, they asked Estela to try the telescope again. She gave out a long low moan and shook her head. Never was a 'NO' more emphatic and frightening. Estela was actually crying. Those were tears rolling down her cheeks.

It embarrassed me to stand there, witnessing this little family drama. What could I say? What could I do? After another half-hearted attempt to cajole her to try the instrument again, the couple gave up, whispering between them. Estella glared at the object with as much loathing as her eyes could show.

Later I learned that they tried again the next few days, but to no avail. Strangely enough, Estela always agreed to try the telescope as if she had no memory of what had transpired before, but her reaction against it was as violent as the previous times. In the end, the very sight of it alarmed her and she would go into spasms of screaming, frantically clawing the air as she reared her head. Defeated, her parents finally put the telescope away and Estela returned to her favorite show: a glittering San Francisco at night as seen through her naked eyes.

As I turned to go back to my room, Dr. Sotto held me by the arm. "Sorry, I never expected this. Let's talk next time, tomorrow maybe. For sure I'll have something definite to tell you."

Like a fool, I had to say, "What do you think are the chances?"

He cut me short. "We'll soon know. Not later than next week," he said softly.

Back in my room, I gathered all the notes I had jotted down, folders in loose leaves, yellow pads, cards tied with rubber bands all filled with words written close together in tiny script, as if there might not be enough space in the paper for all the words I wanted to write. Now the words stared back at me as I tried to decipher some of them. They made no sense.

At this point it was easy to indulge in self-pity, cry over the waste of time and energy and the day-to-day subsistence on hope, walking up and down what must have been once-upon -a-time a pristine hill now constantly being violated. I shall miss Diamond Heights and the lovely people who had sheltered me all this time, including Estela who could have been the loveliest of them all. Where would be my next stop? The pity of it was that, whichever way I turned, it wouldn't be towards home and that's where I knew I truly belonged.

This was the time to make other plans when the final word was given. That night I lay in bed, tossing, unable to sleep for a long time. When sleep finally came, I, unaccountably, dreamt happy dreams. In one of them I found my father at last and his first words to me were: "Son, this is one hell of a city."

179

47

TRUE TO HIS WORD Dr. Sotto called me up before the following week was over. It was a Wednesday, the day I usually played a set or two at the Golden Gate Park, so I had to tell Tingting that I could not play that day and set up another date for the weekend. Dr. Sotto wanted me to be free that evening because he wanted to have a long visit with me. He and Imelda were inviting me for dinner upstairs.

"Too bad I have to say the news isn't any good, David," he said, sounding really sad, almost contrite over the phone. "Anyway, let's talk about it later tonight, okay?" He hung up before I did.

I put back the receiver on its cradle, wondering why I felt no excitement, no sensation of despair or anguish. I had just been told to stop dreaming of ever putting out the magazine I had been working on all these months. It meant the end to a lot of things that had begun to take shape in my mind, things that had become part of my life. This was rejection of the bitterest kind for a writer like me, looking for an anchor to hold on to—and yet I felt nothing. No tremor in my voice as I echoed back, "okay," long after he had hung up, no trembling in my hands. There was no happiness either, no thrill, no sense of relief, no joyous ringing of bells. I had expected it but at the same time prayed that my expectation would not be fulfilled. I couldn't see myself without a job in San Francisco and I had definitely made up my mind not to return to the Philippines. I had dreaded this day and yet now that it was here, I felt nothing. Was this numbness a prelude to a deepening pain?

While waiting for the couple to send for me, I spent time looking over my papers, lined or plain, which I had put away in folders. Notes, reminders, comments, running accounts of events, thoughts, feelings. There were several sheets full of figures. I was trying to come up with reasonable estimates of my own, reducing the rather ambitious project to the barest minimum (just so I could have a magazine to edit for Filipinos abroad). Some of my notes fascinated me. I couldn't remember having written them; they sounded too good, I couldn't have written them myself. Surely, not all of these things I had written were for the magazine. Not all of them were magazine material. Was it possible I had been writing stories and sketches without the magazine in mind?

Sorry. The word had been spoken. I stared at the jumble of words on sheets scattered on the table. All these—for nothing. I couldn't even feel sorry for myself. No, that wasn't true. I was sorry for myself. I was wallowing in self-pity and there was something cold and familiar in the feeling. As in the past, I felt stirrings within me, a burgeoning self-hate.

It was Imelda herself who came down to get me. I could not tell whether she was wearing a house dress or a formal gown. She had on a long lavender outfit that looked like a toga draped around her loosely, making her look slimmer than she actually was. I was not sure whether my old brown cardigan over a beige shirt with no tie was all right for the occasion. Then it occurred to me that women, especially the Filipino wives whom I had met at parties on Diamond Heights, tended to overdress while their husbands, except those coming straight from the hospital or offices where they worked, wore casual clothes. I hoped that Dr. Sotto would not be in a business suit, which would make me look shabby.

In the narrow corridor leading to the stairway that spiralled upwards, Imelda paused, bidding me to go ahead. No, I didn't want to go ahead of her. It didn't seem proper.

"Go ahead, please," she said as I stopped at the foot of the stairs. From the tall ceiling overhead hung a cluster of Capiz shells that looked like oversized wafers, but these were aglow with many electric bulbs that shone brightly within the clusters.

"No, please, you go ahead," I said diffidently, feeling like a calf being led to slaughter.

"No, you do. I insist. If you miss a step I'll be right below you to keep you from falling."

"I should have said that," I said, taking a step up. Without thinking, I added, "Then you would fall into my arms."

She chuckled (God, even the way she chuckled!). "I'd be too heavy for you."

We were still smiling when we walked towards the dining hall bright with chandeliers. In most Filipino homes in the States, the more festive the occasion, the brighter the glare of the lights, unlike in most American homes where it's almost dark and only candles light up the dining table.

The hall was ablaze. Estela didn't need to watch the city below before she went to bed. Dr. Sotto had a gray sweater vest over a plum-colored plain shirt open at the throat. He met us half-way, extending his hands to me.

181

"David, welcome. We seldom get a chance to visit."

"Thank you, you're very kind," I said, looking at both of them as I took the chair he had indicated.

It was a smaller dining table we were using but even then it was too big for the three of us. Dr. Sotto sat at the head of the table between Imelda and me.

"How's Estela?" I asked.

"She's much better now," Dr. Sotto answered quickly. "As a matter of fact, she has just turned in for the night, earlier than usual, but, yes, she has had a glimpse of her favorite sight. She was unusually happy tonight."

We all looked towards the window below which the city lay like a sheet of sparkling jewels. From where we sat, we could see only parts of the skyline and what looked like an overcast.

Over soup the couple talked about Estela. She could now make intelligible sounds and there were things they now understood apart from what she liked or didn't like. They could tell when she was just trying to communicate something instead of mistaking her sounds for moans or cries of pain or disgust. She was improving as well as could be expected. They agreed they should have brought her along with them when they migrated to this country.

"But we were quite poor then," Imelda said. "It would not have been easy to have her around."

"We couldn't have given her what we can now afford to give her, the care she needs. I think we've brought her here just at the right time, all other things considered," Dr. Sotto said.

"How I missed her then," Imelda said softly as if we were not supposed to hear.

While the old woman was removing the soup plates, Dr. Sotto turned to me, patting my arm. "Sorry, you had to miss your tennis game this afternoon. If we had known earlier, you could have gone ahead and played and have a late dinner afterwards."

"That's all right," I said. "I get enough exercise anyhow walking the streets of San Francisco. Besides, I can't seem to beat the guy."

"I was never good at it. Never learned to swing my backhand," Imelda said, looking at her husband.

"Besides when she saw the big muscles and veined playing arm of one of the current women champions, she was afraid that would happen to her. So she quit playing. Women's vanity."

She slapped his arm gently, it was like a caress.

"That's true," I agreed, "but us guys don't mind."

"You told me once you play this Pinoy guy Tingting. He's called Cesar and very popular around the Golden Gate Tennis Courts. They say he's fabulous."

"He's great, goes after every ball, is all over the court. He's so steady he'll run you ragged unless you can serve and volley or play the net and put away everything he sends you back over the net. And this guy's clever, too. He passes you or kills you with his lobs."

"How old is he?"

"Old enough to be my father. But he's wiry. Oh, you'd love this: he doesn't believe in doctors."

"I don't blame him," Dr. Sotto said. Imelda smiled.

"What does he do aside from tennis or is that all he does?" she asked.

"He lives and works in a small rundown hotel. Easy work, according to him, 'it's a steal.'"

"Have you seen the place?"

"Oh, yes. He's also a good cook. And he loves to go fishing. He cleans and puts the fish he catches in deep freeze, and he eats fish all the time, I mean, almost all the time."

"The secret of longevity," Dr. Sotto said, pretending to shudder over the huge tenderloin steak we were now busy cutting and eating.

"The wine is good," Imelda said.

"Very good," I agreed, taking another sip.

"I hear you're looking for your father," Imelda said, watching me over the brim of the goblet on her lips. Putting it down, she added "Any success?"

What else did they know about me? I never told them I was looking for my father. Or did I?

"You're surprised that we know," Imelda said. "Someone told us."

"Well. . ." I began hesistantly, not knowing exactly what to say. "Well, no, I haven't found him yet. Besides, I haven't been looking lately."

"Have you considered the possibility that perhaps he's dead now?"

"That has crossed my mind, but I have a feeling he's still around. He couldn't be much older than Tingting."

"Have you tried the Tolosas in the phone directory?"

"Yes, including those from way back."

"No success, eh?"

"Most of the Tolosas who answer me are Hispanics. The Filipinos never heard of my father. You see, he was a poor man, maybe he never had a telephone in his name — a nobody."

"Isn't that what most of us were in the past in the Philippines?" She sounded very sincere.

"That's not the impression I get, talking to other Filipinos in this country. Most of them seem to be well connected. They seem to be related to most of the Big Shots in our country. Perhaps they simply want to put me in my right place."

"I don't blame you for feeling the way you do, David," Dr. Sotto said.

"But you should know by now," Imelda was saying, "that there are many Filipinos around who brag a lot. Name droppers. I hate to admit it, but I'm ashamed of some of our countrymen. They're loud, they call attention to themselves. They're always trying to impress others either with their money or connections or both."

"Well, frankly, they look and sound phonies to me. When I feel they're trying to tell me I don't deserve their company, I say to myself, good riddance. Both ways."

God, I was praying silently, don't let me talk about my father. It's bad enough that I feel guilty about seeming to have given up looking for him. But now, I have all the time. From now on, I can begin the search all over again.

"Professor Jaime should be able to help you," Dr. Sotto said, adding before I could say anything, "How did your teaching go at City College?"

"Not bad. In fact, it was good," I said trying hard to suppress an impulse to brag about my students in Philippine Culture.

"I understand it pays very little," Imelda said.

"Can't Professor Jaime help?" Dr. Sotto asked.

"He has been very helpful already. Yes, he's trying to help. Have you met his wife? A great lady."

"No, we seldom meet the Jaimes. They live in San Jose, don't they?"

"Yes. They own a two-story house. A great couple. They want me to stay with them."

"No, no. You stay here. This is your home," Imelda said.

184

"Thank you," I said, remembering another Imelda in another season. "You've been very kind to me. But I think it's about time I start moving on."

"David, I feel responsible for you. It was I who started you on this. Too bad . . ." Dr. Sotto paused.

"What happened?"

"Frankly, nothing. Nothing happened."

We were just starting on desserts. There were a number of choices, but when I saw the *leche flan* burnt at the edges just the way I liked it, I ignored the blueberry cheesecake and the chocolate mousse.

The whole matter could be summed up in a few words: the backers backed out because they didn't see any money in it. The couple heard first from the wives. They didn't like the idea of a magazine that was not a money-making venture. Even assuming it might make money after the first year, they were afraid the losses might go beyond the following year and the next. Imelda herself thought it was too ambitious, almost too grandiose a project and she feared Dr. Sotto would have no time for it and I would be saddled with all the responsibilities. Furthermore when the Board learned there was a need for a staff involving adequately salaried experts in various departments, they knew the startup capital would be eaten up by that and they could not afford to put in more, what with their incomes tied up in other ventures. Then problems began cropping up, personal and family problems. Among the doctors, already high insurance premiums against malpractice soared even higher. So, actually, it was not the final report from Mr. Segal that frightened them off. They had already given up the project even before that.

Dr. Sotto kept hoping it was not so. He kept praying for some kind of miracle that would save his pet project. He was even tempted to go ahead with it all by himself, but Imelda thought that would be quixotic. That was her term. But he was tempted in spite of her opposition. He wanted the magazine. The longer we were together in it, the more faith he had in me and the magazine. Yet perhaps now was not the time for it. He was keeping my report in his files. Who knows, there might be another time? He would not admit it, much less say it outright, but he had been shouldering all the expenses lately. He was not complaining. It was his sole responsibility since the magazine was his original idea in the first place.

"Stick around, we might yet be able to work out something together. I like working with you." He was, without doubt, much concerned about me. So was Imelda.

"Please stay with us for as long as you want to, David. I repeat, this is your home." I detected a sadness in Imelda's voice and when she touched my arm, the big sentimental fool that I was, I wanted to cry. At last the numbness was gone, giving way to a hurt deeper than I ever thought possible. Good God, it was not the end of the world.

"Thanks to both of you," I said, trying to hold back emotion. "But please don't worry about me. Something will turn up. Something always does."

"But not just anything, David. I hope not," Imelda said.

"You know, it's easier in a way, in this country. I have been in similar, well, not exactly, but quite similar situations before. And I've always managed to survive."

"You're not intending to return to the Philippines, are you?" He seemed to know my answer.

"Of course not. I have less chances there, being the kind of writer that I am, what with martial law . . ."

"I don't doubt it," Dr. Sotto agreed. However, I wondered whether he really understood what I meant when I said, "being the kind of writer that I am." Frankly, I wasn't sure myself. I felt I would not be able to write there the way I really wanted to.

I said good night to Imelda before returning to the basement.

"This is not goodbye," she said, holding my hand in both of hers. "I'll be seeing you again. Good night."

Dr. Sotto saw me to my room, but he did not stay long. We talked a while. He kept repeating he was responsible for me and I kept saying, "You've done everything possible, doctor. As a medical doctor, you know you can't win all the time." He insisted I should stay in their house for as long as I wanted to—there would be no change in the arrangement. I said, "Yes, yes, doctor. I'll do that."

As he was about to leave after saying goodnight several times, Dr. Sotto said what he must have wanted to say all this time. "Well, David, one thing, though, you got to admit, it's better that it ended this way before you've been able to do anything. At least, you haven't started anything yet. So nothing's wasted."

"Yes, doctor," I said, "it's perfect timing—nothing is wasted. Good night. And thanks a million."

He mumbled something I didn't quite hear, waving his arm as he disappeared into the corridor outside my door, then up the stairs. I watched him go and heard him turn off the lights. Maybe I didn't actually hear but I saw the darkness swallow him up and what remained of his presence, the goodness in the heart of the man, his innocence.

48

FOR THE FIRST TIME in a long while, I visited the condemned building. Not that I had forgotten it, but there were other pressing concerns which never seemed to give me the leisure I needed. Besides, most of the things I had to attend to took me away in the opposite direction of the city far from that shoddy part of Market Street. I walked past it without recognizing the dark main entrance that appeared as forbidding as ever. What I was looking for was the sign on a piece of cardboard which contained one word: CONDEMNED. There used to be a carbon copy in blurred type of the order from city hall glued to the front door. The sign was no longer there. It could have been removed by some of the transients in the building.

In its present state, abandoned and in disrepair, only those who needed it for shelter knew where it was. They visited the place and after a few trips, they became familiar with the location and found it without fail, sign or no sign. It remained a well-known secret because only a few sought refuge there and their number did not fill the one floor which the tenants occupied. It came to be known by word of mouth and only those who had friends among the more or less "permanent" residents had access to it.

Judy was on my mind. I had not seen her for so long, I missed her. There had been times when I was afraid that the building had already been razed to the ground and I wondered how I could see her again.

It was dark when I started the long climb to the floor where I had been before and darker yet inside the building. There were really no lights except in the evenings and late into the night when the illumination from the street lights reached out into the build-

187

ing casting shadows and light in the darkened interior. There were the usual bodies like heaps of rags on the floor in different corners of the room. But not that many yet. The rest of them arrived late beyond midnight.

I knew my way and when my eyes got used to the dark, I found the spot that "belonged" to Judy and whoever she brought in for the night, man, woman or child. For a brief while, I stood there with growing doubts. I could be wrong. This might not be it. Every space seemed to be occupied, at least that section of the floor that I remembered so well. Maybe Judy had changed her spot, or worse, she had moved on to another city. I felt a great loss, oh, God, don't let me lose her now. Not tonight. I could not bear to be alone, this night of all nights, not with this pain in my chest like a knife.

"Is that you, David?"

The once-familiar voice sounded strange, almost eerie in its softness, coming from somewhere in the half darkness. It was Judy. I moved towards the sound, feeling a sense of relief surge through my body, anticipation, a great weight lifted from my chest. She had sat up and her arms, a sudden flash of whiteness, were outstretched towards me.

"Judy, it's me, Judy," I whispered, trying to keep calm.

I went into her arms and almost fell on top of her as she drew me to her with an eagerness that astounded and thrilled me. Her scent of something old and earthy enveloped me in her embrace.

"Missed you, where have you been?" she asked in a whisper between kisses.

"Among the proud ones," I said, sounding vague. The meaning in my mind was clear.

"What made you come back?"

"They have humbled me too much over there, Judy."

That night, Judy made a place for me beside her, to her right. To her left away from the window, someone else lay who had not stirred even when I snuggled close to Judy.

We spent the night whispering words which meant so much to me but didn't quite make sense to Judy. Yet I felt she understood me to a point where it didn't matter whether she did or not.

As I felt the warmth of her body, she whispered, "Sleep well, David."

I did.

49

IT WAS THE DARKEST NIGHT I ever experienced in the condemned building. The lights on Market Street must have all gone out. I felt disoriented, unsure about where I was until I caught a whiff of the odor of closets and closed lockers, long unopened drawers suddenly pulled out, unvisited caves in my childhood that I had learned to associate with Judy. Groping towards her, rather towards the wild animal smell that held me while it repelled my finer senses, I touched her hand and her fingers closed over mine, soothing and warm. "Judy," I was going to say, but her lips stopped mine as though she could see in the dark. "Hush," she whispered. She turned her white face, barely visible in the thick darkness that seemed to have devoured us, to the ceiling. My hand moved towards her crotch and felt the rough texture of jeans. Her hand caught mine and held it there.

"Missed you," I murmured more like a child than a lover.

She was silent and I waited for her to say something. Maybe she had fallen back to sleep.

"This man beside me to my left is your father, David."

I made a move towards the body immobile on the other side of her, but the darkness held me back like a solid wall.

"Father, is that you?"

"Yes, David."

"Why are you here, Father?"

"Waiting for you. You have been away for a long time."

"No, Father, it's you who have been away a long long time."

"Yes, son. This is one hell of a city."

"You have said that before."

"I say that all the time."

"Why did you stop writing Mother?"

"Had nothing more to say. After a time words refused to come."

"You should have continued sending her money."

"I did."

"I didn't know that."

"You don't know many things, son."

"Teach me."

"You have nothing to learn from me."

"Yes, I have."

"I have nothing to teach you."

189

"Oh, yes, you're my father."

"No. You're my father now. Teach me."

"Isn't it too late now? Besides, what can you learn from me?"

"You know words."

"So do you."

"Oh, if you only knew."

"What?"

"Nothing. You teach me."

"What, for instance?"

"What is love?"

"I don't know, Father."

"What is hate?"

"God, I don't know."

"Why can't I ever win? How can I handle loss?"

"What the hell are you talking about?"

"You should know. You have the words."

"Is it really you, Father, have I found you at last?"

"You have found me."

"No, I have not. I'm still looking for my father."

"I'm your son, Father, I have found you!"

"Father!"

The inky darkness bore me down to a deeper pit and there was nothing more to say. Nothing more to feel. A complete nothingness like death.

50

ON THE DAY I left Diamond Heights for good, nobody seemed to be home. I thought at least Estela would be in her room with the old woman who was always with her. I wanted to say goodbye to someone, yes, especially to Estela. How would it feel to touch her hand, if I could catch it and hold it long enough, how would she take my bidding her goodbye? She would understand. There was no need of telling her what I felt in my heart which I could not put adequately into words. I paused in my tracks, putting down the two suitcases I carried. There was enough time to catch the next bus which stopped down the hill. I had not gone far from the Sotto mansion. Now I wanted to return, run up the stairs

190

and call out without shame and regard for propriety, "Estela, Estela, I have come to say goodbye to you, dear child!" I should have visited her more often, thought of her even more.

What was she to me, why was I so concerned now, feeling I would miss her even more than I would miss her parents who had been very kind to me, this Estela, their true child, the only child, forever a child, unable to control the movements of her body, the secretions of her glands, head and hands twisting, blabbering, salivating, her eyes always bloodshot turned towards you with the intensity of a probing lance; the closest to a word is Mommy long drawn out or spilled in a shower of saliva, the nearest to laughter is an eerie cry, demoniac, wrung from the breast of some wounded beast.

The feeling didn't last long. I turned back to where the suitcases stood and picked them up as I moved faster than I intended to on the walk downhill to wait for the bus that would take me down the now familiar streets of San Francisco. The darkness came with a suddenness that never failed to astonish me, the quick burst of lights and the day was gone; it was actually night, no lingering dusk of evening.

Look close, Estela, under the stars; see us little brown men and women, walking the streets of the city as they wind and turn and climb upward, without warning about sudden corners and dark alleys on the downward bend.

There are no stars blinking at our feet, no encrusted jewels, such as you might imagine, winking over our heads. We are flesh and blood, tired before the day is over, seeking to find after the rains, a welcome door, a smiling face, both the familiar and the strange. Surrounded by strangers, we look for friends in a continuing search against despair.

We have left native land but our hearts are still there, not here, Estela, not in this golden city by the bay. We like to think we gain a lot from day to day in hope, that we are not as we often suspect we are, sentimental fools. But we believe in love, that's all we live for, love. But what the hell is that? And like you, Estela, we carry our own deformities as nobly as we can, but unlike you, we hide them well.

We have names, too.

Father Belarmino wanders the streets of this city, often lost and uneasy, begging for alms to rebuild a crumbling parish church in San Juan, not far from the main street named after his great grandfather.

191

The Professor and his wife think of the daughters they have driven away from their lives, as they walk hand in hand near the Union Square, passing the time of their sorrow, looking into shop windows and seeing their daughters' faces wherever they turn their eyes and wondering, where are they now? God, where have we gone wrong?

You see us all, don't you? At least, your heart knows we are here—that's why you love to look down from Diamond Heights on this city blazing up at you.

A special prayer for the others, too, Estela, strangest of friends— for your parents waiting for a miracle, for Judy the mysterious girl with scars all over her body, and Tingting whom I love like my father.

Then there are the nameless ones.

They have found this city, their city now, nurturing them like a mother sitting on the hills, the fog in her bosom, the salty breezes chasing the clouds beyond the reach of your naked eyes, Estela.

There is fear in our hearts as we listen for tremors under our feet and against our will we look back to that home faraway now lost in the late mists of evening and the long years. Pray that life give us another chance for each loss we suffer as we walk and live on these sullen streets among rusting wharves, smelly canneries and loud fish markets far from the vineyards spilling with bubbly wine.

Dear Estela, good night.

NEW DAY LITERARY TITLES

Alabado, Ceres. *Kangkong 1896*
Albis, Abelardo S. *The Bell Ringer and Other Stories*
Alcantara, Adriana C. *Life of Jesus in Verse*
Allego, Antonio M. *Telling Triple*
      This Time Yesterday and Other Stories
Avena, Mauro. *Tatlong Dula*
Ayala, Tita Lacambra. *Pieces of String and Other Stories*
Bautista, Paulina F. *Find Me Another Jewel*
Becker, Truman. *The Revolution*
Bernad, Fr. Miguel A. *The February Revolution and Other Reflections*
      The Lights of Broadway and Other Essays
Brainard, Cecile M. *Woman with Horns and Other Stories*
Brogan, Isabel. The SAGA OF THE DEAD SEA SCROLLS: Book One, *The Novice of Qumran;* Book Two, *Qumran!* ; Book Three *Naomi:* Book Four, *Masada*
Bulosan, Carlos. *The Philippines Is in the Heart*
Casper, Leonard. *Firewalkers: Literary Concelebrations 1964-1984*
Casper, Linda Ty.   *Fortress in the Plaza*
      The Hazards of Distance
      The Three-Cornered Sun
Cruz, Isagani R. *Beyond Futility: the Filipino as Critic*
Daroy, E. Vallado. *The Drumbeater and Other Stories*
      Nobody Gathers Seashells and Gun Shells Anymore
De la Costa, Fr. Horacio. *Five Plays*
Demetillo, Ricaredo. *Barter in Panay*
      Lazarus Troubadour
      Major and Minor Keys
Deriada, Leoncio P. *The Dog Eaters and Other Plays*
      The Road to Mawab and Other Stories
Diaz, Manuel S. *Rice for the Moon and Other Stories*
Edades, Jean G. *Onstage and Offstage*
Enriquez, Mig Alvarez. *House of Images*
      Three Philippine Epic Plays
      The White Horse of Alih and Other Stories

Espino, Federico Licsi, Jr. *Geometries Bright and Dark*

Espino, Jose Ma. *Into the White Hole*

Fernandez, Doreen G. (ed.). *Contemporary Theater Arts; Asia and the US*

Garrido, Wilfredo, Jr. *Stolia*

Guerrero, Wilfrido Ma. *My Favorite 11 Plays*

Hidalgo, Cristina P. *Ballad of a Lost Season and Other Stories*
Sojourns

Hosillos, Lucila. *Originality as Vengeance in Philippine Literature*

Infante, J. Eddie. *Affairs*

Jose F. Sionil. *My Brother, My Executioner*
Two Filipino Women

Lanot, Marra PL. *Passion and Compassion*

Lim, Paul Stephen. *Some Arrivals, But Mostly Departures*

Lim, Paulino Jr. *Passion Summer and Other Stories*

Lora, Maria Luisa Lumicao. *Gaddang Literature*

Maayo, Geraldine. *The Photographs and Other Stories*
A Quality of Sadness

Madrid, Renato E. *Southern Harvest*

Mella, Cesar T. *A Priest to the World and Other Prose Works*

Montano, Severino. *Selected Plays* (3 vols.)

Moore, Lina Espina. *Cuentos*
Heart of the Lotus
A Lion in the House

Morantte, P.C. *God Is in the Heart*
Remembering Carlos Bulosan

Murphy, Denis. *The Pope's Confessor and Other Stories*

Noriega, Bienvenido N., Jr. *Pares-Pares* (6 Plays)
Soltero (Movie Script)

Peralta, Federico C. *Love Poems*

Queano, Nonilon V. *Ang Katutubo at Dalawa Pang Dula*

Reuter, Fr. James B. *Plays for Children*

Reyes, Gracianus. *The Uncommitted*

Reyes, Jun Cruz. *Tutubi, Tutubi . . .*
Utos ng Hari at Iba Pang Kuwento

Roperos, Godofredo. *The Bald Mountains and Other Stories*

Salanga, Alfrredo N. *The Birthing of Hannibal Valdez*

San Juan, E.P., Jr. *Ang mga Mangwawasak*

Santos, Bienvenido N. *Dwell in the Wilderness*
The Man Who (Thought He) Looked Like Robert Taylor

> *The Praying Man*
> *Villa Magdalena*
> *The Volcano*
> *what the hell for you left your heart in
> san francisco*

Tiempo, Edilberto K. *Cracked Mirror*
> *Finalities*
> *More than Conquerors*
> *Rainbow for Rima*
> *The Standard-Bearer*
> *To Be Free*

Tiempo, Edith L. *His Native Coast*

Tiempo-Torrevillas, Rowena. *Upon the Willows and Other Stories*

Valeros, Florentino et al. *Filipino Writers in English*

WOMEN. *Filipina I*
> *Filipina II*

Build up your own literary Filipiniana collection by checking with your favorite bookstore in Metro Manila for the above titles, or contact NEW DAY Publishers (P.O. Box 167, Quezon City 3008, or Tel. 99-80-46). Subscriptions to the UPPER ROOM (English, Cebuano, Tagalog, and Ilocano editions available) also accepted.

In the United States, the official distributor for New Day books is: The CELLAR BOOK SHOP, 18090 Wyoming St., Detroit, Michigan 48221.